They love each other. Will the rest of the world let them?

Reluctantly on her way to a blind date, second grade teacher Maureen detours into her mechanic's garage because her brakes are squeaking. Her regular mechanic isn't there but his very intriguing brother Michael is. Michael tells her that he can't let her drive home with her brakes in that condition and offers to take her out to dinner in his 1972 Plymouth Satellite. Maureen can't believe how instantly and powerfully she's attracted to this grease monkey and neither can any of her friends, but since he's only going to be in town for a week, she doesn't want to waste an instant.

Except that grease monkey is no grease monkey. He's Bear D'Amato, rock n' roll drummer and in a week he's headed back to get ready for a world tour with his band, Touchstone. When he first meets Maureen, he just wants to go out with her a few times like a normal guy, but as the relationship deepens, he realizes he wants more than just a couple of dates. He wants a lifetime.

Maureen is shocked by his revelation, but she realizes she wants a lifetime too. Now all they have to do is convince the rest of the world.

Books by Christa Maurice

Drawn to the Rhythm Series
Satellite of Love

Arden FD Series
Three Alarm Tenant
Struck By Lightning
Spark of Desire

Weaver's Circle Series
Secrets Everybody Knows
Long Memory

One Ring to Rule
Melody Unchained

Published by Kensington Publishing Corporation

Satellite of Love

Christa Maurice

LYRICAL PRESS
Kensington Publishing Corp.
www.kensingtonbooks.com

To my own loyal band: Trisha, Roxanna and Jacki

Chapter 1

Maureen dropped her head to the steering wheel in front of Tony's Garage. She was not going to make that blind date, and depending on the repair bill, might be happy about that. One of these days she had to tell her friend Linda no when she came up with another man. So far they had all been wasted evenings.

She really needed to try to meet some decent men on her own. So far the strategy of school all day and sitting home all night planning for school the next day wasn't working so great for the social calendar.

At least the screaming brakes gave her a good excuse to cancel. The sign said closed, but when she pushed the door, it opened. The bay to the right was empty, but further back, in the bays behind the building, she could hear clanking and a radio playing. Tony must be working late.

"Hello?" Maureen peered through the short hallway from the obsessively clean waiting area to the back repair bays. The far door stood nearly closed so she could only see a sliver of the room. A tire, a black fender with a piece of masking tape on it, a work light, a black hood propped open. "Tony? Are you back there? It's Maureen Donnelly."

Feet shuffled and the radio's volume lowered. What if it wasn't Tony? Maybe one of his assistants had stayed late. Rusty or...the high school kid...Eric, that was his name. Did Tony trust his high school work-study assistant enough to leave him alone in the garage after hours? "I'm having some trouble with my brakes. They're making a lot of noise. You probably heard them when I pulled in."

What if it wasn't either one of them? What if it was some total stranger? What if it was somebody dangerous? She fumbled in her purse for her cell phone then stopped.

What was she going to do? Call 911 so they could listen to her screams for help without being able to do anything because they didn't know where she was? Tomorrow's headline could read: *Second Grade*

Teacher Slain In Garage, Too Stupid To Know Responders Couldn't Track Her Cellphone Signal. She should have gotten one of those apps that broadcast her every move. Then she could have just posted to Facebook. *Being murdered. Call Police. Tony's Garage.*

The door to the back bays opened and a bulky silhouette that didn't really fit Tony, Rusty, or Eric filled it.

She took a step back toward the outside door. "Hi, sorry I bothered you. I can come back in the morning." *Teacher's Body Found Rolled In Rug Behind Convenience Store, Cell Phone Still In Her Hand.*

"It's okay." The man walked through the dark hall and into the waiting area. His broad, friendly face seemed familiar. He wore his long brown hair in a ponytail and had a smudge of grease on his cheek. "I heard you pull in. You want me to take a look?"

"No." She bumped into the door. "I mean, you don't have to. I'll just leave it for Tony in the morning." The mechanic didn't look at all threatening, but adrenalin interfered with rational thought. *Memorial Service For Murdered Teacher Tuesday, Local Garages Offering Free Brake Checks. Says Tony D'Amato, owner of the garage where her car was found Friday, "If she'd just gotten that squeaking noise checked when she first heard it, all of this could have been avoided."*

"They sounded pretty bad. You might have worn down to the rotors. Let me take a look." He crossed the room.

Honestly, he looked about as threatening as the Easter Bunny. If the Easter Bunny had amazing shoulders. "It's okay." Before she announced that someone was picking her up, she stopped herself. The neighborhood wasn't the greatest and calling for a ride meant standing around in it, increasing her chances for ending up in that rug. Better the devil she had just met than the one who might be lurking in the dark. "Who are you?"

He had been reaching out, hopefully to grab the door because his hands were filthy, but pulled back when she asked. "I'm— I'm Michael, Tony's brother."

"Michael. No wonder you look familiar. Sorry. I wasn't sure." Too much caffeine and too many murder mysteries. She needed to lay off both for a while.

"That's okay." Michael pursed his lips. Nice lips they were too. Full, red, very kissable for the Easter-Bunny-slash-killer. "You want me to take a look at those brakes now?"

"Sure. Thanks. I know it's after hours, but they started to sound really bad." She held out her keys. "I guess you'll need to put it up on the lift or something."

Michael nodded, ripped some paper off the roll inside the door to protect the interior of her precious ten-year-old clunker and crossed the lot to her car. She wouldn't mind having that body in her driver's seat. The way he filled out his coverall was a sight. Broad shoulders, narrow waist, nice tight butt. Very nice.

She turned away from the window before he caught her staring. Good thing she wasn't going on that date in this frame of mind. From murdered and rolled in a rug to sweaty sex on the hood of a car in ten seconds flat, and all she'd needed was his name.

Oh. Date.

Her phone was still in her hand so she located the latest bachelor on her list of calls as she walked through the hallway to watch Michael pull her car in. Tony didn't like customers in the bay. He claimed it was dangerous. The only danger she could imagine was brain damage from the stench of oil, gasoline and exhaust. Brain damage be damned, she wasn't going to pass on the chance to ogle.

"Hello?"

"Hi—" Crud, what was this bachelor's name? "It's Maureen. I wanted to let you know I can't make it tonight."

"Sorry to hear that." He didn't sound sorry. Maybe Linda's sales pitch hadn't been that good.

"My brakes are making a horrible noise. I'm sure you can hear it." Michael had just pulled through the door and the squeals echoed beautifully on the cinderblock walls.

"That sounds pretty bad. Um... I guess you'll need a ride."

"No." That was it. No more of Linda's blind dates. "I'll be fine."

"Okay. I guess I'll talk to you."

Not if I recognize your number before I answer the phone. "Yeah. Okay. 'Bye." She closed her phone. At this very moment she could be at home watching TV in sweats, grading math tests and deciding to bring the car to Tony tomorrow. She'd washed her hair, shaved her legs, put on makeup and dressed up for whatshisname. The sexy dark blue jersey dress she'd selected needed somebody who'd appreciate her effort. Hands on hips to hold her coat open, she sauntered behind the car. Michael was operating the lift, but he gave her a once over when she passed.

"Well?" she asked.

"They aren't supposed to sound like that. I'll have to pull the tire off to see how bad it is, but it's not going to be good. Does Tony do all the maintenance on your car?"

"Most of it. He told me to go to the quick lube places for my oil changes." Lube, hehe. She really needed to mix with adults more often.

"Has your transmission fluid been clear?" Michael walked to the front driver's side tire, so she followed him.

"I guess so. The guy at the lube place said I needed to have it flushed next time I go in. Why?"

"Felt to me like your transmission was slipping." He popped the hubcap off and used a loud tool to loosen the lug nuts.

When she flinched away from the noise, she bumped into the car he'd been working on. It was black except for the trunk, which was orange. Just sitting there, hood up and orange trunk lid, it seemed to say, "Hey, baby, wanna ride?" She sidled toward the front. On the fender a strip of masking tape said *Satellite of Love*. "Is this your car?"

Michael looked over his shoulder, yanking the tire off as if it weighed less than a duvet. "Yeah. That's my baby."

"Satellite of Love?"

"My sister-in-law's idea of a joke. It's a '72 Plymouth Satellite."

As if that meant something to her. As far as she could tell, it was a car that might or might not run. She leaned on the Satellite's fender. Her car always looked so helpless up on the lift. More so now that it was missing a tire.

"You headed someplace tonight?" Michael asked.

"A date."

"Sorry."

"Naw, if I'd really wanted to be there I could have continued to ignore that squealing." She grinned, but he didn't turn around to see it. Another wasted effort. "So what are you doing here?"

"I'm visiting my brother and his family." Michael glanced over his shoulder frowning, clearly absorbed with the car thing in his hand. Men and their obsession with inanimate objects. "This is bad."

"What's bad?" She stepped forward.

"This piece?" He held up a dirty, holey piece of who knew what in his large, strong-looking hand. "This is the shoe. This is what stops your car and it works best when it isn't full of holes."

Her grimace, such an attractive expression, he did see. Of course. "Is it expensive?"

"Expensive?"

Why did he sound like money was no object to him? "Yes, is it going to cost a lot to fix?"

"It's not cheap, but it's a lot less expensive than plowing into a wall or another car." He shrugged. "Tony's pretty busy tomorrow, but if he can't get to it, I'm sure we can do it Sunday so you can have it back for Monday."

She clenched her fists behind her back. As if that would keep the money from flying out of her wallet. "Will somebody call me and tell me when to bring it in?"

"Oh no." Michael dropped the worn brake shoe on the floor. "You can't drive out of here like this."

"If you put the tire back on, I can."

"No, you can't." Michael folded his arms, which accented those fantastic shoulders and did incredible things to the muscles in his upper arms. "I can't let you drive this car in good conscience. You'd be a danger to yourself and anyone else on the road."

"Great." Maureen stared out the bay door into the waning light, thoughts of fantastic shoulders ebbing. She'd have been better off going on the stupid date. A whole weekend without a car? The price was too high. "How am I supposed to get home?"

"I can give you a ride or you can call a cab."

Her stomach growled. On the top of her To Do list for tomorrow was buying groceries. Until she could get out to the store, she was eating oatmeal and crackers with jelly. "Great."

"You know, if you're hungry we could stop for pizza on the way." Michael smiled. He had a warm, playful smile that gave her a glimpse of the little boy in this big hunk of man. "My treat since I know Tony is going to gouge you on the repair. I'll even kick in a ride in the Satellite of Love."

Well, that did make the bill a little more manageable. "You had me at pizza."

He nodded. "I'm known for overplaying my hand. Let me clean up and we'll get out of here." Switching off the work light hooked to the Satellite, he set it aside and closed the hood. Then he headed toward the little hallway. "It'll only take me a minute."

This had to be one of her more irrational moments. Fifteen minutes ago she'd been convinced he was going to murder her and dump her body in an alley and now they were headed out to grab a pizza? In his car yet. Insane much? "Hey, you aren't going to turn out to be a serial killer, are you?" she called after him.

He turned at the mouth of the hallway. "A what?"

"Never mind."

He chuckled, a deep rich sound. "Don't worry. I'm not a serial killer." Then he ducked through a door in the hall that was always closed.

She should probably be concerned about the way he emphasized the word *not*, but somehow couldn't summon the desire.

No, she was busy desiring something else.

* * * *

Bear stripped off his coveralls and hung them on the door of the extra locker. He'd been hoping to get a little more work done on the Satellite, but this was a lot more interesting. Pulling on the Tesla t-shirt he'd worn in this morning, he wished he'd dressed a little better. Of course, Maureen Donnelly thought he was an auto mechanic, so the old concert t-shirt and jeans might be a better way to sell the illusion.

His phone had five messages. One from Sandy, one from Candy, one from Jason and two from Marc. Sandy was probably mad he hadn't called in since last week. Going off the radar like he had, especially with a tour looming, must be driving Sandy nuts. Candy wanted him to do some publicity thing. Her job was getting them publicity, but she never had understood the word *vacation*. Jason, if Jason was still acting the way he had been for the past couple of weeks since he'd gotten dumped in *People*, was just calling to bitch. He called Marc and pinned the phone between his shoulder and ear while he scrubbed grease off his fingers.

"Yo."

"What?"

"Nothin'. When are you coming back?"

"Ten days." He checked his watch as if it measured days. Ten short days, until he was stuck in a room, and then a series of rooms, with the rest of the band and their melodrama.

"Good. Jason is selling the New York apartment."

"Beautiful, so he's going to be in Malibu all the time now?"

"I guess. Ty has taken up grass boarding."

"What the fuck is that?"

"Just like snowboarding, but on grass."

"He can still sing when he falls and fucks up his wrists. Did you call for a reason or just to give me a newsy update?"

"Why? You got a hot date or something?"

Bear didn't answer. He'd hoped to already be tooling down the road with Maureen Donnelly headed for a simple pizza between two people who'd just met. Two totally normal people.

"The suits just want to make sure everything is on track," Marc said. "The album is still moving up the charts but the single is slipping. The next single is coming out Tuesday and it would really help if you would pick up a little promo."

"I'm. On. Vacation."

"I know, but we owe the company a fortune and if this record tanks, we are never going to record another one. The label will drop us and we'll all end up managing a fast food joint."

"Yeah, I know. I took Rock Star 101 with you." His head started to throb. "We did all that promo when the album came out. The thing for MTV and that Canadian show. And we're doing that casino to kick off the tour. All I asked for was two fucking weeks."

"And all I'm asking you to do is take two hours out of your vacation and hit a radio station."

"Marc, they're getting the next ten months of my life."

"It's the job, man, and it's the best fucking job in the world." Marc's tone remained pleasant and even.

"I know. Is that what Sandy wanted?"

"No, Sandy wants to know where you are and that you're healthy."

"Tell him I'm right where I was the last time he talked to me and in about the same shape."

"Great. Jason has been busting his ass on promo."

The last thing he wanted to hear about was what a superhero Jason was. Not with a sweet thing like Maureen Donnelly waiting. "I gotta go."

"Oh, that's right. The hot date. See ya in ten days."

Bear snapped his phone closed as he pulled on his leather jacket. He should have skipped this whole music thing and gone into business with his brother.

Then both of them could be trying to scratch a living out of this little three bay garage.

He snatched the keys off the locker shelf and hurried out to see if Maureen Donnelly had hung around while he was getting scolded.

She stood in the filthy repair bay behind her car, holding her purse with both hands. Cocking her head, she gave him a little smile.

For about ten seconds, he couldn't take his eyes off her. The minimal makeup she wore accented the simple prettiness of her features instead of them being obliterated under raccoon eyeliner and some wild shade of lipstick. Her brunette hair was cut in a bob and pulled back off her face. He hadn't seen what with yet, but he bet it was a bow or some kind of flower. The dark blue dress crisscrossed over her perfect, unenhanced bust, creating some really intriguing cleavage.

Really intriguing. He couldn't see her legs around the bumper of the car, or her shoes. He wanted to check out her shoes and, more importantly, the legs that led into them. As he recalled, the hem fell right to her knees.

"Sorry I took so long." He tore his gaze away from where he could have seen her legs if he had x-ray vision, and met hers. She didn't seem to be on to him. "I had to make a call."

"No problem." She shook her head and her cute little bob bounced around her shoulders.

"I'll lock up and we can go." He ducked into the waiting room to lock the door and turn off the lights. The sooner he got out of here, the sooner he was going to get a look at her legs. "Which pizza place do you like better? Napoli or Mama Lena's? I like Napoli's."

"So do I, but I don't like to eat there." She sounded sorry as she followed him to the car door.

He glanced over his shoulder. Her pretty, small mouth was drawn into a frown. "Why?"

"They're always screaming at each other, did you notice? The food is wonderful, but the brothers who own the place are always arguing or yelling at the kids waiting tables." She shivered. "It just makes me uncomfortable."

"Tony always gets carry out. I guess there's a reason." He opened the passenger door of the Satellite. "Mama Lena's it is."

She sat down on the seat sideways and twisted forward like a lady. His mom used to get into cars that way when she wore a dress and he'd never seen any other woman do it. Swallowing at the unfamiliar rush of mixed heat and uncertainty, he opened the bay door so he could back out. This woman was not a score-seeking groupie. Maureen Donnelly qualified as a nice girl.

And he was already lying to her.

Not lying really, but not filling her in on a few details. Like he wasn't an auto mechanic and in a couple of weeks, he'd be off on the one ring circus currently known as the Bayonet Ball Tour. Like the next time she saw him after this, he'd probably be on MTV. If she even watched that. She struck him as a History Channel type.

Did it really matter? He was taking her out for a pizza, not marrying her. For one night, he could just be Michael, the guy who was buying her a pizza, taking her home and maybe getting a kiss on the doorstep instead of Bear D'Amato, drummer for Touchstone.

He backed the car out and closed the garage door. "So what is it you do?"

"I'm a teacher. I teach second grade at Wilson."

"Really?" Teacher. Little kid teacher yet. That fit. "You like it?"

"Yeah, it's great, but I'm looking forward to summer vacation."

"Oh?"

"February is kinda long and Spring Break is late this year so we've had this really long stretch with no days off. It gets a little tiring, for the teachers and the kids."

"I always thought the teachers were annoyed when we had days off." He glanced at her. She had half turned toward him with her purse in her lap, as if she were interested in the conversation, not as if she were amortizing him.

"Nope. We're all shooing the kids out the door and making plans for our days off."

"And what do you like to do on your days off?" What did regular people do on their days off? Most of his time was spent in the studio, on tour or in between and in between was only a couple of days here and there. Not that it was bad, he did have the greatest job in the world, but it was a twenty-four seven gig. Even last year's sabbatical had been spent analyzing what had gone wrong with the previous album so they could avoid it this time.

"The usual stuff. I read, watch TV, garden a little."

"Go out on blind dates."

She groaned. "Yeah. I should have given that up for Lent. My friend Linda means well, but she's not very good at it. I think next time I'm going to be washing my hair or something pressing like that."

"So it is an excuse."

"Like you've ever gotten it."

"Once or twice." A long time ago. Now all he had to do was pick a girl from the line up, which was frustrating in its own way.

Her laugh was light and musical. "So what do you do, other than fix cars?"

Damn. How to answer this question without flat out lying? "I travel and play music." That sounded good. Like they were two separate things.

"Travel. I've always wanted to travel, but never had the money. Where have you been?"

"All over." He clenched the steering wheel. He'd never seen much of the places he'd been. Travel, perform, sleep, repeat.

"That sounds wonderful."

Not the word he'd use. "So you have a garden?"

"Yeah. I bought a house last year so I spent last summer gardening. I'm really looking forward to my tulips and daffodils coming up this spring."

He pulled into the parking lot of Mama Lena's. The place was jammed. Great, now he had to use his fame to pull a few strings for a table, blowing his cover, or stand around like a jerk waiting for one. "Here we are."

"Wow, they're busy tonight." She checked her watch. "Let's hope the theater at the mall has a showing time soon so we don't have to wait long. I don't know about you, but I'm starved."

Oh yeah, she would *expect* to wait for a table. She wouldn't be disappointed when he couldn't magically make one open up for her. Man, he was so out of practice for this regular dating thing.

She climbed out without waiting for him to open her door and strode toward the restaurant, giving him the chance to fall back and check out the rear view, what he could see of it above and below her black raincoat. Her calves were slender and well shaped, practically insuring fantastic legs. The three-inch heels she wore put a beautiful glide in her stride. Her hair clip wasn't a bow or flowers. It was a gold Mickey Mouse. Mickey freakin' Mouse. This woman was so real, she was surreal.

He pulled open the door. Nobody lingered in the tiny waiting area and a blonde in a white t-shirt and black pants with a little red waitress's apron wrapped around her waist bounded over before the door even fell shut.

"Hi, Miss Donnelly, you need a table? Benny's clearing one now." The waitress's gaze shifted over Maureen's shoulder and her eyes went wide. He had about ten seconds before his cover went up in hysteria.

"Thanks, Tara. How's your sister doing?" Maureen scanned the restaurant. When she returned to the waitress, the girl's gaze pinged back to her, still wide eyed.

"My sister? Um, Ellie's fine. Um... I'll, um...check on Benny." The waitress spun around and all but sprinted for the back of the restaurant. Probably headed for the kitchen where she would tell the entire staff he was here.

"Tara's little sister was in my class two years ago." Maureen turned and frowned. "You have grease on your face."

"I do?" Bear watched over her shoulder for the kitchen staff to come boiling through the swinging doors to check out the visiting celebrity.

"Yeah. Do you want a Kleenex?" She dug in her purse.

"No, I'll just go wash it off in the bathroom." He lunged past her in the direction the waitress had gone, crossed the dining room without touching the floor and burst into the kitchen.

The entire staff huddled around Tara. They turned as a unit to stare at him. All of them in Touchstone's target audience range.

"I told you!" Tara shrieked.

"Hush," an older man hissed. The only one not in the crowd. "The customers will hear you."

"Listen, I just want to have a nice quiet dinner." Bear held up his hands. "I'll sign all the autographs you want in here, but out there I'd really appreciate it if you treated me like anybody else."

"But you're not anybody else," a girl with black hair and black rimmed glasses whimpered. "You're Bear D'Amato from Touchstone."

"You know Brian Ellis," another girl said.

"And Jason Callisto."

That broke their spell and they rushed him, order tablets out for autographs, babbling about how much they liked the album and the single and were they going to be doing a show anyplace close? He started signing. "I'm going to be in town for a few more days and I really want to keep it quiet. I just want to have dinner like anybody else. If everyone could just keep this between us until I leave, maybe I can talk the band into swinging by here while we're on tour. But seriously, if there's a breath of a rumor that I'm here, I can't promise anything."

The whole group gasped, exchanging conspiratorial glances. Hopefully, it would be as easy to arrange as it had been to promise. Sandy was going to murder him.

Tara stood in front of him with bright eyes. "Are you dating Miss Donnelly?"

"I'm having dinner with Miss Donnelly." Eventually. If he ever managed to get back to her. He'd been gone a really long time and still had grease on his face.

"I bet she doesn't even know who you are." Tara clutched her autograph to her chest. "She's so tragically unhip. I'll go seat her."

"Not a word," he cautioned as she scooted through the door. Now he was lying. Flat out, no doubt, lying.

But if he told her, she'd either run screaming or latch on tighter for all the wrong reasons. He just wanted one night. Not even the whole night. For the next three hours, he wanted to be nobody special.

Chapter 2

By the time he parked in her driveway, Maureen had been wrestling with the idea of coffee for five minutes. If she invited him in, he might take it to mean something more than the offer of a hot beverage on a chill night. Worse, she wasn't sure if she didn't mean it to be something more, which was completely out of character.

Dinner had been nice. Weird, but nice. Michael could recite whole episodes of *The Simpsons* with voices. He'd claimed he was working on the movie, but hadn't had time to study it yet. That made up for the fact that the entire wait staff had gone crazy.

Tara hung around the table so much, Maureen had no idea how much soda she'd drunk. Every time her glass dropped below two thirds full, Tara swooped in to refill it. Jenny Riggs argued with a customer over their check until she was screaming and Joe had to come out to settle things. Jenny had stood in the middle of the dining room clutching her glasses in her fist so she could rub tears out of her eyes with both hands. Odder still, it appeared they hadn't been arguing over the price, but the paper it was written on. Then Benny tripped over the jukebox power cord, unplugging it, and no one bothered to plug it back in.

"This the place?" Michael asked.

"I know it's not much to look at." What did he see when he looked at her tiny house? A one story yellow brick box on a postage stamp lawn? But hers, all hers. "I had a nice time tonight."

"What are you doing tomorrow?"

"What?"

He turned in his seat, leaning toward her. "What are you doing tomorrow?"

Why was he asking about tomorrow? "Well, I was thinking about doing some laundry."

He reached for her, but instead of stopping at her hand like she expected, he ran his fingers up her arm, over her shoulder and around the back of her neck. The electric sensation continued down her spine causing her thighs to clench and her nipples to tighten in sympathy. So out of character. "That sounds like one of those excuses," he murmured.

"It's not. I can't really go anywhere. No car, remember?" She tried to draw a breath, but her lungs didn't seem interested.

"I'll take you anywhere you want." Michael brushed his lips across her cheek.

A whimper escaped her. "Anywhere? What if I said Paris?"

"I'd take you to Paris. Get your passport." He kissed the corner of her mouth.

"I have to be back on Monday for school."

"The Concorde is really fast."

"The Concorde doesn't fly anymore."

He pressed his lips to hers.

Maureen closed her eyes. Her fingers clutched his leather jacket. This was not like her at all. First dates ended with a chaste kiss at the door followed by a minimum one week interval before the second date. Michael was so unlike any man she'd ever dated. Something about him made her feel like she was standing at the edge of a volcano, considering hopping in to test the temperature of the lava.

His tongue brushed across her lips.

She pulled back. "Slow down there, cowboy."

Michael stared at her. His heavy breathing was the only sound in the car.

Cowboy? Urg. Well, it had been nice while it lasted. Before she screwed it up, she'd had the focused attention of a really sexy guy for a whole evening.

He bit his lip and shook his head once. "So what are you doing tomorrow?"

"Are you serious?"

"Absolutely."

"But I'm a prude," she blurted out.

Michael shrugged. "I can work with that. How about I pick you up around noon? We'll grab some lunch and go see what there is to do." He jumped out of the car and hurried around to the passenger door.

Maureen looked up at him when he opened it. "You're serious."

"I said I was." Michael held out his hand.

As he guided her from the car, she protested, "There really isn't a lot to do around here."

"I'm sure we can find something." He stopped in front of the door and looked at her expectantly.

Her mouth went dry. What was he waiting for? An invitation in? Another kiss? Either one would be nice. Not her, but nice. What would he do if she stepped forward, wrapped her arms around his neck and kissed him?

Dumb question.

"Are you going to unlock the door?" he asked.

That, on the other hand, was an excellent question.

Maureen dug through her purse for her keys. She unlocked the door quickly as if it would make up for standing on the porch like a thunderstruck teenager. "So you'll come over tomorrow?"

"Noonish, and I'll see what I can do about getting your car finished." He kissed her cheek. "Good night, Maureen."

"Night." After she'd closed her front door, she leaned against it trying to remember how to breathe. She'd lost her mind. That was the only explanation. Too many blind dates and she'd gone gaga for the guy who fixed her car. Check that. The brother of the guy who fixed her car. The way she was acting, he was a movie star.

Well, as long as she managed to keep her head, it wouldn't be so bad. Once he went back to wherever he lived, it would fizzle. Long distance relationships never worked for her. The two times she'd tried, they'd imploded in months and both of those had been established before the separation.

No, this would be short and sweet, emphasis on sweet because she wasn't going any further with some guy she was never going to see again. Especially since she had to face his brother every time her car broke down.

* * * *

Bear went straight back to Tony's house. He wanted to turn in early so he could work on Maureen's car before he went to pick her up. If he could get the parts, he'd have it done by the time he needed to pick her up. The Satellite wouldn't be finished before he left town anyway and the lure of being her hero was enticing. He was already imagining the expression on her face when he pulled into her driveway with her car.

"You hung out at the garage late," Pam said as he walked in the front door. "You get much done?"

"No. One of the regulars showed up with bad brakes so I took her to dinner." Bear walked through the living room headed for the rumpus slash guest room they put him in when he visited. "Wake me up in the morning. I want to get a head start on her car before I pick her up."

"What?" Tony floundered off the couch like a turtle trying to turn off its back. "What did you just say?"

Bear stopped at the end of the hall. "One of your regulars came in with a brake problem. I want to get it taken care of so I can take her car back when I pick her up tomorrow."

"Pick her up?" Tony put his fists on his hips. "You asked her out on a date?"

"Yeah."

"Bear." Pam stood too. "What are you doing?"

"Don't screw with the locals, Bear. These are my customers," Tony said.

"I'm not screwing with the locals. She doesn't even know who I am. I just want to have a nice normal couple of dates before I have to go back to the circus. Trust me."

Tony glanced at Pam and scowled at him. "Who is it?"

"Maureen Donnelly."

"Miss Donnelly?" Tony folded his arms.

"Bear, that's the teacher we're hoping to get for Nicky next year." Pam wrung her hands.

"So?" Bear looked from his brother to his sister-in-law. They were clearly peeved, but why? Other than a momentary loss of reason in the car tonight, he'd been on his best behavior. The whole night, he'd been a perfect gentleman and he planned to continue. "What's the big deal?"

"This is not some groupie you can walk away from," Tony said.

"I'm not treating her like a groupie. We went to dinner. Tomorrow we're going to go to lunch and then we're going to go do something in the afternoon. And I'm hoping to get up early enough to take care of her brakes before I pick her up. Is that okay?"

"No, it's not."

"Well, that must suck for you." Bear dropped his keys into his pocket. "I'm gonna go out with Maureen a couple of times while I'm in town and then I'm gonna leave and you all can get back to your regularly scheduled programming. She never needs to be the wiser and we can just be those two ships who pass in the night. See ya in the morning."

Inside the guest room, he sat on the foot of the sofa bed. If on that day, freshman year of high school, when Brian and Jason had walked up to him in the hall and one of them had said, "We heard you play drums" if he'd said no, he could have had this life. The mortgage, the business loan, the regular programming. He could have met Maureen when she brought her junker in for a repair and taken her out for dinner without Tony and Pam freaking out. Hell, by now he might have been sharing that mortgage with her. As shaky as the car was, she must have had it in a lot. The repairs could have served as a courtship.

Bear put his elbows on his knees and buried his hands in his hair. He'd promised Marc he would do a drop-in next week. He was going to have to be a rock star for one day in the middle of playing regular guy. Greatest job in the world.

* * * *

Maureen scrubbed the makeup off her face. It looked ridiculous and she didn't know where they were going. Studying herself in the mirror, she discovered she'd splashed water all over her shirt. Super. Any second, he was going to be here and she'd gotten herself drenched.

She ran into the bedroom, yanking the yellow, long sleeved knit shirt over her head as she went. Her second choice was a turtleneck with tiny flowers all over it that screamed elementary school teacher. Most of her clothes screamed elementary school teacher. They might explain her dating track record. What man wanted to spend time with a woman who dressed like she might launch into a lesson on fractions at any moment? She pulled on the back up and ran her fingers though her hair, which promptly stuck up in all directions.

The phone rang in the kitchen. At least she hoped it was in the kitchen. She kept forgetting to put it back on the charger.

"Hello?" she answered it.

"Hey, how did the date go last night?" Linda asked.

"Oh my God, last night was fantastic." Eyes closed, she recalled Michael sitting across the table from her, drumming his fingertips together and saying *excellent* just like Mr. Burns.

"Really?" Linda sounded dubious. Why?

"Oh wait. I didn't actually meet the guy you fixed me up with. I had car trouble."

"And car trouble was fantastic?"

"Yeah. I met my mechanic's brother. He was at the garage working late." On the Satellite of Love.

"Your mechanic's brother?" Now Linda sounded more dubious.

"My brakes were making a horrible noise so I stopped in and he said they weren't safe to drive on so he offered to take me out for pizza and drive me home."

"Oh, please. You fell for that?"

"For what?" Maureen smoothed her shirt over her hips. The clock said straight up noon, but he had said around noon.

"Every mechanic in the world uses that it's not safe to drive line. That's how they get you for more money."

Maureen twisted the ends of her hair around her finger. "He showed me the thingy and it looked really bad. Besides, if he just wanted to get more money out of me, why did he take me out to dinner?"

"Let's see, you wore the blue dress. Do you think he might have been trying to get a look at your cleavage?"

Well, her turtleneck would be a test then. Cleavage didn't exist in it. "I thought that was the point of the dress."

"It is, but do you really want to waste it on a grease monkey?"

"I didn't happen to be using it for anything else. That guy you fixed me up with wasn't too upset when I called him to tell him I couldn't make it."

"Greg isn't the type to show his emotions. I know he was looking forward to meeting you. You ought to give him a chance."

A shape slowed on the street, but she couldn't make it out through the sheers. It wasn't dark enough to be the Satellite. Nobody else was supposed to drop by today. "Listen, I hafta go."

"Another clandestine meeting with your mechanic?"

"I'll call Greg and try to reschedule for next weekend." *If I remember his name long enough.* "But I really have to go right now. I'll see you Monday." Before Linda could get in another zinger, she hung up the phone. Michael walked past the front window and her heartbeat stammered. He wasn't just a grease monkey but funny, sweet and interesting. Sexy. Mustn't forget sexy.

When she yanked open the door, he had his hand poised to knock.

"Hi." He raised one eyebrow. "Waiting long?"

"No, I was on the phone and saw you through the window so I figured I'd just get it before you knocked and—" And babbling like an idiot. What was it about this grease monkey that made her gibber like a teenage girl?

He held up her keys. "I brought your car. I got the brakes done this morning. It needs a tune up, but I didn't have time to get to that. The garage is closed tomorrow, but say the word and I'll take care of it for you."

"That would be great. Did you bring the bill? I can write you a check if it isn't ruinous."

"No bill," he said with a shake of his head. "I took care of it."

"You took care of it?"

"Sure. The part was cheap and I did the labor myself." He grinned, and the way his eyes sparkled did funny things to her insides. "Of course, I would take a kiss in payment."

"A kiss?" The memory of their kiss last night assaulted her. Her body throbbed as she remembered the moment she would have given in and a split second later when she'd known she couldn't. Did he remember it as clearly? Especially the couldn't part?

Michael turned his cheek to her and tapped it. "Come on. I think I earned a kiss. It was a lot of work."

Okay, maybe he did remember the *couldn't* part. Laughing, she pecked his cheek. "Alright, but we're going to have to establish some rates if you're going to continue to work on my car."

He caught her around the waist, hauling her against his hard chest. "I'm willing to negotiate on a case by case basis." Then he dipped in, gave her a quick kiss on the lips and released her.

She tottered backward. There was way more to this guy than grease monkey and whatever it was short-circuited her decision-making abilities. Like right now, she should be annoyed that he'd grabbed her, but wasn't. Last night she should have been more careful about going anywhere with a stranger in his car, but hadn't been. In a few minutes she was going to head off to who knew where with the same guy even though logic, good sense and Linda told her it was a bad idea. "So where are we going?"

"I was hoping you'd have some ideas. I'm not very familiar with the area."

Maureen clasped her hands. How was he going to take this idea? If he didn't like it, he'd probably endure the day and never talk to her again. Outside of tomorrow when he was tuning up her car. He'd already committed to that. How much did she care? He wasn't permanent date material. He wasn't even local. But he was really— Interesting. Regardless, this dating option didn't carry the same weight it might have. It wasn't like she was destroying a perfectly good specimen with a really stupid choice. "How do you feel about dinosaurs?"

"Dinosaurs?"

Linda's expression while talking to her on the phone a few minutes ago had probably looked a lot like Michael's did now. Textbook dubious. "Yeah, dinosaurs. The natural history museum has a special exhibit. Some recent finds from China. If you're interested." She chewed the inside of her cheek. He didn't. Look interested, that was. If anything, his expression had shifted to baffled.

"Dinosaurs," he repeated.

"The exhibit is going to be there for another month so if I don't make it this weekend, it's no big loss. Besides, I'm going on a field trip with the kids in two weeks. I was just hoping to get a preview."

"No, that actually sounds fun." Michael frowned like he couldn't believe he was saying it. "I haven't done anything like that in ages. Do you want to take your car or stop at the garage for the Satellite? I'm afraid it still has a mismatched trunk, but it purrs."

If he was going to give on the museum, she could give on the funny looking car. "That's fine. I'll grab my coat and purse and we can go."

Muttering about the timing and the transmission, and finally extracting a promise from her that she'd bring it in tomorrow for a tune up, he drove to the garage. He parked around back and she followed him to the bay where the Satellite was parked. Tony stood behind the car with his arms folded.

"Hello, Miss Donnelly." His barely pleasant tone turned hard when he spoke to Michael. "Where are you going?"

"A museum." Michael's voice was equally tense.

"A museum," Tony repeated.

The two men stared at one another. In the garage, Rusty peeked around the hood of the car he was working on. Maureen stuffed her hands in her pockets. What was it about this that bothered Tony? Did he disapprove of his brother taking her out? Or of her going out with his brother?

"You be home for dinner?" Tony asked.

"I doubt it." Michael reached back and took Maureen's arm. "See ya tonight."

As she let him escort her to the car and open the door, panic crawled through her chest. Tony had a son going into second grade next year. If he didn't like her dating his brother, he might talk to other parents. If enough of them decided they didn't want their child in her class the school board might not renew her contract. That was probably a lot of wild paranoia, but having a class full of kids with hostile parents wasn't. Linda had a pack of them this year in third grade and they were making her life hell. Two years ago Jenny Gilchrist had six kids fail and those kids' parents drove her so crazy, she'd ended up in the hospital with panic attacks and had quit at the end of the year.

Without a word, he backed the car out of the garage. By the time he'd pulled onto the street, she couldn't bear spinning scenarios anymore. She turned sideways in her seat. "What's going on?"

"What?" Michael stopped at the light and glanced at her.

"With your brother."

"Nothing."

His features were set in hard planes. Had the question or the incident spawned his irritation? Since she didn't have a lot invested in this relationship yet and it might be too hot for her to handle anyway, her need to know was more important than his delicate ego. "It didn't look like nothing."

"Trust me. It was nothing." The light changed and he turned onto the main road.

"Really? Because I saw something and I'm still seeing something. Something really grumpy. I've never dated any of the seven dwarves before, so I might be wrong, but it really does look like Grumpy."

He struggled to hold on to his stiff, annoyed expression for a few seconds before caving and grinning at her. "Grumpy?"

"Yes. So are you going to tell me what was going on or do I have to reference a few more kids' movies?"

"My brother doesn't think I should be seeing anyone local since I'm not going to be around long."

Hands clutching steering wheel. No effort made to meet her eyes. Carefully chosen words. There was at least half a lie in there. Instinct demanded she run it down, but that could be another reason her first dates so rarely turned into second dates and those almost never turned into third dates. Michael was not nine and her natural suspicion needed to take a hike. "You're going to need to go over a block. This street doesn't have an exit onto the highway."

Now he made an effort to meet her eyes. "You don't care that I'm... not local?"

See, this was where she was growing as a person. That little hesitation should be driving her nuts, but it wasn't. Or it was and she was ignoring it. Personal growth. "It's a date not a courtship. Besides, I'm not sleeping with you."

Michael turned onto a side street, but didn't hit the gas. Instead, he let the car coast. A wise decision since he was staring at her. "You're not?"

"No. Were you under the impression I would?"

The car drifted to the right, but he corrected it without looking. "I was still working on where we were going to eat lunch."

"Anywhere's fine with me. There isn't a lot around the museum though and it's going to take almost an hour to get there, so we should probably eat before we get out of town." Maureen fixed her gaze out the windshield. He still stared at her with about the same expression he'd had when agreeing to go to the museum. He stopped the car at the end of the block without looking at the sign or the traffic. When he made no effort to pull out, she turned to him. "There's a Subway about a block that way. If you're in the mood for a burger, there's a great local place called The Station, but it's kinda out of the way."

"I don't mind out of the way."

"Then go straight to the next stop sign and turn right. We have to go over the highway to the other side of town."

* * * *

Bear squeezed Maureen's hand and studied the artistically arranged bones. Definitely a dinosaur. He had to take them at their word that it came from China. That she'd wanted to go to a museum still warped his mind a little. A museum. He hadn't been in one since he got out of school. More proof Maureen wasn't your average, ordinary, everyday girl.

Then again, maybe she was and he'd just been steeped in wacko, weird girls for too long. To flat out announce she wasn't having sex with him couldn't be what regular girls did. He hadn't even thought that far ahead.

That was a lie. He'd been thinking about it since the moment he'd glanced over his shoulder and seen her leaning against the Satellite, her dress accenting her trim little waist and the swell of her breasts. A lotta dreams last night had his greasy handprints all over that dress. And her creamy flesh.

Yeah, that would be the woman holding his hand in a natural history museum, wearing jeans and a turtleneck, who had announced on the way here she wasn't having sex with him. He studied her profile as she read the plaque. No way he was getting any of that unless he played the fame card. Which might only get him a slap in the face. That would suck.

No matter what he did, this experiment was going to be a failure. Sure, he had a couple of days when he got to pretend to be a guy with a girl, but he wasn't going to get the girl in any way. He got to enjoy the illusion without anything else.

"The kids'll love this." Maureen sighed. "They are going to go bonkers."

Bear admired the glow to her face. She was already excited for the kids. Once upon a time, he'd had that glow about his shows. When he knew how excited the fans would be to see them and he'd been excited for them in advance. Someday, he hoped to get that back.

"So, do you want to see the rest of the exhibits?" Maureen asked. "There's a really cool fish."

"Well, if there's a really cool fish." Bear draped his arm around her shoulders. "Are you wearing perfume?"

"No."

"What is that sweet scent?"

"Probably shampoo. What does it smell like?"

"Lemons."

"That's the body wash." She guided him out of the special exhibit and past the planetarium.

"Lemon scented body wash?" Why was it perfect that Maureen would use lemon scented body wash? He brushed his nose across her velvet cheek. Yep, lemons.

"I have one or two indulgences."

"Really?" Really? Beater car, cheap lunch, tiny house. What could she be indulging in? Better question. What did she consider an indulgence? And how difficult would it be to fulfill those indulgences? "Like what?"

"Why?" She stopped in the middle of a display of volcanoes and looked at him. Her eyes sparkled. "Do you plan on bribing me for some reason?"

Busted. "Maybe I'm just trying to learn what makes women tick."

"I don't know that I'm the best one to study for that."

"Why?"

She quirked one corner of her lips. "Don't you think I'm special?"

"Of course."

"Then why are you using me to figure out what women in general are like?"

"Got me. Maybe I am trying to bribe you."

"Now I have to wonder what for."

He hooked his finger under her chin. "Life is better with mystery."

"Is it?"

Out of the corner of his eye, he saw something glittering. "What's in there?"

"That's the gem room."

"Let's look." He towed her into the gem room. Hundreds of stones sparkled under pinpoint spotlights. Several cases held semiprecious stones the size and shape of eggs. Bear leaned over a case full of different colored diamonds. This was more his element. "This is pretty cool."

"They're neat." Maureen stood beside him with her head cocked.

"Which one would you want?"

"I'm not much of a jewelry person."

"You're not?" His eyes went out of focus for a second. A woman who didn't like jewelry? When he could see straight again, he turned to her and realized that, other than a watch, she wasn't wearing a single link, stone, or bead. "You don't wear jewelry at all?"

"I used to, but when I was student teaching I leaned over a kid to help her with something and my necklace got caught in her hair. After that I stopped."

"But nothing at all? I can't imagine a woman who doesn't love jewelry."

Maureen shrugged. "Has nothing to do with loving or not loving, it's just not practical. Necklaces and bracelets catch, rings scratch, earrings get lost, but I have a lot of barrettes." She reached back and touched her hair, which she hadn't pulled back today.

"So barrettes are one of your indulgences?" The gems lost interest for him. The woman in front of his was too much of a gem for them to compete.

"No, I get most of them from the kids. Early in my career I was warned that if I didn't plant an idea for Christmas presents, I was doomed to get half a dozen coffee cups every year. Instead I get a half dozen barrettes every year."

Damn, jewelry was his best girlfriend gift. He knew how to shop for it, how to give it and how it would be appreciated.

Of course, it was meant for a girlfriend. Maureen wasn't a girlfriend. She didn't know who he was and was willing to let him take her out a few times while he was in town. Bear kissed her cheek. "At least they're something you can use."

"That's what I figured."

Bear guided her out of the room. "So what are these indulgences of yours?"

"Why are you so interested?"

"Because you're not telling me."

"That makes sense," she muttered.

"Of course it does." He'd ignore her sarcasm. "Why don't we just end the run around? Tell me what these indulgences are."

"You're not letting this go."

"No, I'm not."

She giggled. "Well, that might make me happy this is going to be a short lived relationship."

"Since it's going to be short lived you have every reason to be completely honest with me." God, he was a hypocrite.

"Don't you think it's a better reason to be dishonest?" she asked. "Then for the rest of our lives we can be the perfect one who got away."

"Hmm. Do I want knowledge or mystery? I've decided. I want knowledge. Tell me."

"Here's the fish."

They were standing in front of a huge case filled by a petrified fish. It looked like a piranha, but six feet long. "That is cool."

"It's my favorite thing in this museum."

"It's not going to get you out of answering my question." Bear turned away from the giant fish so he could study her. As much as he enjoyed this little game, he wanted answers.

She stared into his eyes for a long time. Hers were dark, the look in them almost challenging and a little smile flickered around her mouth. In the accent lights, her lips shone too temptingly. He tried to consider the consequences for kissing her here, right in front of the fish, but thoughts of what her lips would feel and taste like kept getting in the way. Then there was what her body would feel like when he wrapped his arms around her.

"Lemon Sugar body wash, Godiva chocolates and *The X-Files*."

Chapter 3

"What?" Bear tried to pull himself back into focus. Twice she'd done that in the last five minutes.

"My indulgences. You wanted to know. Fresh Lemon Sugar body wash, Godiva chocolates and *The X-Files*." She cocked her head and smiled up at him. "Happy?"

No. He kinda wished he'd skipped the answers and gone for the kiss. Even with the fish watching.

"Miss Donnelly! Miss Donnelly!" A little girl with long blond hair ran over and grabbed Maureen's hand. "What are you doing here?"

"I came to see the dinosaurs. What are you doing here?"

"I'm with Daddy this weekend." The girl turned in the direction of a medium sized guy walking toward them. "Daddy, look, it's Miss Donnelly. I told you she was pretty."

"Yes, honey, you did." The guy held out his hand. "Nice to meet you, Miss Donnelly. Lindsey talks about you all the time."

"She's an excellent student. I graded the math tests this morning and you did very well."

"She likes being in your class," Lindsey's dad said. While the man kept his gaze on Maureen, his focus on Bear was so tight it felt like a smothering pillow.

"I like having her in my class. Lindsey, are you studying for your Monday spelling quiz? You have an unbroken streak to protect."

"I know." Lindsey pulled a scrap of paper out of her pocket and waved it around. "I look at it all the time."

"Unbroken streak?" Lindsey's father asked.

"I give the kids their spelling words on Friday and we have a quiz on Monday. If they get them all right Monday, they get free reading time on Friday when the other kids take the spelling test. Lindsey hasn't had to take the Friday spelling test since Thanksgiving."

The proud father beamed. "Really? Lindsey, you didn't tell me that."

The way this guy was eyeing Maureen, he was going to be taking a much bigger interest in his daughter's school career.

Lindsey's father turned to him in obvious appraisal. The expression on his face reminded Bear of beta fish glaring through their little glass windows at any other fish around, except this guy wasn't flashy enough to be beta fish material. He was more of a plain lake trout. A nice local lake trout who wasn't going to be going on tour for the next nine or ten months or how ever long this fucking tour was supposed to last.

"You haven't introduced us to your date," he said.

"This is my friend Michael. Michael, this is Lindsey Conner and her dad, Mr. Conner."

"Hi." Bear held out his hand. Conner had an I-can-take-him gleam in his eye that made him want to turn this handshake into arm wrestling. Right. Conner had no clue what he was dealing with. Not only could he not take Bear, he wouldn't be able to handle a woman as hot as Maureen. Of course, Conner was also part of her realistic dating pool and it wouldn't be fair to scare off the competition before she had a chance to size him up.

Conner had no such qualms and gripped him like his hand was a boa constrictor and he was fighting for his life. Bear started to squeeze back, but the other man yanked his hand away before he could get a serious grip going.

"Nice to meet you," Conner said, backing up a step, proving himself to be more of a guppy than a beta fish. "We should leave you alone."

"Aw, Daddy," Lindsey whined.

"Honey, it's Miss Donnelly's day off. We should leave her alone with her boyfriend." Conner put his hand on his daughter's shoulder and pulled her away. "It was nice meeting you, Miss Donnelly."

"'Bye, Miss Donnelly," Lindsey said over her shoulder as her father beat a hasty retreat.

"Well, that was a little weird," Maureen said, after father and daughter had disappeared around another display. "For a minute there I thought we were going to end up on a double date. I wonder why Lindsey's father suddenly got the attack of manners."

Bear shrugged. The whole pissing contest had only taken about two and a half seconds. Not long enough for her to even notice. He hadn't been the one to start it either. His conscience was clean. Conner wanted the battle. He'd also realized he was in over his head and retreated before it got obvious.

Conner was also going to be here in two weeks and had a good reason to visit Maureen. He'd lost the battle, but he had a better chance of winning the war.

"Cool dinosaurs," Bear said, pulling Maureen toward the T. Rex skeleton looming over the next room.

* * * *

At her house, Maureen found herself contemplating coffee again. He'd indulged her for hours at the museum, wandering around, looking at everything with more than polite interest. While she wasn't paying attention, he'd gotten a restaurant recommendation from a staffer. Not the kind of place she frequented. Cloth napkins, crystal stemware, multiple utensils. The last time a date tried to impress her, he'd taken her to Red Lobster—and she'd been impressed.

It made her wonder what he expected.

And, if she wouldn't give it. The way she'd been tingling in front of the bonefish, he didn't have to try so hard. If Lindsey and her dad had shown up five minutes later, they might have rushed away a lot faster. Her resistance only lasted so long.

Michael was just so darn delicious to look at. Add that to how polite, nice and patient he was and the way his scent made her blood sing and resistance really was futile. What was the point of resisting anyway?

Oh yeah. Michael's brother Tony had a first grader and she didn't need that kind of reputation, considering some of the busy bodies posing as parents. Life was difficult enough without inviting trouble.

Did trouble always have to come in such marvelous packaging?

"So do you want to come in?" She kicked herself the moment the question was out. Of course he did. Based on the gleam in his eyes at the museum, he wanted to come in for coffee and stay for breakfast.

He frowned at her. "Um, okay." Reaching for the door handle, he hesitated. "Just so we're clear, you're inviting me in for a drink or something, right?"

Shoot, the packaging was really good. "I was thinking along the lines of coffee, yes." *Ha! More like coffee, tea or me.*

"Perfect." He jumped out and ran around the car to open the door for her. All day long, she hadn't been allowed to open a single door for herself. Michael *had* to be gentlemanly on top of everything else.

Maureen allowed him to usher her into the house. What about asking him in for coffee was perfect? He hadn't sounded sarcastic and if he was being sarcastic, why had he accepted? What man in his right mind was happy to find out that coffee wasn't a code word for horizontal mambo?

She shrugged out of her coat and threw it over the back of the chair. "I'll get the coffee going."

"You need help with anything?"

You could help me by not being so perfectly, weirdly normal. "No, I've got it."

In the kitchen, she started the coffee pot and debated breaking out her cream and sugar set. It distracted her from debating what was going on with Michael. He wasn't acting like any other guy she'd ever dated and seemed really happy about it. Why was he happy that she'd put the brakes on last night, announced she wasn't sleeping with him this afternoon and spelled out that coffee was just coffee tonight? Coffee. She was supposed to be thinking about that so she didn't have to think about Michael and his mysteries.

"So what did you think of Lindsey's father?"

Maureen turned away from the cupboard. Michael stood in the kitchen door with a curious expression on his face. "What?"

"Lindsey's father. What did you think of him?"

There he was, doing mysterious stuff again. Asking weird questions out of left field. To be honest, she'd done it to him, so this was fair play. "What about him?"

"Would you go out with him?"

"I couldn't. He's the father of one of my students." Maureen took out her cream and sugar set so she would have something to do with her hands. The small pitcher and sugar bowl were shaped like a bucket and a watering can.

"So?"

Maureen poured milk into the watering can. "It's unethical to date the father of a student."

"What about this summer when she's not your student anymore?" Michael leaned on the counter.

"It's still an ethical gray area and I try to stay out of those." She put the milk back in the fridge. "Is there a reason you're trying to fix me up with another man?"

"Just wondering what you'll do when I leave."

She faced him. This was weird behavior. Really weird. "I was thinking about throwing myself off a tall building from grief. Would that be too much?"

Michael stared at her.

"It was a joke," Maureen said. She took two coffee mugs out of the cupboard. The coffee pot gurgled to a finish.

"I figured," he said after a too long pause.

A terrible joke. "Where is it you live anyway? You never said."

"California."

"North, south, someplace in the middle?" She could handle a bit of mystery in her life, but so far all she'd managed to find out about him was his passion for muscle cars and what he liked to watch on TV.

"South. Malibu."

The name rang a vague bell, but she couldn't place it. That only meant it wasn't a state capitol. "Malibu? Isn't that near Los Angeles?" She poured the coffee and held out a cup. It had bears holding up a sign that said, *Teacher, I love you beary much.*

"Yeah." Michael took the cup and looked at it suspiciously.

"I know where I've heard of it now. Famous people live there." Maureen put milk and sugar into her cup. "Have any famous neighbors?"

"Famous neighbors?" He held the cup like he'd forgotten what it was for.

"Yeah, famous neighbors. Do you want cream or sugar?" She shouldn't have bothered. Now she had to wash them.

"No, thanks. I take it black." Michael sipped from his cup. "I buy groceries at the same place as Rick Allen."

"Oh, really? Is he an actor?"

"He's a drummer."

"He wasn't in *Toy Story*?"

"No, he's in Def Leppard."

"Oh." Maureen nodded. "That must be interesting. Do you want to go sit down in the living room?"

Michael stared at her for another beat. "Sure."

She sat down sideways on the couch and curled her feet under her so she could face him. "Where are you from originally?"

"Detroit."

"How did you end up in California?"

He shifted the cup around in his hand. "Work."

"You didn't want to go into business with your brother?" Maureen relaxed into the back of the couch, willing him to follow suit. He sat with both hands clutching the cup and both feet on the floor, looking less comfortable than if he were on the wrong side of the principal's desk.

"No. What about you? Are you from around here?"

She shrugged. "Pretty close. I grew up in a little town about a hundred miles south of here, but they didn't need any teachers when I needed a job."

"You like it."

"I love it. I wouldn't do it otherwise. It's too hard."

Michael shifted toward her. "Really? Why's it hard?"

"Lots of planning, lots of effort and sometimes that horse just won't drink."

"That little girl today seemed pretty excited about you."

"She's one of my fans. They aren't all like that."

Michael took a drink of his coffee and gestured to the bookshelf in the corner. "You have a lot of dinosaur books."

"I like dinosaurs and I work with little boys who also like dinosaurs. What about you? Other than cars and *The Simpsons*, what do you like?"

He took one hand off the coffee cup, reached over and brushed his fingers down hers. "I'm liking you a lot."

"You know that wasn't what I meant." Her whole being centered on his touch, making following the conversation difficult.

"It wasn't?" He worked his fingers under her palm and started drawing circles on the back of her hand with his thumb.

"I was thinking about hobbies and interests." She couldn't manage a decent breath. Only the top third of her lungs were operating and it was making her dizzy. Or maybe it was his touch making her dizzy. Either way, she needed to put down her coffee cup before she dropped it.

"You're interesting." He leaned over, set his coffee cup on the table and when he sat back, turned toward her.

"Not that interesting."

"You'd be surprised." He brought her hand to his lips.

The fingers around her cup got very jealous and distracted, but just as they mutinied, Michael caught the cup and put it on the table. Maureen shivered as he leaned in closer.

"I think you're fascinating," Michael murmured just before pressing his lips to hers. He cupped her cheek, and still held her hand.

Maureen parted her lips under his gentle assault. Her free hand strayed across his chest, exploring the tempting hardness she'd been sneaking peeks at all day. Exactly as hard and molded as she'd thought. He groaned against her mouth. The sound vibrated through her and raised her temperature. The turtleneck was a bad choice. Too hot. She needed to take it off right now. Bunching her fingers in his shirt, she decided his shirt was too hot too, and she needed to know what his bare skin felt like. No other man had ever made her feel this reckless. She couldn't decide whether she should push him onto his back or lean back, pulling him on top of her.

Michael made the decision for her. He sat back, still holding her hand and blinking. "Well, that's some coffee."

"Yeah." Was he up to innuendos about dessert, and was she really up to offering? This was a second date. She had a reason for resisting. Was she prepared to toss that reason out the window?

"I should probably go." Michael stood, a little unsteadily. "Are you coming to the garage in the morning?"

"Only if you come get me. My car is still there." She stood too. There was still time to offer dessert. It would save him a trip.

"Great. I'll get you for lunch again."

"I'll have to bring some work with me."

"Oh." He frowned. "I am being a big time suck, huh? Do you—are you sure you can afford to lose the time? I can just bring the car over tomorrow afternoon when I'm done. You don't have to be there."

She knotted her hands behind her back. Dang it, he was doing it again. Mixing his signals. Assuming she wanted to be at the garage and then telling her she didn't need to be. Push, pull. That alone should have been enough to make her remember she was fixed here probably with his nephew in her class next year while he'd be leaving. Imagine the parent teacher conferences with Tony and Pam D'Amato sitting across the desk from her.

Imagine missing out on Michael. "Don't you want me at the garage?"

"Yeah, but not if you don't have the time. I mean, I don't want to get in the way of your job."

"I can bring what I need." Except the computer to put the grades into. Lugging her desktop to the garage would be overkill. It was early enough to get some done tonight.

And after he left town, she'd have plenty of time.

"I'll just bring along what I need. Unless you don't want me there."

He gave her a crooked grin. "Baby, I'm starting to want you everywhere." Dragging her into his arms, he kissed her again, bending her back.

Maureen sunk her fingers into his shoulders as a tide of heat engulfed her. Parent teacher conferences with the D'Amato's were a long way away and her personal life wasn't any of their business. She wanted this, now. To hell with the consequences. Maureen wrapped her arms around his shoulders, pulling herself up his body until he groaned. His fingers clutched the back of her shirt.

"You are no average, ordinary girl," he murmured, brushing his lips along her jaw.

"I never claimed to be anything I wasn't."

"No, you didn't." He lifted his face from hers. "I better get out of here before this gets out of control. I really am trying to be a good guy here."

"Is that what you're doing?" She'd tried to sound playful and did manage a smile to go with it, but the question rang through her mind with anguish.

"Can't fuck with the locals." He put his hands on her shoulders and took a step back. She thought she heard the sound of Velco separating, but she might have been imagining it. "Tomorrow. Lunch, and then you can hang out at the garage while I tune up your car."

Maureen followed him to the door. "I'll be ready."

"Good." After he opened the door, he kissed her forehead. "I'll see you tomorrow." He pulled the door closed behind him, leaving her staring at it.

Can't fuck with the locals? What did that mean?

* * * *

Bear backed the Satellite out of the driveway. Early evening again. Maybe not for her, but nine o'clock was pretty early for him to end a date.

If he hadn't ended this date when he had, he would have to regretted it. Damn, two days into this charade and it was already rubbing him raw.

He wanted her. In fact, he was starting to think he wanted her every day, morning, noon and night in a permanent, legal kind of way. Lust was part of it. That cute little bob and flowered turtleneck look covered a hot chick. The body, the responses, the innocent delight in her eyes. Such a turn on. Way past the fuck-me heels and nothing left to the imagination cleavage he was usually treated to.

Another component too. One that upped the ante into something he didn't recognize. This settled quiet, a calm center. There had to be a word for what she had, but he didn't know it. She knew who she was. Really knew.

That went well beyond the fact that she didn't know who Rick Allen was. Which meant she might not know who *he* was. Not that he was in the same league, but she wasn't going to know anything about his band. She seemed to be clueless about any pop culture that didn't impact little kids. A quick scan of her living room while she'd been in the kitchen had revealed lots of dinosaur books, a coffee table book on Disney World and a stack of gardening magazines. She didn't appear to own a single compact disk. Not even a soundtrack.

If he'd told her who he was last night when she walked into the garage, she probably would have cocked her head, told him it must be interesting and asked if he could still fix her brakes. He'd really screwed himself there. If he'd just 'fessed up in the first place, he could have been doing all this aboveboard and maybe had a chance at something real. But no, he'd decided to be a genius and pretend to be someone he wasn't. Someone ordinary. Now if he told her who he was, she'd think he was either insane or a liar.

Tony and Pam would have killed him if he hadn't come home tonight. They might anyway. Watching Maureen with that little girl today, Bear could see why they wanted her to be Nicky's teacher. The kid had come at her out of left field and she'd been nice and attentive. Not at all bothered by them bugging her on her day off. Nicky would shine under that influence. If Bear got in too deep with Maureen, she wouldn't be teaching Nicky. She'd said dating the father of a student was an ethical violation. Dating an uncle probably was too.

He'd rolled his own loaded dice and still managed to get snake eyes.

* * * *

Maureen peeked down the hall to the garage and tried to figure out what she was doing here. The obvious reason—getting her car tuned up. Important regular maintenance. Then there was the less obvious. Hanging out with Michael. What did she hope to gain, other than the tuned up car, from spending her Sunday at Tony's garage working on lesson plans while Michael worked on her car? This wasn't going to turn into a relationship. How could it, after next weekend?

She sat down on the stool behind the counter where she had all her work spread out. Everything was finished and recorded in her grade book. Tomorrow she had recess duty, so she'd need to commune with the copier after school. Unless Michael was free. If he was, she might have to go in early so she could leave right after the last bell.

Michael walked in, wiping his hands on an oily rag. "How's the work going?"

"I'm done." She leaned on the counter. Something about being near him made her arch her back and lick her lips. My, he was fine to look at. Beautiful broad shoulders that made her think about hanging onto them. Dark eyes that always made him look ready and willing. Last night's kisses suggested all kinds of wonders.

"*The X-Files*," he said.

"What about it?"

"I've been thinking about that. It doesn't make sense."

"Why not?"

He slouched on the counter and looked at her sideways, giving her a nice profile of his flat abs. Most of the guys she dated were not in as good shape. Desk jockeys a little on the soft side. Nothing soft on him, except his gaze, especially when he looked at her like he was now.

"You don't like mysteries, but from what I heard *The X-Files* was all mystery all the time. It doesn't fit," he said. His gaze traced the jutting curve of her hip.

"Maybe I like my mysteries in small controlled portions I don't have to live with."

His gaze traveled back up her body and her temperature rose too. When his eyes met hers, they were dark and warm. "I guess I can take that answer."

Licking her lips didn't help. If anything, her tongue was drier than her lips. "So how goes the tune up?"

"Finished."

She nodded, trying to maintain some cool. "That leaves us most of an afternoon free. What shall we do with it?" Bad question. The images blossoming in her mind were not PG.

He smiled like he had the same thoughts. "The first thing I need to do is wash up. I wouldn't want to get grease all over you."

The images in her mind went straight through R on their way to X. With grease. On the hood of his car. This counted as a third date, didn't it? There had been a meal involved. Maureen followed him into the hall. "So I guess the first thing we should do, after you wash up and change, is take my car back home."

"Sure." He stopped in the locker room doorway, letting his gaze skim over her again.

Pink sweater, jeans, sneakers. She wouldn't be winning any fashion awards any time soon. Still, the look in his eyes was appreciative.

He shifted away from the door. "You know, we haven't discussed payment."

"No, we haven't." Maureen bit her lip and shifted her weight to one foot. "I believe last time it was a kiss on the cheek for a brake job, but a tune up isn't quite as involved, is it?"

"No, but my rates may be going up." Michael took a step closer.

"Isn't that how it always is?" She leaned on the wall. "They hook you with a deal and then jack up the prices."

"Sorry ma'am, it's the way business is run."

His coveralls were filthy. So were his hands. Her clothes would be ruined and everybody would be able to see why. She should be concerned about that. Heat coursed through her as he moved closer. No way she should be doing this.

"You aren't going to try to haggle me down?" He brushed his lips over hers.

"Quality work comes at a price." As his mouth covered hers, she closed her eyes. Only his mouth touched her, but she could feel the heat of his body. The wine sweet taste of his kiss made her knees want to collapse so she could slide to the floor and pull him down on top of her.

The dirty floor. She shouldn't be getting involved in this.

"Michael." She planted her hands on his chest.

He took a step back. "Yeah. I'm gonna go change." He walked into the locker room without turning back.

Maureen went back to the front desk and gathered up her stuff. Her head spun from their brief encounter. When did he say he was leaving town? Next week? How in heaven's name would she resist him until then? If only he was going to be around.

Or if she could go to where he'd be. He said he lived in California. They had schools there.

Was she honestly planning to move to the other side of the country based on the fact that she couldn't keep her hands off a man she'd just met? Crazy. She couldn't sell her house and switch jobs for a guy she'd met two days ago. The long gap between Christmas and spring break was obviously getting to her. She slid her planning book into her book bag. Time off, that's what she needed. Maybe she should take a personal day.

Next week.

Before Michael left town.

Friday.

A locker door banged closed. Should she tell him she was taking a day off? If things got weird before then, she'd had a long weekend to recover and if they didn't, she'd have a long weekend to enjoy him before he left.

Michael came out still wiping his hands. He tossed the paper towel in the trash. "So what would you like to do with the rest of the day?"

"I think first we should get my car to my house. I'm going to need it in the morning."

He nodded. "I'll follow you. Are you sure you got everything you needed to do done?"

"Sure." She sucked her teeth. "Why are you so worried?"

"I don't want to take up all your time." He laced his fingers through hers. "I don't want to leave town and have you all pissed off at me because you're way behind on the rest of your life."

"It's not like you're ever going to see me again. Why do you care?" Why did he care? Even if he came back it wasn't like they had a chance in Hades of anything developing.

"I'm trying to be a good guy here." His phone started to ring. He pulled it out of his back pocket, glanced at the screen and shoved it back into his pocket. "I don't want to screw up your life."

"Don't you need to get that?"

"No." His phone stopped. He pulled her closer. "So after we take your car home, what do you want to do?"

"It looks like you might have a plan."

"I might."

His phone started ringing again.

"Are you sure you don't need to get that?"

"Positive. It's not important." He wrapped his arm around her waist. As soon as she was pressed against his hard chest, she forgot everything beyond him.

Until his phone rang again.

"Fuck." Michael yanked his phone out of his pocket. "Give me just a minute."

Maureen hung onto the counter so she wouldn't slide to the floor as he walked down the hall. Everything moved way too fast with him. Hadn't she said something about ethical gray areas the other day? Yesterday. That had been yesterday. Yup, things were moving way too fast with Michael.

"Vacation," he said loud enough for her to hear from the garage. He wasn't shouting, but he had a hefty roar. She'd never heard him get mad before. Of course the last three days had been all wine and roses. Well, pizza and museums. With nothing to lose, what did they have to fight about?

"I told you I'd do it and I will. Just fucking back off."

Maureen peered down the hall. He was pacing between their cars, his face an alarming shade. Maybe he was concerned she was blowing off work because he was. Well, he'd have plenty of time to do whatever he was supposed to be doing while she was in school tomorrow. No way she could tell him she'd be taking Friday off. At least not until she ascertained whether she'd be spending a long weekend with him, or spending it licking her wounds.

Still on the phone, he came toward her. "Relax. Sales will pick up. Give me a couple of days and stop acting like an old woman. I'll be back soon enough. See ya then." He snapped the phone closed, all his annoyance disappearing. "So, what do you want to do tonight?"

Chapter 4

"I'll go get lunch." Bear pulled open the door of the Satellite.

"You buying?" Tony grumbled.

"Sure." He backed the car out of the garage. Lunch was a small price to pay to escape Tony's endless foul mood. Friday's irritation had become Saturday's grouse, which turned into Sunday's growl. By the end of the week he'd be spitting flames. And why? Because they wanted Maureen to be Nicky's teacher next year. What exactly was stopping them? By the time Nicky started second grade, he'd be touring Europe and Maureen would be dating some damp sponge like Conner.

Bear glared at the light, considering the guy Maureen might be dating next fall. He wouldn't appreciate her. How could he? Conner didn't have any basis for comparison, while *he* had a great one. Between the girls he'd dated and the girls the other guys had dated and the mobs of groupies he'd met, he had an excellent basis for comparison. Maureen came out head and shoulders above them all. She had this sweet hot thing going on that threatened to cook his engine every time he got near her. And she was smart and so practical. Most women seemed to think he had at least a twenty percent stake in the moon and they expected their expense account to reflect it.

Too bad he couldn't box her up for take out.

Passing the elementary school, he caught sight of her car. He turned around at the next intersection and went back. The three story red brick building looked like it had been popped out of a mold in the early fifties. He and Tony had gone to a school a lot like it in a different state. Switching the radio off, he cruised through the parking lot. Definitely her car.

The playground behind the building overflowed with screaming kids. They seemed to feel obligated to burn up as much energy as possible before the whistle blew. Bear parked the Satellite at the end of a row and peered through the windshield at the two teachers standing on the steps.

One of them was a hot pink puffball in a knee length parka. The other was Maureen.

A hundred feet away in a coat and hat and he knew it was her. Damn, she was hot.

His phone rang. He dug it out and checked the number. Marc. "What now?"

"I wanted to know if you'd scheduled that drop-in."

"What are you? My mom? I told you I would and I did. Happy?"

"Yes."

He tried to make out the expression on Maureen's face, but she was a little too far away. She'd been happy last night. Very happy. So had he, and he couldn't remember the last time he'd been that happy not getting off.

"Are you even listening to me?"

"No."

Marc sighed. "Look, I know we've been bugging you a lot this break, but there's a lot riding on this album."

"And you know what? All the promotion in the world isn't going to help until the tour starts."

"The tour isn't selling."

The last album had sucked, but not so bad it should be killing the new one. "What exactly do you mean, the tour isn't selling?"

"I mean we start touring in a month and we don't have a single venue even half sold."

"You're kidding."

"I wish I was."

Maureen was turned toward the far side of the playground. That woman was too good for a one-night stand. Too good for a one-week stand. Damn, he'd miss her. "I'm doing a drop-in Friday. See if Candy can scare up an interview in the same city and I'll hit the forum."

"The forum? You know all those folks already got their tickets. Plus they're crazy."

"I know, that's why we need them. They're crazy about us so they'll talk up the album, request the songs and convince their friends to go to the shows."

"True. Good to hear you thinking again."

Thinking. Yeah, about how he should have been staying away from Maureen Donnelly. She was a nice woman who deserved a stable romance, not some gypsy musician who was going to rip her life apart like a time bomb when somebody realized who he was and who she was to him. Some of the women on the forum, for instance.

* * * *

"So how was your weekend?" Linda asked, surveying the playground with her hands stuffed in the sleeves of her coat.

Maureen hadn't noticed the chilly weather all weekend. Okay, she hadn't noticed anything. "Great." She caught herself grinning. Great almost defined it.

"Great?" Linda turned to study her. "Did you call Greg?"

"Oh, I forgot." Forgot to call Greg, forgot to do laundry, forgot to get groceries. But she'd gotten her brakes fixed and her car tuned up. Yesterday afternoon she'd almost gotten a tune up of her own on the couch. Her mouth curled into a dizzy grin again.

"What did you do all weekend that was so great?"

"Michael." Her mouth snapped shut as Linda's eyes went round. "No, I mean I spent all weekend with Michael. I mean—" Maureen pinched the tip of her tongue between her teeth as if that would make the words come out right. "I was hanging out with Michael every day. We went to the dinosaur exhibit. The kids are going to love it."

"Yeah." Linda pulled her hands out of her sleeves and folded her arms in the 'you're in trouble' pose she used on the kids. "Who is Michael? Not that mechanic."

Her face now frozen in a ridiculous grin, she nodded.

"I can't believe you spent an entire weekend with a mechanic."

"What's wrong with it? I got my brakes fixed and my car tuned up for free."

Linda cocked an eyebrow. "Free, huh?"

As the subtext sunk in, her grin melted. She should have guessed what people would think. Who was she kidding? She had guessed, she'd just been pretending it didn't matter.

If they found out. Who said they had to find out? It was called a personal life for a reason.

"He fixed my car and took me to the museum and we hung out and watched TV. I like him, okay? Besides, he's not even going to be in town for long. Just a week."

Linda snorted. "That sounds like a really going somewhere relationship."

"Well, looking for Mr. Right hasn't gotten me anywhere so I'm taking a break."

"J'maya Drake, I see you climbing that fence! Down. Now," Linda bellowed before turning back to Maureen. "I just don't understand why you're wasting your time with this grease monkey."

"Because I want to." Maureen half turned, pretending to survey the far side of the playground for infractions. She liked Michael. He made her feel hot and shivery and oh so enticing. Every time he said he was trying to be a good guy his voice got huskier. It made her wish she had another reason to wear the blue dress.

It made her want to go out and buy a whole wardrobe of stuff that would make him grind his teeth while he tried to be a good guy. "Linda, it's my life and I'm tired of safe bets."

"It's your life until it blows up in your face and you're crying over coffee in my kitchen."

She shrugged. "So, have some coffee ready, and bake some of those cinnamon chip cookies to dunk in it. This cry is going to be a bad one and I'm going to love every minute of earning it."

* * * *

Her leg ground against his cock and he shuddered. Returning the favor, he brought his knee up tight between her legs, making her moan. He slid his hands under her shirt and up her bare back. This was as close to naked as he'd gotten with her and he was pretty happy with it. Frustrated as fuck, but happy.

The X-Files theme started to play. Tonight, like every other night this week, they'd gotten dinner, returned to her house to watch TV and ended up necking on the couch. For the rest of his life, that theme was going to make him hot and sweaty. "Baby, you are killing me."

She started kissing his neck and giggling.

God, this woman was amazing. The way her soft body rubbed him in all the right ways made him never want to get off this couch. He smoothed his hands down her satin skin. "You are going to make me stop being a good guy."

"Maybe that's what I want." She teased his ear lobe with her tongue.

His body tensed and snapped like he'd grabbed the jumper cables at the wrong time. "What?" he asked.

She arched up over him, her eyes dark. "I said, maybe that's what I want."

He bit back a whimper. *Don't fuck with the locals.* "What do you mean?"

"I want you, Michael. I have totally inappropriate thoughts about you in the middle of the day." She brushed her lips along his jaw. "I'm being aggressive and asking for what I want. Give me some positive reinforcement."

"Positive reinforcement?" *Don't fuck with the locals.* "Maureen."

"I have a surprise for you." She started working her way down his neck again, roaming his sides with her hands.

Surprise? She had no idea.

"I took tomorrow off. Since you're leaving Monday, I thought we could have a long weekend."

Long weekend. Very long. He couldn't do this. He couldn't sleep with her if she didn't know the truth. "My brother is going to kill me."

"Your brother?" Maureen hesitated. Then her hesitation turned into a full-blown pause. She sat back looking like the recipient of a bucket of cold water in the face. "Ah. I forgot about—well, I forgot about the whole rest of the world for a couple of minutes there. Can't always get what you want, right?"

If the Stones were right, you could always get what you needed and he needed Maureen. Bear sat up. She was still straddling his knees and well within reach. "You took tomorrow off?"

She shrugged. "I thought I'd either want to spend the weekend with you or need the mental health day to recover." She poked his nose with the tip of her finger.

He stroked her cheek. Her warm soft spirit flowed into him. At this moment he wanted a lot more than a long weekend. She was such a genuine, sweet woman. So true, so real.

And he'd been lying to her since the minute he met her. "I have surprise for you too."

"Really?" She cocked her head. "Am I gonna like it?"

"You're either going to like it or you're going to slap me really hard." Bear gritted his teeth.

Her pretty grin melted off her face and she suddenly looked a lot more like a teacher. "You did promise me you weren't a serial killer."

"I'm not a serial killer." He swallowed. The slap was a more likely outcome. In about ten seconds he was going to get a lesson in never lying to a woman. Especially one who might turn out to be more than a passing fancy. "I'm not a mechanic either."

"What did you do to my car?"

"I fixed it. I know how to fix cars. That's just not my day job."

"You're starting to make me really nervous." She leaned back like she was about to bolt.

Bear grabbed her hands. Her body weight bent his knees backward, which wasn't the most comfortable position in the world, but he was afraid if she moved away he'd never get her back. "Wait. I'm sorry. I never meant to lie to you. I thought it would be one evening and a pizza and that would be it. Then it turned into the weekend and now it's—"

"I did mention that you were making me nervous." She was letting him hold her hands, but that was it.

"I'm a musician."

"A musician."

"Yes."

Her frown deepened. "And what is the problem with that?"

"Well." What was the problem with that? "I'm kinda famous and I really wanted you to like me for me."

"I've never heard of you."

"There's a signed picture of my band up in the garage."

"There is?"

"There was. I took it down Saturday morning because I didn't want you to see it." His hands started sweating and not in a good way.

"Because you didn't want me to know you were famous?"

"Yeah."

She pulled her hands out of his, stood up and walked across the room. Picking up a pop up book of dinosaurs, she flipped through it before putting it back on the shelf. "I really dislike being lied to."

Her brittle tone made him wish she'd just slapped him. He turned to put his feet on the floor and debated standing up. If he walked over there, it might piss her off enough that she'd hit him, which would end the Arctic blast, but she'd probably also throw him out on his ass which would end everything else. Better to hold the beachhead he had. "And I'm sorry. I was sorry as soon as it started, but I didn't think it would matter."

"Why did you do it?"

Maybe fury had made her deaf. Hadn't he just said that? "I didn't think it would matter?"

"No, why did you do it at all?" She turned to face him and folded her arms.

He looked at the floor. Why *had* he done it at all? "I'm sorry."

"Well, so am I, because that isn't a good enough answer."

Her well-deserved attitude grated. He shoved himself to his feet. "Don't treat me like a kid."

"I'm sorry. I'm just not sure how to treat you. I thought I knew you, but now you tell me you've been lying to me since we met. What am I supposed to do?"

"Forgive me? You liked me well enough a few minutes ago. You were ready to have sex."

"That might not be the best thing to remind me of right now."

"True."

"I feel like an idiot. All this time I thought I was seeing Michael D'Amato, mechanic from California and now I find out you're a—what did you say you did?"

The DVD menu started to cycle through again. He grabbed the remote, switched off the television and threw the remote down. "I'm a drummer in a rock band. We just released a new album and this is my vacation before I have to go back for rehearsals and the tour."

She nodded.

"You know, I'd feel a lot better if you'd scream at me or hit me or something."

"I'm sorry if I'm making you uncomfortable."

He dropped back onto the couch. Lying to her had to be one of the biggest boneheaded decisions of all time. "Maureen, I'm really sorry I did this to you and I wouldn't have told you at all—"

"That doesn't make me feel better."

"And I'm sorry." Bear drew a deep breath. This was like stepping off a tall bridge not sure if the bungee cord was secured. "But I really like you. I really *love* you. I don't want to leave town Monday and never see you again. What I really want is to see a lot more of you."

"If you're just saying this to get me in bed..." She grimaced.

"No, I'm pretty sure I could have gotten that without the drama. Besides, playing the celebrity card wouldn't have worked with you." That was one of the things he liked about her. The celebrity card might as well have been the four of spades. The level of her shoulders didn't look like knives anymore. Her expression had softened too. Now he had a very small chance of winning this one. He stood again and crossed the room. At the last minute, he decided not to touch her. He didn't want her feeling pressured even though every fiber of him wanted to. "Give me another chance. This time as me. I have to do a promo thing tomorrow. Come with me. I'll show what it's really like to date a rock star."

"I don't know, Michael."

Not the right answer, but not the wrong one either. "Please?"

A little smile started to play around her lips. That was getting to the right answer.

Bear dropped to his knees, clasping his hands up to her. "Please?"

She laughed. "Stop that. Stand up. You're embarrassing me."

"So you're not going to tell me to take a hike?" He stood and draped his arms around her shoulders.

"Not this time. I'm a firm believer in three strikes before you're out." She fixed him with a mock stern look. "But don't test your luck."

Bear kissed her. He didn't plan on testing anything.

She obviously didn't either. Hands planted on his chest, she pushed him back a step. "Why don't we take a little intermission?" She headed into the kitchen. "Coffee?"

No. "Sure," he said, and followed her.

With sharp and quick movements, she went through the cupboards, letting the doors smack against the frames. On the surface, she'd forgiven him, but she still wasn't happy. She had the right. He'd thrown her a hell of a curve ball.

Maureen jerked open the refrigerator and then slammed it closed. "Well, you're out of luck because there is no coffee. I am now out of everything that vaguely resembles food. I have half a bag of flour, some sugar, a tube of anchovy paste and one cherry Poptart. I guess the Poptart counts as food, but we have to share."

"Why don't you have any food?" He ventured into the kitchen as far as the table. Her cupboards had been pretty bare.

"Because I was supposed to go grocery shopping last weekend and didn't."

He'd known the amount of time he was spending with her would come back to haunt him. What else hadn't she been taking care of? How mad was she going to be when he left town and she had to play catch up? "Do you want to go grocery shopping?" That was the last thing he wanted to do, but it would be something to do with her and might win him points.

"I'm not going to drag you grocery shopping." She chuckled and walked around the table. "But thanks for offering."

"Hey, I'll throw myself on that grenade if I have to." He settled his arms around her waist. Her hands rested on his shoulders. Nothing like an embrace. Miles from where they'd been on the couch. So far she hadn't kicked him out, but she hadn't totally taken him back yet either. Kind of an odd sensation, this not being granted extra breaks because of who he was. At least she wasn't holding it against him. "What about Starbucks?"

Her arms slid around his neck and she rubbed her nose on his. "Starbucks it is."

Chapter 5

Maureen picked up their empty cups and carried them to the kitchen. She still wanted him. All week long her wishing had gradually become plotting until she was ready to have him to breakfast tomorrow and every day until he had to leave town, damn the torpedoes. But his announcement still had her staggering. She'd never kept up with popular culture. Among her friends, it was a joke. Her car radio was fixed to NPR and when she played music for the kids it was classical or ethnic. They came in with new bands, but she never listened to the music. She wasn't sure the kids did either. For them it was mostly about having the right binder or t-shirt.

Now she was dating a famous rock and roller. Well, it had to be a step up from grease monkey. Linda would be impressed. Might even know who he was. What kind of life must he be leading to feel he had to lie to her about who he was? She tossed out the cups and paused in the kitchen door to look at him.

His revelation had derailed her for a long time, but coffee, giant cookies and another round of Mulder and Scully and she was back on track. Warm, willing, and now with twenty-five percent more curiosity.

He was still incredibly sexy. Those shoulders, those hands, that mouth. What did he say he played? Drums? That just spawned a lot of cheesy jokes from her id about natural rhythm.

No school tomorrow.

Maureen chewed her lip. In the middle of his confession, he had used the word love. He'd also kept using the word "really." She'd heard enough kids falling back on that word when they were desperate to get their point across.

She'd never intended to get into a serious relationship with her mechanic's brother, whoever he was, but it was all headed that way like an overloaded train on a steep hill. He was funny, sweet, sexy as anything. Instead of expecting her to watch his every entertaining move, he paid attention to her. Michael was the first guy she'd met who didn't make her feel like she was along for his ride. Maybe it wasn't her school marm wardrobe that drove all her other dates away but the fact that she wasn't willing to be their audience. How was it that the first guy she'd met who didn't want her to be his audience and chief cheerleader was a professional performer?

The way he looked at her brought her temperature up a few degrees and when his hands got involved, she went straight into fevered. She wasn't exactly a hussy, but something about Michael made her more than willing to experiment with the role.

She slid onto the couch next to him and trailed her fingers up his arm. Now she understood the phrase iron hand in a velvet glove because it applied perfectly to his arms. "You know I have this problem with my brakes."

"They giving you trouble again?" He glanced at her hand, looking puzzled. She'd left him in the doghouse too long.

"I'm talking about my personal brakes." She shifted closer, her breath shortening in anticipation. "I seem to be having trouble stopping."

"That so?" He raised one eyebrow, smiling. "I'll have to take a look under the hood."

She straddled his legs. "You know that was a cheesy line, don't you?"

"You started it, sugar." His hands wrapped around her waist, proving he had iron elsewhere too.

"I suppose I did." She leaned in and kissed him. Over the past week she'd totaled at least a couple of hours kissing him, but it never got old. The softness of his mouth always intrigued her when everything else about him was so hard. His taste was magic too. Flavored now with coffee and chocolate, she could still detect his dark spice. Utterly indescribable, but this was what had been driving her crazy all week. This taste and the things she imagined he could do with his mouth, especially when she woke up in the middle of the night.

Sliding under her shirt, the touch of his hands brought an electric sizzle. His hands woke her up in the middle of the night too. The strength in his fingers and the way he pulled her tight like he couldn't stand as much as an atom's separation between them.

Maureen shivered and felt it echo through him. "So you're some kind of famous person."

"I am." He pushed the neck of her shirt aside and kissed her chest. Her nipples ached for attention.

"And sex with a famous person is supposed to be lots better than average." She put her hands on his cheeks to make him look at her.

His eyes were dark, but amused and a little hazy. "I can promise you a private performance with at least one encore."

"That sounds delightful. How about we move to a different stage?"

"A different stage?" He frowned.

Maybe that was the wrong word for it. Some research was called for. "Let's go to the bedroom."

"As you wish." He stood, carrying her with him.

Squealing, she grabbed his shoulders. God, he had great shoulders. Based on her inspection, he had great everything. He turned into her bedroom without having to ask and dropped her onto the bed, falling on top of her. The moment his lips slanted across hers again, she forgot to wonder how he knew which room was which. Heat spiraled through her. She needed to shed some clothes. So did he. She pulled his shirt over his head. Cloth broke his kiss for a second and he gave a frustrated grumble. The expanse of bared skin distracted her from her own heat. So slick and perfect. Sliding her palms down his back, she luxuriated in him.

"Are you sure about this?" he asked through heavy breathing. He propped himself up on his elbow.

"You wouldn't be here if I wasn't. Why?" Maureen trailed her fingers down his chest. The pause was annoying, but she knew she should be appreciating it. He wasn't as hairy as she'd thought he would be, but the dusting of dark hair across his tanned chest still seemed perfect.

"I've already screwed up once and I want to make sure I don't screw up again." He smoothed a lock of hair off her face. Every inch of him strained for her.

Every inch of her was straining for him too, but his hesitation kept her from rushing forward. Why was he doing it? All week long they'd been barely able to keep their hands off each other, now twice he'd stopped her. Did he have some other deep dark secret he needed to share with her? Something else he should have admitted and didn't? Or was he just more neurotic than average? "I hope you don't too."

"It's just—" He broke off and kissed her soft and sweet. Totally at odds with the urgent need of two minutes ago. What was wrong with him?

"Michael?" She tangled her fingers through his hair. "What is it?"

"I know we haven't known each other very long and I don't want to make you nervous or anything, but I really like you. You're special."

"Like short bus special?" Maureen tried to smile, but it warped and melted before the expression fully formed. Hadn't know her long?

Make her nervous? What was he going to do? Propose marriage? Propose something super freaky?

"No." He stroked her cheek. "Just special. I don't want to mess things up by moving too fast, but I don't have a lot of time."

"Spit it out, Michael."

"I love you."

Maureen blinked. She thought she'd been ready for that, but the way her lungs emptied and her gut seized, she obviously hadn't been. It wasn't just the words. The expression on his face, the tone of his voice, the fact that he was still trembling. This wasn't a light declaration for him. He meant every letter.

Why did he have to mess it up by making it momentous?

"Maureen?"

She kissed him to buy time to summon up an appropriate answer. Nothing was coming. If she didn't give him something, she was going to poke a hole in his ego that would have it flying around the room like a runaway balloon. "Show me," she whispered. "There's a box of condoms on the dresser."

"The dresser?" He made an attempt at focusing his eyes on her and then on the dresser across the room. "You stocked up?"

She traced her finger across his lips and down his chin. He had a good chin too. Strong, determined. "I stopped on the way home from school."

"Smart woman."

"I like to plan ahead." Relief washed through her. He was off the issue of love.

He pulled her shirt over her head and tossed it off the bed. Her skin sizzled as he traced with his fingers along the cups of her bra. "I never had you pegged for the leopard print bra type."

"Only on special occasions."

Placing his lips where his fingers had been a moment ago, he tasted her leisurely.

Eyes closed, she savored the sensation washing over her. Every inch of her clamored to be next for his attention. She moaned, tangling her fingers through his hair.

Unhooking her bra, he pushed the material away with his mouth, searching for her nipple. An instant after his hot breath brushed her aching flesh, his lips covered her. She arched. "Michael."

He chuckled, already working open her jeans.

As she disentangled herself from her bra, the cool air in the room made her skin tingle. His hot hands and mouth made her skin ache in a completely different way. Most maddening of all was the hunger between her legs that he didn't seem to be in any hurry to satisfy. He laved beneath her breast with his tongue. "Michael."

"Can I help you with something?" he asked in a maddeningly cool tone.

She wanted to tell him in no uncertain terms that she didn't appreciate his behavior. Teasing wasn't nice. Unfortunately, no words came to her lips.

He pulled her jeans off, moving out of reach, and she clutched the blankets. Trailing kisses up her leg and over her hip, he slid his palms up her calves. She grabbed his shoulders, dragged him on top of her. All his coolness of a moment ago was lost the moment his lips met hers. His tongue tangled around hers. His erection dug into her stomach. So close and yet so far.

Working her hands between them, she opened his jeans and tried to push them down, but couldn't get them far enough. Michael dragged himself away from her, shucked his jeans onto the floor and then seemed intent on falling right back on top of her.

"Condom," she said, a hand raised.

"Condom." He peered over his shoulder at the dresser like it was in another state and he might have to take a connecting flight to get to it. "Condom." He crossed the room in three strides and returned in two, ripping the condom open as he did. Slipping it on, he climbed back on the bed to kneel over her.

Other than the one word, all her language skills had vanished. She wished for a few more words so she could tell him what she felt. How lush and rich he made her feel just by looking at her this way. How beautiful and special his hands made her when he touched her.

"You're so beautiful," he said, cupping her cheek, and thrust into her.

Arching, she welcomed him, wrapped her arms around his back, digging her fingers into his muscles. The deep movement of him inside her engulfed her. She wanted to twist herself up in him and never be free. His strong arms could keep her pinned here forever. Face buried in her neck, he thrust harder. Her soul split open and love spilled out, warm and liquid. Her body clenched and released in a tidal wave. "Michael, I love you."

He gave a strangled cry and collapsed on top of her.

Maureen stroked her fingers through his hair. Well, she'd done it now. Even if he had been too busy to notice her declaration, she wasn't. In the past, her relationships had followed a regular path. Date for a few weeks, leading up to heavy petting. Four times she'd allowed a relationship to move into the bedroom and it had never been sooner than two months. And *I love you*? That never showed up until somewhere in the heavy petting phase during the second month.

Last Friday, she'd met him. By Sunday, they'd been into heavy petting. Now, inside seven days, they'd had sex and she'd said those three little words. What was wrong with her?

He kissed her cheek and climbed off the bed. "Back in a minute."

Pointing out the trashcan on the other side of the bed would have been easy, but she needed the time while he went to the bathroom. All her behavior for the past week had been weird. She'd rushed headlong into a relationship she knew had a very close expiration date. When it had turned out to be the relationship she'd thought, instead of hightailing it for the border, she'd plunged in deeper.

Only one answer. She was crazy.

The catalyst for her psychotic break walked back into the room and stretched out beside her. Nuzzling her neck, he said, "So do I get reviews?"

"Reviews?" As soon as his skin came into contact with hers, she wondered what the big deal had been about how fast things had gone. The warm weight of his body dragged her closer to him, but she honestly didn't need that. He had his own gravity that drew her to curl up with her head on his chest and her leg draped across his.

"For the performance." Sweaty skin stuck to sweaty skin as he wrapped his arm around her shoulders.

"Oh, are we continuing that metaphor?" Being crazy wasn't so bad. Kinda nice actually. At the moment, she was hoping to be crazy at least one more time tonight. "It was a great performance. I was on the edge of my seat."

"Next time I hope to have you jumping out of your seat, screaming."

She giggled.

"You have off school tomorrow."

"I do."

"So, will you come with me on my promo thing? We could spend the weekend in the city and get a hotel room. We'll do the town rock star style."

"You make it sound like a roller coaster."

"It is." He rolled over, pinning her under him. "Now leaving on track two, the Rock Star Express. Please keep your hands and arms inside the car at all times."

Maureen giggled again, letting her hands slide down his back to his butt. "Is this a good place for my hands?"

"Pretty good, but feel free to experiment."

* * * *

Bear tried to slip into the house without waking anyone, but Tony was waiting for him in the living room.

"Do you know what time it is?" Tony growled.

"Midnight?" After the encore, they had lain in bed talking until she announced she needed to get a little sleep before tomorrow. Now that he thought about it, it had been after midnight when he left her house. Getting from the bedroom to the door had taken, um, a little while.

"One o'clock."

"Really? Wow, it's late and I have a lot to do tomorrow. 'Night." He wanted to get behind a closed door so he could reminisce. The week of frustration had been worth every second with her.

"What the fuck do you think you're doing?" Tony's voice rose from a whisper to normal and kept going.

"I was going to bed." Bear headed for the stairs.

"I told you to stay away from her."

"I like her." Like was such a useless word. The closest thing he could come to what he really wanted with Maureen involved permanent bonding. He hadn't even wanted to leave tonight, but he'd figured if he didn't come home at all, Tony would rip his beating heart from his chest and serve it up on a platter. Looked like he planned to do that anyway.

"And have you thought about what's going to happen when you leave town?" Tony shouted.

"She can visit me."

"Now doesn't that sound like the life. She can stay here and keep teaching school until you call for her. You are just as self centered as when we were kids."

"Tony," Pam snapped from the stairs. "You're going to wake up Nicky."

"Did you hear what the genius has done?" Tony demanded, still at the top of his lungs.

Pam glared at Bear and then turned back to Tony. "What's done is done. Don't wake Nicky." She stomped up the stairs.

"I can't believe you." Tony's voice dropped to a whisper. "Did you even think before you decided to scratch your itch?"

"Yeah, I did. I thought about it a lot. I really like her, Tony. Whether you believe it or not. Relax. You're taking this way to seriously."

"She isn't like those other girls you date."

"I know. That's why I like her." Nope, nothing like the other girls he'd dated. Sweet, kind, genuine. A girl like Maureen was a mythical creature where he came from. She was everything he ever imagined wanting.

"You're going to ruin her life." Tony clenched his fists. His voice had a raw hiss of desperation.

"That's a little dramatic." Bear rolled his eyes.

In the split second he took his gaze off Tony, his brother crossed the room and slammed him into the wall. The family photos rattled and one of them fell. Glass tinkled onto the floor. "You are a total asshole."

Bear shoved Tony back. "Let me go. I am not going to ruin her life."

"Tony!" Pam snarled from the stairs. Behind her, Nicky called for her from upstairs. "I swear to God if the two of you don't cut it out I'm going to call the cops and have you arrested for disturbing the peace. *My* peace. I'm coming, Nicky. It's okay. Daddy and Uncle Bear are talking."

Tony stalked across the living room and turned around. "I think it's time for you to go."

"What do you mean, *go?*" His brother's tone and posture suddenly registered. Tony hadn't looked that freaked out since Nicky ended up in the hospital with some kind of virus when he was eighteen months old. All week he'd been getting more and more ticked off, but honestly, how ticked off could he be? Bear wasn't going to con Maureen out of her life savings and skip town.

"I want you out of my house."

"You're kidding. Because I had sex with my girlfriend?"

Tony clenched his jaw. "I asked you to leave her alone and you didn't. You had to make things worse. You know what's going to happen now? You're going to leave town and she's going to moon around the garage for months trying to get in touch with you. Then she's going to get mad because she never hears from you and since you're not here she'll take it out on me. And next fall, she's not going to be Nicky's teacher."

"Wow, that's quite a story you have going. Are there explosions too?"

"In the morning, I want you to pack your shit and go back to California."

"You are kicking me out." His stomach tightened. Tony was the only family he had left. He'd known his brother would be mad, but this went straight into enraged.

"I am. I want you away from my family before you do any more damage."

"What makes you think I'm doing damage? You don't know how I feel about Maureen."

"I don't need to." Tony glared at him for a second and then started for the stairs.

"Wait a minute."

"No." Tony stopped at the top. "You can stay tonight, but you need to be out of here tomorrow."

"Tony."

As he turned into the hall, his brother hit the light switch, which plunged the house into darkness.

Sure, he'd known Tony was going to be mad. Really mad. They wanted Maureen to be Nicky's teacher next year. She took her car to the garage, so there was a business relationship to think about too. And she was a nice person and Tony always hated to see somebody nice getting screwed over.

Dammit, he wasn't going to screw her over. Tony wasn't even giving him a chance. He really loved her. He wanted to be with her for—for a long time anyway. Tony should be happy for him. He'd always hated the gold diggers Bear ended up with. Maureen was about as far from gold digger as this twerpy little burg was from Mumbai, India.

Fuck.

He stomped up the stairs and down the hall to the rumpus room. Tony wanted him out? Fine. He'd be out. Throwing his clothes in the suitcase, he snapped it closed and hoisted it off the fold-out bed. In the car, he started the engine and tried to think of where the nearest hotel was. He'd never paid attention to that kind of stuff. When he came to town it was to visit Tony.

No more of that.

There were a bunch of hotels out along the interstate. He'd have to try there.

* * * *

Maureen brushed her teeth and tried to figure out what a rock star's girlfriend would wear to a radio station. Not that she had any of that stuff in her closet. It was a crisp pink blouse and blue jeans or nothing. Though Michael might prefer nothing. Come to think of it, she might prefer that too. He said they had to be at the station at one and it only took an hour and a half to get there. Plenty of time.

Depending on when he showed up. He hadn't been too clear when she'd finally motivated him out the door last night.

Why had she done that? What harm would there have been in him staying the night? They could have swung by his brother's house to pick up what he needed on the way this morning. She walked through the kitchen, wiping down the counters. No good reason to. There hadn't been any food on them all week. With the last Pop-Tart heating in the toaster, she took out her grocery pad. She'd already half filled it, but couldn't summon the desire to finish. She'd go shopping Monday after school. Michael would already be gone.

She threw the list back in the drawer.

What was she doing, getting involved with this guy who had lied to her from the get-go and was leaving in three days? Who could say if she'd ever see him again? He could disappear Monday.

In the living room, she peered through the curtains as if she expected the Satellite to come cruising up the street at her beck and call. He'd said morning, but technically that was anytime before noon. His lifestyle was a mystery, but she doubted it involved a lot of early mornings.

Throwing herself on the couch, she allowed one fit of pique before deciding it was silly. What had she lost? When she first met him, she'd only wanted to be admired by a good-looking man. She'd gotten that. In spades even. After spending time with him, she'd wanted more. That happened too. In fact, even if he didn't show up today she hadn't lost anything. Her expectations had been low and he'd far exceeded them. Everything after last Friday night was gravy.

She sniffed, wringing her hands in her lap. She'd start believing that when she started believing in Santa Claus again. Right now, eyes open, she could remember every detail of his face, the tenor of his voice, the way he smelled under the industrial strength soap from the garage, and she really didn't know anything about him.

Of course as a famous person, a lot of information should be available.

After checking out the window to make sure he wasn't headed toward her at that very moment, she went to her office. She'd forgotten to ask him last night how he knew which room was which. Usually both this door and the bedroom door were closed, so he must have snooped.

She pressed the Start button on the computer and made herself comfortable while it came on. Couldn't really blame him for snooping when she was about to do the same thing on the World Wide Web. She typed his name into the search engine and came up with more than fifteen pages of links. She clicked on the top one and ended up on the Wikipedia. It showed a couple of pictures of him with four other men, all quite good looking in their own way. His parents were both deceased and he had one brother. He collected muscle cars. According to this he was dating a woman named Julia. No photograph of her, though.

How could she subtly ask if he was dating someone? He didn't seem like the kind of guy to two-time, but then, she didn't know him that well.

Clicking the band link, she studied yet another photo of the band. They were onstage and there were only four of them. All she could see of Michael was his face over a set of drums, but he looked very happy in an intense, focused sort of way. Much the same way he did when he worked on the Satellite. The other guys were laughing so they must be having fun too. According to the article, they had released seven albums including one that had just come out. Another link would take her to the tour dates.

Tour dates. Michael was going to be traveling all summer. She followed the link and corrected herself. He was going to be traveling until December. Such a long time away from home. Poor baby. And so many places. They were in a different city every day.

A knock interrupted her. No one else it could be. Excitement bubbled through her. She shut the computer down and ran for the door. She yanked it open, beaming, and his expression made hers crumble. "What's wrong?"

Michael stepped inside, shaking his head. He gathered her into his arms and pulled her tight.

"Michael?" she asked and wrapped her arms around his neck. Standing so still and holding her so tight, he felt fragile, which seemed silly. He was too broad shouldered and strong to be weak. "Did something happen?"

"You know I'm not going to hurt you, right?" he asked into her skin.

"Hurt me?" Maybe this was about Julia. He'd left last night after midnight and it was not even nine in the morning. Had he even had time to talk to the other woman? Was there even another woman to talk to? "Why would you hurt me?"

"My brother is being a dick." He released her and strode to the middle of the room, where he ran his hand through his hair and rubbed his face before turning to her. "Tony is convinced I'm going to screw you over and dump you. He's totally out of his mind. I thought he'd be happy for me." Michael paced in front of the couch.

She closed the door and waited.

"He's always bitching about the leeches I end up with and I finally meet somebody nice. Somebody I really like, and he freaks out because he thinks I'm going to be a dick to her—to you." He stopped. "It's just fucking insane."

"I'm sure if you give Tony a couple of days to calm down, he'll relax." Maureen resisted the impulse to jump up and down and clap her hands. Last night, pre-sex, *I love you* had caught her off guard. This morning his *I really like* carried more weight with less terror.

"He won't. He's really pissed. All week he's been telling me not to fuck with the locals and I did it anyway. But it's not like that. I'm not playing games here. He's making me pick between my family and somebody I want to be my family."

When she'd registered the last thing he'd said, she'd been reveling in his latest declaration of *like* and calculating how long before he'd wear a hole in her carpet and how much it was going to cost to get it fixed. "What?"

"He's mad because him and Pam wanted you to be Nicky's teacher next year, but if we're dating you won't because it's an ethical gray area. And if I screwed you over and left town you wouldn't because you'd be mad. I see his point. Nicky needs all the help he can get. I love the kid, but he's no genius. He needs a good patient teacher. But I need that too. Not the teacher part, but the good patient part."

"I'm sure we can make sure Nicky gets the teacher he needs. All the other teachers at the second grade level in my building are good. I could steer him into the most suitable class." Maureen clasped her hands in front of her. When was Michael going to slow down? His pacing made her legs hurt and he kept snapping his hands open and closed. Maybe she should try to stop his tantrum. He just seemed to be getting worse.

"He wouldn't have a problem with it at all if I wasn't who I am. If I was just his brother and his business partner, he wouldn't care who I dated. But because I'm in the band, he's all bent out of shape. I don't even want to be in the fucking band. I wish I'd never joined them."

Of the pictures she'd found, except for one shot where the band looked rather stern, they really seemed happy. Honestly, how horrible could it be to be worshipped by thousands for playing music? Not exactly back breaking labor. His entire tantrum reminded her more and more of the kids when they claimed they didn't want to go out for recess.

"I don't want to go on tour. Being dragged around like a piece of furniture. Doing this promotional shit all the time in the hopes that we can sell enough records to pay back the record company. I just want to stay home with you."

"Stay home with me?"

He stopped pacing and crossed the room to her. Taking her in his arms, he kissed her. "I love you, Maureen."

"I love you too, Michael." She leaned her cheek on his chest. At least he wasn't pacing anymore. "I'll talk to Tony about Nicky. He could still end up in my class. Class lists won't be settled for a couple of months yet." That required working around her relationship with Michael, but she'd burn that bridge when she came to it. "He's just worried right now. Once he sees there's nothing to worry about, he'll be fine. You are already committed to this tour so you might as well make the best of it. If you hate it at the end, you could still quit, right?" She looked up at him to see if the flames in his eyes had gone out yet.

His face had settled into the lost expression he had appeared at her door with. He hadn't shaved this morning either. Somehow that fact had escaped her despite her scratched cheeks.

"When did you have this fight with Tony? This morning?"

"Last night. He threw me out."

"Where did you sleep?" She had visions of him hunched in the backseat of the Satellite.

"I went to a hotel. I figured you wouldn't be too happy if I showed up here."

She stroked his cheek and felt some of the tension drain out of him. "You could have showed up here if you wanted to. If this happened last night, Tony might already be regretting it. People don't think straight when they're tired. He was up late waiting for you and got upset. Maybe we could stop by the garage on the way and talk to him."

"Marry me."

Chapter 6

Maureen blinked. Stress was making her hear funny. It sounded like he'd just proposed, but he couldn't have because that would be crazy. "What?"

"Marry me."

He *had* proposed.

She'd only met him a week ago.

She didn't know him at all.

He lived on the other side of the country.

He wasn't even going to be at that home for months.

What about her job?

Marriage wasn't something to be rushed into.

"Yes."

He picked her up and swung her around. "I love you so much. I am going to make you so happy."

"I hope I can make you happy too." Her feet dangled above the floor and her heartbeat still hammered from the suddenness of being swooped into the air, but she felt safe, protected. As if it wasn't such a bad idea to marry a rock star she'd met a week ago. Michael would make it right. Everyone had to see that they were perfect for each other.

"You already make me happy." He grinned with more brightness to his face than she'd ever seen on anyone and leaned her into the wall. "Everything about you makes me happy."

As his hard body pressed into her, she moaned. She kissed him, relishing his flavor. That rich, exotic, wonderful flavor. This was what movies were always going on about. Two people meet and fall madly in love at first sight. Destiny. No need to ever think about anything because when it was right, it just was. Everything else was details.

His phone started to ring. He cursed, pulling the phone out of his pocket, but didn't release her. "What?"

She could hear the person on the other end as clearly as if she'd had the phone pressed to her ear. At this proximity, she practically did. "Just checking to make sure you were on your way to the radio gig."

"I'm kinda busy here." He caught her eye and his frown turned to a grin. "Hey! Guess what!"

"What?"

"I'm getting married."

Breath caught in her throat, she waited for a response.

"Married?"

"Yeah." Michael kissed her cheek.

"To who?"

"You'll like her. Maureen."

"This woman you just met?"

"Yeah, but she's fantastic. Here, talk to her." He twisted the phone to her ear. "Talk to Marc."

"Hello?" she said.

"You're Maureen?"

"Yes, it's nice to meet you, Marc."

"How did you meet Bear?"

"Bear?"

"The guy you're apparently marrying."

"I met him at the garage. My brakes were making a terrible noise so I took it in and he happened to be there working on the Satellite."

"The Satellite?"

"His car."

"So you're going to marry Bear."

Utter joy welled through her body. She met Michael's gaze. This guy. She was going to marry this guy. Whatever his name was. "Yes, I am."

"Well, good luck. Can I talk to Bear again?"

She handed the phone to Michael, who stepped away this time. "She's great. You're gonna love her." He paused beside the coffee table, but she didn't need to be near the phone to hear Marc this time.

"Are you out of your fucking mind? You just met this woman and you're going to marry her? You haven't even told Tessa about her, have you?"

"You don't know her." Marc's voice dropped out of her hearing, but Michael looked angry. "Well, you married a stripper, what did you expect?"

"This is not about me!" Marc bellowed.

"Like fuck it's not. You know what? I just got engaged. Somebody should be happy for me."

Her heart ached for him. He sounded so forlorn, but Marc was right. They had just met and they were talking about forever. To keep herself from trying to go to him and fix it, she knitted her fingers together. How was unclear, but in any case, she shouldn't be. This was his fight. She couldn't start diving in to rescue him every time things got difficult. It set a bad precedent.

"Fine. I'll talk to you when I get back." He snapped the phone shut and then opened it again.

"Your friend not happy?"

"He's in the middle of a divorce. He's jealous." Michael fiddled with his phone for a minute and then stuck it in his pocket, grinning. "Now where were we?"

Though she ached to take him back to the bedroom and get a repeat performance, she'd had enough time out of direct contact that reason was kicking in. "Michael, are you sure he isn't right?"

"He thinks you're trying to steal my money. He doesn't know you."

Oh yeah, money. Since he was famous, he probably had some. No wonder every time she mentioned how much something cost he sounded baffled. "We have only known each other for a couple of days though. It's not even going to be a week until—" She checked her watch mostly because she couldn't stand the shattered expression on his face. It reflected her own turmoil too well. "Six thirty tonight."

"So?"

"It's very fast. Don't you think?" Maureen chewed her lip. "Shouldn't we get to know each other better?"

Michael put his hands on her shoulders and leaned his forehead on hers. His eyes bored into hers. "I know you. I love you. That's all I need."

Emotion choked her, and she swallowed hard. His absolute certainty was hard to resist. The weight of his hand anchored her to the ground and to him. She couldn't imagine anything better than to be wrapped in that love forever. She put her hands on his cheeks. "That's all I need too, but we have to get going if we're going to stop at the garage on the way."

"I'm going to have to hire you as a road manager. You're ruthless." He kissed her lightly. "Where's your bag?"

"On the bed."

He bowed and bounded down the hall after it. God, she hoped his confidence stayed with her. He made it sound so simple.

When he returned, he ushered her into the car and started talking about his plans for the weekend. After the radio show, he wanted to take her out to a restaurant she'd never heard of. Where he'd gotten the recommendation, she didn't know, but guessed it was several degrees better than the one he'd taken her to last weekend. Saturday there was a concert he wanted to go to, but he had all day free and he was willing to go back to the natural history museum. After he let her out of bed, of course. Sunday, he needed to show up at a record store. It was a surprise appearance and he didn't have a set time he had to be there.

"I don't understand how it's a surprise if you plan to be there," she said and twisted sideways in the seat. All the better to stare at him.

"It's a surprise for the people who shop there." He brushed his fingers over her cheek. "The owners may have told a couple of people, but otherwise nobody knows. We do these hit and run things sometimes. It's fun."

She nodded and glanced up the road. They were getting close to the garage. Hopefully, Tony had cooled off after last night. She didn't want to get caught between the two of them. Most of her life was designed around avoiding tension.

"You don't have to do this," Michael said. "We can just go on our merry way."

"You were very upset this morning."

"I got over it."

It was a lie. He wasn't over it. She spoke enough body language that she could understand the tenseness in his jaw and the stiffness in his back. For whatever reason, the argument with his brother bothered him a lot and she didn't want him to have to carry that around. "We'll give him a try before we go. You don't want him to hear secondhand that we got engaged, do you?"

Eyes bright, he turned a grin of pure glee on her that made her heartbeat leap. "Oh yeah. We got engaged this morning. Maybe that's what we should do tomorrow. Go hit a couple of jewelers for a big, fat rock."

"It doesn't need to be that big." Her face heated. What were the other teachers going to say when she showed up Monday morning sporting a flashy engagement ring?

Michael pulled into the side lot and shut off the engine. "Ready?"

"Are you?"

He leaned across the parking brake and kissed her. "Now I am."

She waited while he jumped out and ran around the car to open her door for her. Not like it was a hardship. No one had ever wanted to put her on such a high pedestal before and she was enjoying the view.

Rusty stood behind the counter. He looked up when the bell rang as Michael opened the door. Without a word, he shambled down the hall to the repair bay. In itself, that wasn't unusual. She hadn't heard Rusty say more than a dozen words in the six years she'd been bringing her car here. Today, his taciturn nature put her on edge. More on edge.

Michael reached for her hand and as he did, she turned toward him. Over his shoulder she saw an empty nail on the wall over the cash register. That must have been where the picture had hung. She vaguely remembered seeing one there, but hadn't been interested enough to look at it. Usually when standing at that register she was too busy gasping at the cost of the latest repair.

Tony walked out, sullen. "Yeah?"

"Me and Maureen are getting married." Michael thrust out his chin.

Tony's eyes narrowed. "That so?"

"It is."

The brothers glared at one another across the reception room. Rusty's shadow filled the doorway to the repair bay, and the sound of Eric shuffling near the door to the side bay came to her. Neither Tony nor Michael were going to move and this reconciliation was spinning down the drain.

"Tony," she said, breaking into their standoff. "Michael said you were hoping your son would be in my class next year."

"Like that's going to happen now." Tony kept glaring at Michael.

"I'll talk to his teacher this year and we'll see who might be the best fit for him. I'm sure we can figure something out."

"Thank you." Tony sounded like the last thing he wanted to say was thank you, but she wasn't going to push him.

"You could be nice about it," Michael said. "She doesn't have to help you."

Maureen squeezed his hand. "It's okay."

"It's not okay," Michael snapped. "He's busting my ass about screwing up Nicky's chance to get in your class and he can't even say thanks when you promise to help? And nothing about us getting married. I told you he was being a dick."

"You want me to congratulate you for popping the question after a week? I should be apologizing to her," Tony shouted then turned on her.

"You do know he won't go through with it. Or if he does it'll be a disaster and you'll be divorced in two years."

Michael took a step forward but when she laid a hand on his arm, stopped. That must mean he wasn't too serious about his threat. "Let's go," he snapped, turning for the door. Slamming through it, he shattered the glass.

"I'm right, you know," Tony said.

"I hope you're not. I do love your brother."

"I do too, but he's a natural disaster. Hurricane Michael, here to destroy your life. Tell him he owes me for the fucking door." Tony stomped toward the hall, but stopped just short. "Oh, and thanks for the help with Nicky. Me and Pam really appreciate it."

"It's not a problem." Trying to get her pulse and breathing under control, she looked at the broken door. This did not bode well.

* * * *

Bear scowled out the windshield. As soon as she'd climbed back in the car at the garage, he'd reached for her hand and kissed her. Other than a few minutes when he'd needed to navigate onto the highway, he hadn't let go and she hadn't tried to pull away. He took that as a good thing, but he wasn't enjoying the sound of her silence at all. First Marc had to be a loon and then Tony.

"He's wrong, you know," Bear said when they got close to the city.

"I know." Her voice was soft, as if she were talking to him from a distance. Then she squeezed his hand, reminding him how near she was. "Maybe we shouldn't tell anyone else we're engaged."

His body froze and he had to resist the urge to clench her hand. If he squeezed too tight, he could hurt her. "You change your mind?" The thread of wild panic that wound through his voice humiliated him, but he couldn't take it back now. He couldn't even stop the beat of panic drumming through his blood.

"No."

Her tone had the flat metallic taste of a lie. He pulled his hand away from her, clutched the wheel. That he couldn't hurt when she finally coughed up her rejection. The world started to swim. Ahead the highway divided in three and the woman who'd given him the directions had warned him that it was tricky. One direction led to the morass of downtown. He could get to the radio station from there, but it wouldn't be easy. A second lane led in the opposite direction. He needed option number three, except he couldn't remember now if option number three was the left lane, the right lane or the middle lane. Traffic wasn't helping either. Every other driver on the road seemed intent on shoving him into a different lane and the semis in front of him kept blocking the signs.

"I just think that it's confusing the issue." She turned to him. Her tone still hadn't changed. "Your friends are going to need to meet me before they find out we're getting married."

Based on the way his phone had been vibrating since he'd hung up with Marc and turned off the ringer, all his friends already knew. "So we're still getting married?" He switched into the left lane at the split and hoped it was the correct one.

"I haven't changed my mind. Have you changed yours?"

"No."

She smiled. "Good."

The world stopped swimming and he took a deep breath. Traffic had cleared and he could now see the signs. The wrong signs. "Shit."

"What?"

"We're headed the wrong way."

"No big deal. We'll find an exit and turn around."

She had the calm tone to her voice again and was staring straight ahead. Maybe that wasn't distance from her. Maybe that's how she handled tension. Marc and Tony were right about one thing. He didn't know her, but it was going to be a lot of fun getting to know her.

"There's an exit." She pointed.

The exit ramp snaked around and dumped them off on a residential street with no sign of an entrance ramp. Bear stopped in front of the elaborate Catholic church at the bottom of the exit. "So now what?"

Frowning, she surveyed the neighborhood. She looked really cute with her lips crinkled with that puzzled quirk.

"I know, let's run into this church right here and get hitched. That would blow their minds, wouldn't it?"

She gave him a long suffering eye roll. "That looks like a Russian Orthodox church. I'm willing to bet they don't marry people who walk in off the street. Even if they did, this isn't Vegas. It takes time to get a marriage license in this state. Though I have to say, running off and getting hitched would be a lot easier than getting my parents in the same room together."

"Then let's go to Vegas. Instead of all that other stuff we were going to do after the radio show, we can hop a flight to Nevada and get married."

She patted his leg and sighed. "No. Now I think I got lost down here once. Make a right."

Bear turned in the direction she indicated. His breathing had gotten a lot easier in the last few seconds. "Why is it going to be hard to get your parents together?"

"They hate each other. They don't even live in the same state."

"Really?" She said it so matter of factly, she might have been talking about the weather. "What happened?"

"They stayed together until I graduated high school. Then they put the house up for sale and all three of us went in different directions."

"That sucks."

"Believe me, it was better than the previous fifteen years. I was the only kid I knew whose parents had separate bedrooms. You need to make, ah—" She glanced in both directions. "Make a right here too. At the next main intersection we can take Ninth back to the highway.

"After that you'd still be willing to get married?"

"I don't plan to make the same mistakes my parents made."

"What did they do wrong?"

"Got trapped into marriage with an unplanned pregnancy and then stayed together for the child. It would have been better for all of us if they'd split up." She reached over and patted his arm. "No unplanned kids for you and even with the planned ones, if things go south we won't be staying together for their sake because I can tell you from first hand experience that does not work." She said it with a smirk, but it left him cold anyway.

How to answer that one? At Ninth Street, he followed the signs to the highway. He really didn't know her at all. "Hey, baby?" he said as he pulled into the radio station parking lot. A couple dozen people hung around the door.

As she tore her gaze from the crowd to look at him, her expression changed from fearful to concerned. "What is it?"

He took her hand. "I just want you to know I'm gonna take care of you. No matter what happens."

Her fingers were light and cold on his cheek. Not at all reassuring. "It's okay, Michael. I can take care of myself."

"I don't want you to have to." The mob had started for the car. A security guy headed for his side of the car. If he didn't hurry up, he wasn't going to be able to stay between her and them. He jumped out of the car and hurried around the front to her door. The security guy met him there. "Keep track of her, would ya?" Bear asked before turning to the fans. Escorted to the door, he answered about eighty questions, signed at least a hundred autographs and had his picture taken a hundred and fifty times.

Inside the station, an intern gushed all over him and pulled him toward the recording booth while the security guy took Maureen someplace else. He hadn't even had time to give her a kiss.

* * * *

"So how was your visit to the radio station?" Michael asked.

"Informative." Maureen clasped her hands. She had no idea why a twenty-minute live radio spot had taken two hours to do, but it had. While she waited, she'd tried to learn about popular music without raising too much suspicion. She was pretty sure she'd failed on both fronts. What she'd managed to figure out didn't make any sense. "Why is it musicians can't spell?"

"I don't know. Not paying attention in school, I guess."

The elevator doors slid open. The bellboy, carrying their two small bags, led the way down the opulent hall to a room, swiped the lock and pushed open the door. With a professional snap, he put down a ledge in the closet and set their bags on it. Then he turned to Michael with the key card held in a none too subtle palm.

She wandered deeper into the room. Decorated in blues and greens, it was by far the biggest hotel room she'd ever been in. The bed alone appeared to be about the size of her living room. She pushed aside the sheers and peered out the window. Their room overlooked the city's main square, probably the best view in the place.

Michael wrapped his arms around her waist and buried his nose in her hair. "So what do you want to do now?"

"I get the impression you have a plan." His hard length digging into her warmed her. Being wanted this much was its own aphrodisiac.

"Hmm, maybe a short term one."

Dropping the curtain, she turned to wrap her arms around his neck. Immediately, he leaned in to kiss her, teasing her mouth open with such gentle heat that she trembled. His flattened palms ran up her back.

"I missed you today," he murmured.

"You were right down the hall."

"I know. I might as well have been in another country."

She tangled her fingers through his hair. "Well, we'll have to make up for lost time then."

He scooped her off the floor and carried her to the enormous bed. Laying her down, he stripped off his shirt. She reached for the buttons of her blouse, but he caught her hands. "Nope, I like to open my own presents."

"I'm a gift now?" The heat of the compliment rushed through her limbs.

"You were a gift the moment I met you." He unbuttoned her blouse with deft fingers and smoothed his hand across her belly.

As his lips met hers again, she closed her eyes and clutched his powerful shoulders. Nothing mattered beyond him. Not his friends or his brother. Not the weird looks the intern gave her or the DJ calling her beautiful when he'd never laid eyes on her. Nothing mattered.

He slid between her legs, the rough texture of his jeans chafing against hers. His member strained against the material. Her body opened for him, arching for his touch. He unhooked her bra with one hand and cupped her breast. "You are the most beautiful woman I have ever seen."

"Thank you. Are you planning on doing more than looking?"

"Maybe." He brushed his thumb across her nipple, sending a spark through her.

Maureen twisted and rolled him onto his back so she was straddling him. She ran her hands up his tight abs. "Maybe?"

"You have other plans?"

She brushed her lips along his skin, tasting the rich, salty flavor of him. Working her way down his chest, she traced the dips and hollows of his flesh with her fingertips. His body was so delightfully fine tuned. Every inch of him, sculpted and tight. Fingering the button on his jeans, she looked up.

He had his hands behind his head, watching her. "Don't let me stop you," he said lightly.

She sat up. "Oh come on. By now you should be putty in my hands."

"Who says I'm not?"

"That smug expression on your face."

"Hmm, I'll have to try harder. You should have worn the leopard print bra again."

She swatted his arm.

"Hey, there's no need to get violent."

"Unless that's what you like," she said, crawling over him. "Maybe you've developed some depraved tastes."

"Depraved? Sounds fun."

She couldn't help giggling, and brushed her fingers along his cheek, enjoying the flush she'd raised.

He reached up and slipped his hand behind her neck, drew her down on him. Her body pressed to his, flesh to flesh, she explored him, raising a moan that vibrated through both of them. He unbuttoned her jeans and slid his hand inside them and between her legs. His fingers found the throbbing knot of her need.

"Ah! Michael," she moaned.

"I'm not just looking anymore."

"You're a bad boy." She rocked against his hand.

"I know." Turning her onto her back, he pulled her jeans down. He reached into his pocket and tossed a condom onto her stomach. "Open this up, would ya?"

While he yanked off his jeans, she ripped open the foil. The sight of that beautiful body made her heart swell. That a wonderful man like him could want her. That he could look at her the way he was looking at her now… She placed the condom over his swollen head and rolled it down his length, gaze locked with his. His eyes were dark and his breathing heavy. Lying back, she held out her arms. Her heart couldn't wait for the moment his skin touched hers. He stretched out over her, kissing her with sweet softness. His hot breath caressed her skin as he sunk into her.

The richness of being filled by him wrung a cry from her. She dug her nails into his back as he thrust deeper and deeper. Every movement a sweet rush. She met each thrust, winding tighter and tighter until she snapped, gasping. Michael groaned and shuddered, collapsing on top of her.

In the glowing aftermath, she stroked his hair, cherishing these moments in his arms. The weight of his body on hers was wonderful. He nestled his face into the curve of her neck, breathing deeply. Eventually the ferocious desire to be with him every second had to go away, or at least lessen, didn't it? This insane desire to never leave the bed. To stay wrapped up in him forever.

"What am I going to do without you?" he whispered, kissing her throat.

"What do you mean?" Tears pooled in the corners of her eyes, so she closed them hoping to stem the flow.

"When I have to go back. No chance of you quitting your job so you can come home with me, is there?"

To keep an irrational yes from popping out, she bit her lip. In this second, she would quit her job and go anywhere he wanted.

But the kids. Her house. Her life. Everything she'd made for herself. She couldn't leave that behind. Not for a man. Not even for Michael.

"I didn't think so," he said. He rolled off her and propped himself up on one elbow. Brushing her cheek with the backs of his fingers, he said, "Boy, did you get sweaty."

Maureen laughed, hoping he didn't notice her pained rasp. Not all of what he wiped away was sweat. "You're quite a workout."

"I'll have to make sure I feed you well. Speaking of which, we never got to have lunch."

"No, we were busy being lost." She laced her fingers through his. She was still leaning toward staying in this bed until they died of starvation, but couldn't figure out how to present it to him so he'd go for it. The last thing she wanted was to get up and get dressed. That would severely limit the amount of his bare flesh she could get her hands on.

"Are you hungry? Our dinner reservations aren't for hours." He cupped her breast. She shuddered. Was his touch actually better now that she knew who he was or was she just imagining it? "We could venture out for food or order room service."

"I'm fine." That was an exaggeration. She wasn't fine. Half of her was already mourning that he was leaving in three days. The other half was consumed with figuring out how to keep as much of him as possible.

"Are you sure?" He trailed his hand down her belly.

"Positive." She put her hand over his to hold it against her skin. If only it were so easy to hold him. To catch him and cling to him.

"Didn't you say you didn't have Easter Break yet?"

She had to swim through layers of her conniving to decipher his question. "What?"

"Easter Break, is that over?"

"No, it's in two weeks. Everyone's climbing the walls."

"Come to LA." His hand tensed, sending a thrill of pleasure through her. "You weren't planning on going to visit anyone else, were you? Come see me."

"Aren't you going to be on tour?" She couldn't keep her eagerness out of her voice. How tough would it be to go on tour with him? Or would she just be in the way?

"No, rehearsals. I'm going to be busy a lot of the time, but I'll be home every night. And you can meet everybody."

"Come visit?"

"Yes." He caught her hands and pulled them over her head. His eyes were bright and excited. "It'll be great. Say you'll come. I'll make it worth your while."

"I bet you will." Maureen licked her lips.

Laughing, he rolled off the bed. "I'll call Jody right now and get your tickets set up."

She reached for him, but missed. He was already flipping open his phone. Go visit. Spend a week with him in Los Angeles.

"You'll have to visit me on tour too," he said, focused on the phone. "You have summers off. You can travel with us for a couple of weeks. It's kinda boring, but at least we'll be together."

Hurricane Michael.

Chapter 7

Bear squeezed Maureen's hand. Next door to the hotel stood the city's premier shopping galleria. Four floors of the very best shops in the state. Marble flooring, gilt scrollwork, a dancing fountain keyed to classical music on the bottom most floor. It was the best he could do under the circumstances. After making love, he'd wanted to take her out and show her off. Unfortunately, there wasn't anyone to show her off to. Most of the people here were women whose watches cost more than Maureen's house, and what was the point of showing off his girlfriend to them anyway? They weren't the target audience.

That was in California, prepared to hate her, if Marc had his way. But the guys in SendDown weren't already against her and they'd be meeting her tomorrow night. He stopped in front of a shop window. The display mannequin wore a short silver dress that hooked around the neck with a silver chain. "I could see you in that."

"Really?" Her pretty pink mouth quirked into a Billy Idol-like sneer. "I can't."

"Okay, how about I say it a different way." He draped his arm over her shoulders. "Can I see you in that?"

She stared up at him, chewing her lip. "I don't think I can afford to even be looking at that dress in the show window."

"I can." He grinned. "I have plastic and I'm not afraid to use it."

"You want to buy me a dress."

"Sure. If it looks good and you like it." He brushed his nose across her cheek. "Besides, if I buy it, I get to take it off you."

She giggled. "Okay, I'll try it if it makes you happy."

Bear steered her inside the store. There wasn't much to it. A pair of ornate arches leading to smaller rooms on either side. A few mannequins here and there. No racks of clothes anyplace. Nothing as crass as a register. An older lady in a neat white suit took one look at them and disappeared though a curtain at the back. A second later a young blond with long skinny legs encased in dark wash jeans walked out. Her exasperated expression evaporated the moment she set eyes on him.

"Bear D'Amato." She gasped. Her gaze flickered to Maureen and back to him. "Oh my God. What can I help you with?"

"I want to see my girlfriend in that dress you have in the window." He cocked his head in the direction of the dress.

"Your girlfriend. Oh. Absolutely." The blond fluttered her hands, stumbling backward toward an archway. "If you'll step this way, I'll show you to the viewing salon. Miss, the dressing room is right through that curtain and I'll bring the dress to you. Mr. D'Amato you can...um, there's a sofa for you to wait on—and coffee— Or I can send someone to get you...something."

Once they'd passed through it, the clerk untied a curtain, shielding them from the main store.

"I'll be fine." Bear gave Maureen a squeeze before letting her go and sat down on the couch. Then shooting him a doubtful look, she disappeared behind the red velvet curtain.

A few minutes later, when she reappeared in the dress, she still looked dubious. Hot, but dubious. The clerk had put her in a pair of matching strappy silver heels that gave her a lovely chewing gum walk, but didn't erase the uncertainty on her face. "Do you have any idea how much this costs?" she asked.

"I'm pretty sure I don't care."

"It feels like I'm naked."

He shifted, trying to control the response that image produced. Good thing the hotel was only a block away. "If you're not comfortable in it, we don't have to get it."

The clerk cleared her throat. "There are a few other things that would look good on you in the back, if you'd like to see them."

"You started this," she said to him with a shrug.

"Let's see what you have then."

"You can— You can have a seat and I'll bring them out... Unless you wanted to change back into your clothes first...I can wait... Are you sure you don't want something to drink? Coffee? Soft drink?" The clerk twisted her hands together.

"I'm fine," Maureen said. "Michael?"

"I'd be better if you were over here." He patted the seat next to him.

The clerk gave a delighted sigh as Maureen walked over and settled next to him, then scurried off to collect the other options. Bear traced his fingertips over Maureen's bare back, and she crossed her legs. Her gaze slid sideways toward him, cool and hot at the same time. "You're being bad again."

"I know. Are you going to make me stand in the corner?"

She raised an eyebrow. "Depends on how bad you are."

The clerk came out, pushing a wooden rack with a bunch of dresses on it. Instead of watching the fashion show, he watched Maureen. She eliminated a couple of things out of hand as too racy and a couple more as too expensive. Within a few minutes, she'd narrowed it down to three, only one of which was backless. The old cow who had dismissed them when they'd walked in, came to stand at the back of the room while the clerk put together complete outfits for Maureen to take into the dressing room. When he glared at the old bat so she would go away, she only returned the look.

"Do you mind?" he asked.

She snorted and flounced out.

Maureen returned, wearing a fluffy blue and purple thing. Its raggedy hem fell to her knees and, though backless, it left too much up to the imagination. "You don't like it," she said.

He shook his head.

She shrugged. "Okay. Next!"

Next looked like something off a sixties TV show. Neat and sleek, it was cotton candy pink, fell just above her knee and didn't show enough cleavage. She looked like she was born in it.

"You don't like it," she said.

"I didn't say that."

She smirked at him. "I'll go change. Maybe third time will be a charm."

Third time was not a charm. Crushed dark green velvet that molded to her form, this dress only fell midway down her thighs and had a high neck and long sleeves. Maureen walked out tugging the hem down. "I bet you like this one," she said, smoothing the fabric over her hips.

"You don't."

She stuck her tongue out at him.

"That a promise?"

She gave him a dirty look before turning to the clerk. "I'm sorry. It looks like we're batting zero today."

"Can I ask what event you're dressing for?" The girl started nibbling her fingernails.

"A concert," Maureen said.

"The SendDown show." That dress made her legs look several delicious miles long. Totally out of character, but delightful to look at. Maybe he could talk her into wearing it at home when it was just the two of them. No, that would get in the way of her being naked.

"Oh, the SendDown concert! I'm going to that show. Wait. I have another idea." The clerk dove behind the curtain.

Maureen shrugged.

"Come here," he said low, waving her closer.

"Why?"

"Because you look fantastic and I want to experience it up close."

She licked her lips and slunk across the room. Stopping in front of him, she leaned over and put her hands on the back of the sofa on either side of his shoulders. "Close enough?"

"Almost." He snaked his arm around her waist and pulled her into his lap.

"Michael! We're in public."

Bear rubbed his cheek on the velvet. "We're alone."

"Someone could walk in any second." She pushed herself off his lap, but stayed next to him. "If you like this dress that much, I'll wear it for you."

"Who says I like it that much?"

The clerk zipped through the room and out the curtain to the front of the store.

"You haven't stopped petting me since I sat down," Maureen said.

He put his hand on her shoulder and forced it to stay still. "You look uncomfortable. I don't want you to wear anything you don't like."

With a soft sigh, she leaned her head on his shoulder, and he rested his head on hers. Who cared what those guys in SendDown thought of her? Who cared what the other guys in the band thought? She was fantastic and if they couldn't see it, they were morons.

"So what do you do in rehearsal?" she asked.

"Sort out the set list and practice the songs until we can do them in our sleep. You'll have lots of time to sightsee."

"And what do you do on tour?"

"Travel, perform, sleep, start over the next day." He ran his fingers through her hair. The velvet was nice, but it had nothing on the texture of her hair. "You'll want to bring a book. Maybe one of those ebook readers so you can bring lots of books."

"You don't sound like you enjoy it."

"It's pretty boring. You spend a lot of time waiting to get on stage and very little time performing."

"What do the other guys' girlfriends do while you're all touring?"

"I dunno. Shop? I guess you'll have to ask them."

The clerk zipped back in with a couple of shopping bags in her hands and stopped in the middle of the room gasping for breath. "I've got...some things...for you to try." She held up the bags.

Maureen slid off the couch. "You didn't have to rush. We're in no hurry."

The clerk shook her head, gesturing with the bags.

As Maureen followed her into the dressing room, he tried to soak up as much of her departing view as he could. She knew how to work a pair of high heels. Something he always admired in a woman. Too bad she wouldn't be wearing that dress again, or the silver one. Neither one really suited her, but the view had been nice. Of the three, the pink conservative one had looked the best. He'd never imagined himself as the kind of guy who would be with a girl in a proper pink dress, but here he was.

The clerk drew the curtain back and Maureen stepped through. Snake skin stilettos. Dark wash jeans that made her legs long and lean. A long sleeved chocolate brown velvet top that hugged her body, but draped loosely between her breasts. A gold chain around her neck with a single music note suspended from it. Hair swept back off her face to show off earrings that matched the necklace. She strode to the mirror and smiled at him in its reflection.

Bear went to stand behind her. The heels made her almost exactly his height. He wrapped his arms around her waist. "Comfortable?"

"Yes. You like?"

"I do." He nuzzled her neck. "You look amazing. Why don't you wear it now? They can put your clothes in a bag."

"Will it make you happy?"

"If it'll make you happy."

She reached back and brushed her fingers through his hair. "Pay the nice lady."

"Yes, ma'am." He trailed his hand around her waist as he stepped back. This velvet slid under his hands like warm water and he didn't want to stop touching it. He fished his credit card out of his wallet and handed it over. "Pack up that pink dress too, with whatever stuff you had with it."

"Why?" Maureen asked as the clerk hurried out.

"Because you liked it."

"You didn't." She draped her arms around his neck.

"I liked you in it."

She brushed his nose with hers. "I guess I'll have to think of an appropriate thank you."

"I look forward to it."

* * * *

"Here, stick this on your jeans." Michael handed her a satiny disk that looked like a sewer cover and had the words *SendDown Street Release Tour* written around it. In the center was a scribble that could have been a set of initials or a pictogram from a lost civilization. She peeled the paper off the back and stuck it on her thigh.

They'd taken a cab the seven blocks to the hall and been let off at the back door, where a small mob was held back by sawhorses and city cops. The guard at the door had recognized Michael and ushered them inside. She wiped her hands on her leg. It wasn't just the guard who recognized Michael. The crowd had and so had most of the people inside the building. At least most of the people inside were men. Outside, it had been mostly women dressed in less than what she'd turned down yesterday.

"They're in the dressing room," the guy Michael had gotten the disks from told him. "You know where it is."

"Yeah, thanks." Michael caught her hand. "They won't be going on for an hour so we'll have some time to hang out."

"These are friends of yours?" Up and down the hall, the white cement block walls were broken periodically by doors and ended in a set of double metal doors. A roar leaked through like there might be several prides of very annoyed lions behind them. Michael pushed open a door and walked in. A couple of guys lounged on cracked black vinyl couches that faced one another across the long narrow room.

"Hey!" A tattooed man with greasy black hair leaped up. "Bear, man, glad you could make it." He grabbed Michael's hand and shook it. Another guy got up and sauntered over, looking only at her. She took a step back and half behind Michael. Everyone else in the room started moving closer.

"Haven't seen you guys in ages," Michael said.

"Yeah, cuz we've been fuckin' touring forever," the first man said. "This must be the new woman." He held out his hand to her. "Trent."

"Maureen." She held out her hand and he didn't rattle her teeth when he shook it as she'd feared.

Michael put his arm around her shoulders, pulling her forward again. "Maureen, this is Trent, Alan, Gian and Rumballs."

"Fuck you," the one he'd called Rumballs said before shaking her hand.

"A pleasure to meet you." Gian cupped her hand, his gaze boring into her.

"A pleasure." She pulled her hand away. Rumballs punched Gian's shoulder. Michael didn't even seem to notice the come on. He hadn't introduced any of the women either. There were seven or eight. One walked over and tapped her on the shoulder.

"Hi again," she said. In the skimpy dress and heavy makeup, it took Maureen a minute to recognize the clerk from the store yesterday.

"Hi."

"I have to say, that outfit looks great on you." She smirked. "I do good work."

"Yes, thanks. You didn't mention that you were with the band." Maureen glanced at Michael, but he was already deep in conversation with Trent and Rumballs.

"I wasn't yesterday."

Oh. Maureen stared at the floor.

"So, hey, you want something to drink?" The clerk took her hand. "Come on."

Maureen considered insisting that she needed to stay with Michael, but decided she didn't want to be an albatross. "I'm sorry, I don't even know your name," she said, following the girl across the room to a table full of food.

"Call me Jenny."

"Jenny, babe," Trent called. "Peel me an orange."

"Comin' up." Jenny grabbed an orange out of a silver bowl and started peeling it. "I'm hoping to be going home with him tonight. Just grab whatever you want. They won't touch most of this stuff. It's all just here in case they get hungry before the show."

Two six foot tables laden with fruit, vegetables and drinks. A lot of food for five guys and their assorted hangers on. She picked up a bottle of water.

"You're with Bear D'Amato?" a girl said beside her.

The girl had short black hair and a tattoo of roses around her neck. She would have been perfectly comfortable in that silver dress Michael picked out yesterday. In fact, it might have been too conservative for her.

The black-haired girl licked her lips. "I did him last tour. He's good."

"Shut up, Cyn," Jenny snapped. "It's not like that."

"Not like what?" Cyn asked.

Jenny tossed the orange peel in the trash and split up the segments on a napkin. "He's off the market."

"Oh, please. He's a man."

"Just don't."

"Now, girls." Maureen stepped between them, holding out her hands to keep them separated.

Michael grabbed her by the shoulders and pulled her against his chest. "Maureen, come on over here and meet the guys."

She almost reminded him that she'd already met the guys, but Trent had an arm around Jenny and was picking orange segments out of the napkin she still held. Jenny looked like she was in heaven and since she was the closest she had to a friend in this room, Maureen didn't want to interrupt. Plus, she needed to have a conversation with Michael. Gian was walking Cyn to the door. Alan and Rumballs were talking to a guy in a black t-shirt wearing a headset. The other girls preened in front of the mirrors. This was as close to privacy as she was going to get until they went back to the hotel and if she didn't ask him now, the question would eat its way out of her chest like the monsters in *Alien*. "Did you have sex with that girl?"

He glanced over his shoulder and frowned. "Maybe. I think so."

The deep breath she tried to draw caught on the steel bands around her lungs. She didn't expect him to have been a saint, but to not remember? Another steel band tightened around her head and the room went a little flat and sideways.

"Listen, baby, those girls don't mean anything. When you're out on the road they're everywhere. It's like exercise." He flushed.

"You weren't jogging with her."

"No." He slouched.

"And you're going to be out on the road soon." She folded her arms to keep her body from flying apart. How had she gotten mixed up in this?

"Yeah, but it's different now. Why go out for hamburger when I've got steak at home?" He stroked her cheek.

"What if you get hungry while you're out?"

"Baby, I'm not going to." He put his hands on her neck and leaned his forehead against hers. Her view shrank to just him. Just his eyes. "I love you, Maureen. Ever since I met you, everything's been different. You're all I need."

"What if the hamburger is particularly insistent?" Cyn looked the type to take no as a challenge. And there were thousands of girls like her. Probably a dozen in the building right now. None of them would think twice about having sex with him. They might not even think of it as cheating. *He* might not think of it as cheating. "If I'm going to marry you, I need to know you're going to be faithful."

"I promise you I will give new meaning to the word faithful."

"That's what I'm afraid of." Maureen bit her lip. If he cheated on her, all of these people were going to know. They would be laughing about how naive she'd been, believing he wouldn't be with another woman when so many willing ones were available.

All she could see was his eyes, and eyes never lie.

"You have nothing to fear. I am forever yours. Faithfully."

Four sweaty guys walked through the door and Michael straightened, draping a protective arm over her shoulders. The first guy in the door stopped so suddenly all the others plowed into him like a comedy routine. "He came," the guy said. "Holy shit, man, it is so cool to meet you." He crossed the room and seized Michael's hand.

The guy in the black t-shirt started yelling that the members of SendDown needed to get their shit together right fucking now. The guys in the other band swarmed around Michael. Though Gian was still hanging around by the couch and the other girls were still there, Cyn was absent. Jenny hooked her arm through Maureen's free one.

"You want to come out and watch the show from the pit?" Jenny asked.

"The pit?"

"The photographer's pit. You can get right up to the stage."

"I don't know. I should stay with Michael." She hadn't thought he was listening, but the moment she said his name he turned to her.

"Go on ahead, Maureen. I'm coming out in a few minutes." He kissed her cheek. "Stay with her though."

Jenny hung onto her arm as they walked out of the room. "Good news. I'm in with Trent. I'm off tomorrow so I can go with him to the next show, but if he wants me to follow along any further I'm gonna have to quit."

"You would quit your job?"

"Oh sure. For a shot at Trent Markov? I'd do anything. Could you imagine if he wanted me to be his girlfriend? We'd get to hang out all the time." Jenny's eyes shone as she pushed through a side door that led into a narrow, dim hallway.

Those girls don't mean anything. When you're out on the road they're everywhere. It's like exercise. Did Trent think of Jenny of exercise? "I don't know if I'd get my hopes up."

"Oh, I know. It's different for you."

She stopped and Jenny stopped with her. Jenny had her hand on the door at the bottom of the hall. Through it came the muffled sounds of the concert hall. They weren't as loud as they had been before, but it still sounded like a lot of people. "What do you mean it's different for me?"

"You're the girlfriend. We're just groupies."

"And that's different?"

Jenny cocked her head. "Sure. We're good for a night or so. He goes home to you. I don't have any delusions about what I am. Not like Cyn."

"Cyn has delusions?"

"She thinks some rock star is going to fall in love with her and marry her, but she's starting to get desperate. She used to be able to get backstage at the big shows and now she can't."

"Why?" Other than a striking lack of ethics when it came to other women's men, she couldn't recall anything in particular wrong with Cyn.

"She's getting too old."

"How old is she?"

"Thirty-two."

Maureen nodded as if this were indeed over the hill, keeping to herself the fact that she was thirty-four.

"Come on. I want to be out there when they get on stage." Jenny tugged her arm so she allowed herself to be led out.

* * * *

"What did you think of the show?" Bear asked. He'd intended to hang around and have dinner with the band, but by the time they got offstage at eleven, Maureen's lights had begun to blink out. At least she wasn't still freaked about that groupie.

"It was loud."

"But you had fun. You looked like you were having fun." He swallowed. She'd hated it. Half of the show, she'd had this look of stunned horror plastered on her face. What was he going to do if she hated what he did for a living? Quit?

Hmm, quit.

"I had fun. I've never been to a concert before." She nestled her head on his shoulder. "You're a wealth of brand new experiences."

"Good ones, I hope." He resisted the urge to clench his teeth. The way she leaned on him, she'd know and he didn't want her to know how anxious he was.

"Mostly. And I get to be with you." She sighed, sinking more heavily into his arms. "Sorry. I'm still on school time."

"That's okay." He squeezed her shoulder. Damn, they weren't even on the same schedule. She was in bed every night at eleven and when they were on tour, he was just getting ready to have dinner at that time. Day shift, night shift.

"So if I came with you on tour over the summer I guess I'd be watching the show every night."

"Not every night. Not if you didn't want to. You could hang at the hotel and watch movies or something."

She nodded. "But the girls would be there every night."

"Girls?" He held his breath wondering if she was going to allow him to play stupid. She twisted to stare at him. Nope. "Oh them. We don't entertain as much as we used to. Marc is— Well, Marc is getting a divorce now, but last tour he was married and Brian's married. Jason was dating that bitch. Ty is sort of like a hummingbird anyway and I...indulged. A little."

"Apparently."

"But I was single and I had been for a while." He wished he could even remember that particular groupie. Last tour he hadn't been celibate by any stretch, but he hadn't gorged either. Most of the time he'd picked one and kept her around for a couple of dates. "Now that I'm with you it's different."

"Different." She settled back into his arms, but the cab stopped in front of the hotel.

He paid the driver as she climbed out. She didn't say anything as they waited for the elevator and it made his skin itch. Usually he had better taste in groupies and took a miss on the more vicious ones. "Seriously, baby, I have willpower and I'm not afraid to use it," he said as the elevator doors closed.

She leveled him with a distant stare. "You keep calling me 'baby' and I'm going to start thinking you forgot my name." Her tone was light and she did smile as said it, but it scared the bejeezuz out of him. She was still freaked about the groupie thing. Very freaked.

"I'm sorry—" He bit his tongue before he called her 'baby' again. He pressed his hands on the elevator wall behind him. "Maureen. I'm not going to cheat on you. I swear," he said, clenching his teeth on a 'sweetheart,' which had to be as bad as 'baby.' Why was everything coming out of his mouth peppered with smarminess? "You're going to have to trust me."

She studied him from the other side of the elevator, and it felt like he could have fit a small country between them. His hands sweated against the wall. Then she stepped across, sliding her hands up over his shoulders. "I do. Dammit."

Bear put his hands on her waist. "Why dammit?"

"Because I have no good reason to trust you and I do."

The door slid open on their floor and he grabbed her hand as she stepped away. Letting her go didn't appear to be a good idea. It gave her too much room to think.

What was he supposed to do when he left town and she had three thousand miles of room?

Chapter 8

Maureen adjusted her carry on strap over her shoulder and squinted down the corridor. He was pacing beside the luggage carousel. As she watched, he rolled one of his shoulders gingerly. He'd told her on the phone that every time someone in the band forgot something during rehearsal they got slugged on the shoulder. Michael, it seemed, was getting more than his fair share of slugs. Boys. They never grew up. "Michael!"

He spun around and she waved her arm over her head to attract his attention. As he bolted through the crowd, people scattered. He scooped her off her feet and swung her around. "Baby, I missed you."

"I missed you too."

He let her slide down to her feet and kissed her deep and slow. She wanted to be lost in that sensation. Being here with him seemed unreal. They'd talked on the phone every night and about everything. She knew all about rehearsals and the set list and the arguments and he knew all about her students, but it still seemed unreal that she would be in warm, sunny Los Angeles in the arms of warm, sunny Michael.

"The Satellite is still in my garage," she said when he allowed her to speak.

"The car?"

"Yes, silly. You said you wanted to store it at my house. I've been going out and starting it up every couple of days so the battery doesn't die." To be honest, she went out to sit in the car to remind herself that she wasn't crazy. He did exist and she hadn't made him up. For some reason, the telephone conversations weren't as reassuring as sitting in his car, parked in her garage, listening to the engine purr.

He smoothed his hand over her hair. "You have to drive it around if you don't want the battery to die."

"Oh, sorry."

"Don't worry about it. I can get a new battery if I have to. It's not important." Bear drew a deep breath. "Come on, let's get the rest of your stuff."

"This is it." She toed the bag she'd dropped when he grabbed her.

He looked down. "You're kidding."

"I'm only going to be here for a few days." Most of the past week, she'd considered what to bring. Jeans, tops, some long sleeves in case it got cold. She'd stashed a pair of nice shoes in there in case he wanted to go out. They were the ones he'd bought for her when they went to the concert. She'd also brought the dress he'd bought her.

"This is all you have?" He picked up the bag and slung it over his shoulder.

"Should I have brought more?" She chewed the inside of her cheek. She probably should have. If she wanted to spend time with him, she was going to have to start reading fashion magazines. That or make a trip to see Jenny for some advice. Provided Jenny still worked at that store and hadn't quit to follow Trent on the off chance he wanted to keep her around.

"Don't worry about it. Let's go. I have a surprise for you." He took her hand and led her through the airport. She tried to take it in, but everything blurred together. Seven hours ago, she'd been leaving school, trying to get to the airport in time to catch her flight, but now her watch read only four hours later and the sun was still up. Her brain wanted to get ready for bed. Her body concurred, but with a different end in mind.

He used a remote to pop open the trunk of his car and dropped her bag in it then led her to the passenger side. The other teachers thought it was terribly romantic that he didn't let her touch a door. When he climbed in the driver's side, he stuck the key in the ignition, but didn't start the car. Instead, he turned to her grinning.

"What?"

"I have a surprise for you." He reached into his pocket and pulled out a credit card, which he handed to her.

"What's this?"

"Look at it."

She stared at the card. Mastercard. Platinum. Maureen Donnelly. "This isn't my credit card. Why is my name on it?"

"It's your expense account."

"My what?"

"Your expense account."

She flipped the card over and checked the back as if it would explain what he was talking about. "What do I need an expense account for?"

He shrugged. "Stuff. It's only got a ten thousand dollar limit, but my office will pay it off every month and if you need more, let me know and I'll get it taken care of."

"What's it for?" Ten thousand dollars? A month? That was almost a third of her annual salary. What in God's name did he expect her to spend that much money on every month?

"Shoes and clothes and beauty shop. Girl stuff." He shrugged again like it should have been obvious.

"Don't you like the way I dress?" She *was* going to have to start studying fashion magazines. She should have known, based on her internet research over the past two weeks, that her second grade teacher look wasn't going to work. No way could she afford to shop at that place where Jenny worked, if she still worked there. Of course, now that she had an expense account...

"I love the way you dress." He kissed her cheek.

"Then why are you handing me money?"

"I'm not handing you money." He frowned. "It's an expense account. For expenses. I always give my girlfriends a credit card. What's wrong?"

"I don't understand why you're giving me an expense account."

"So you have money if you need it. I'm taking care of you, baby."

She resisted the urge to remind him she could take care of herself and spent the time studying the credit card again as if its true meaning might have appeared on its surface.

He put his hands over hers, covering the card. "Maureen, I don't care what you do with it. I don't care of you spend it or if you toss it in the bottom of your suitcase and forget you have it. Use it for clothes or groceries or jewelry or house payments or coffee. I don't care. Just let me give it to you."

She nodded. For whatever reason, it was important to him that she take it, so she might as well. She didn't have to use it. She really needed to talk to Jenny. "So do you have to rehearse all weekend too?"

"No, we take weekends off." He started up the car and backed out. "Marc wants to get together for dinner tomorrow. Is that okay with you?"

"Sure." An uncontrollable yawn escaped her.

"He's probably going to interrogate you. He's getting a divorce and it's making him nuts. At least you won't be stuck with Jason too. His girlfriend broke up with him a few weeks ago and he still hasn't replaced her."

She nodded and rested her head on the seat. She hadn't slept much last night because she'd been worrying if she'd packed everything and how she was going to make her flight. When she did, her dreams had been filled with vivid images that woke her up reaching across the bed to find him. She should have spent more time worrying about meeting his friends. They couldn't be worse than his brother, could they? Her eyes slid closed as he worked his way into traffic.

"Sandy needs to size you up too. Sorry." He kept talking and his words blurred together until she felt his fingers brush her cheek. "I guess you're pretty tired."

"Pretty tired." She caught his hand and pressed it to her lips. "But I missed you."

"It's gonna take a while to get home. Why don't you try to sleep so I can keep you up late?"

"That sounds fun." She let herself relax. She was here. She hadn't missed the flight and if she'd packed the wrong stuff, Michael would be happy to take her shopping again. Everything after that first pizza was gravy, and this was some very nice gravy. A week here with him, away from the cold gray weather. If she did nothing more than hang out at his house waiting for him to come home, it would be lovely.

"Baby? Maureen?" He shook her shoulder. "We're home."

"Home?" She blinked and stretched. The car was parked in a two-car garage. In the other bay sat another blunt, heavy car in a color she could only describe as dragon spit green. Along the front wall stood a professional workbench. She yawned. "Did I sleep all the way here?"

"Yep." He climbed out, popping the trunk.

She stretched and opened her door, but before she could climb out he was there, reaching for her hand to help her. He led her through a door into the kitchen. Small and neat, a table was crammed against one wall and a litter of notes on the fridge door. "I take it you don't spend a lot of time at the grocery store where Tim Allen shops."

"What?"

"You said you shopped at the same grocery store as Tim Allen, but I challenge you to eat a meal at that table." She pointed to the table heaped with junk mail and miscellany.

"Oh, no. I eat out a lot." He dropped her bag on the floor and gathered her in his arms. "I missed you so much," he murmured, kissing her throat. "I wish you could stay forever. I wish I could stay forever."

Maureen bent back in his embrace. She arched her neck for him, tangling her fingers through his hair. Breathing deeply, she inhaled his spicy, exotic scent. If she never made her return flight, that would be okay. If she could just stay here with him. "Me too."

He leaned his forehead on hers. "The guys are all still pretty wound about the whole marriage thing."

"Don't worry about it." No one at school even knew.

"What?"

As many times as she'd used the trick of getting in close to get the truth, she'd never had it used on her. It wasn't a comfortable feeling. Over the phone she'd been able to keep her private drama to herself, but he obviously wasn't going to allow it in person. "Everybody at school is pretty upset I came to visit."

"Why?" He straightened, but only gave her a few inches between his eyes and hers. He still held her tight enough that she could feel his heart beating.

"Linda wasn't happy when I told her who you really were. She said if you started out lying to me what would you do later?" That was the abbreviated version. Linda had been lecturing on that theme for the past two weeks.

"I explained that. I know it was a mistake." Muscles tensed, he pulled her tighter, as if she might try to get away.

"I know," she said, a finger over his mouth. "I understand. I can even see why you did it." *Sort of.* "I just can't make her understand."

"And all the other teachers think the same thing?"

The other teachers? Kathy kept saying she had to make her own mistakes. Lauren couldn't decide whether she was the luckiest woman breathing or an idiot. Kaitlyn wanted autographs. Everyone else fell somewhere in the middle. None of them thought the relationship was going anywhere. Hence the reason she hadn't told them about the engagement. Why make things worse? "The vote is still out."

"And my brother?"

His brother. "I talked to Nicky's teacher and she thinks if for some reason Nicky can't be in my class, he would do well in Kaitlyn's so she's going to note it in his record. Kaitlyn's pretty young, but she's a good teacher. Tony seemed pleased with that when I stopped at the garage Monday."

"Did he say anything about me?" His lips pressed into a thin line.

She swallowed. She'd been hoping he had talked to Tony and not told her. A thin hope, but she'd been holding it with both hands. Apparently she wasn't going to be able to Tinkerbell this into existence. "I told him I was coming out here. He said to enjoy the sunshine."

Christa Maurce

He let her go and picked up her bag. "Let's take this into the bedroom so you can relax."

She followed him through the dining room, which had a drum set where the table should have been. Behind the drums, sliding glass windows overlooked a small yard with a kidney shaped pool. The living room boasted a dark blue couch and matching chairs, a rectangular coffee table and a closed television hutch. A short dark hall led past two closed doors. At the end, an open door led to the bedroom, also unremarkable, with a queen sized bed and a dresser. It was all very upper middle class. The clips of *MTV Cribs* on YouTube had misled her.

He set her bag on the end of the bed. When he turned back to her, his mood had brightened again. "Can we get to the serious reunion stuff now?"

"I need to hang up one thing before it gets too wrinkled." She unzipped the bag and pulled out the pink dress. "I know you don't like this one, but you bought it so I thought you might want to see me wear it."

"I never said I didn't like it." He touched the material as if he were afraid his touch would stain it. "I just prefer you naked."

She opened the closet and found a spare hanger. "Well, I figured there might be a couple of important introductions on this trip and naked might not make the best impression."

"Hey, you're pretty smart." He peered in the bag. "Anything else you need to get out of here right away?"

"No." She took it and dropped it on the floor in front of the closet. "You realize if you don't keep me up I'm going to be awake at something like four in the morning."

"Is that a challenge?" He slid his arm around her waist.

Wrapping her arms around his neck, she leaned backward, dragging him onto the bed on top of her. He pulled her to the middle of the bed, the weight of him crushing her into the mattress. Every night for the past two weeks she'd woken up from this sensation and been disappointed to be alone.

"You are so beautiful," he murmured, kissing her throat.

"Well, it is a really nice dress."

"No, I mean just you. Everything about you." He lifted his head to study her, and she lay back on the bed, studying him in turn. The setting sun made him a shaggy silhouette haloed in gold. "You're beautiful. Your face, your body, your personality, your sense of humor. Being with you makes me feel so damn good."

Tears stung her eyes, and she blinked them away. "Why, Michael, that's poetic. I love being with you too." She kissed him, wishing she had more words to tell him what he meant to her. Opening the buttons of his shirt, she slid it off his shoulders and ran her fingers up his arms. His skin contracted and became pebbled under her touch. He shivered. His member strained against her leg as he moved down her body, taking her left nipple onto his mouth.

She gasped. None of her dreams had been this complete. Being near him made her dizzy and hot. His tongue rasped across her tender flesh, sending tendrils of joy through her. One week wasn't going to be enough. One lifetime wasn't going to be enough. "Oh Michael. That feels so good." She laced her fingers through his hair. Long dark strands tangled around her hands. "Make love to me. Please. I want your whole body on mine. I want to have my legs wrapped around you while you thrust into me. Please. I need you. I missed you."

He stood up. For a minute he hesitated at the side of the bed, breathing heavily as he studied her. Then he shoved his jeans down and kicked them off as he located the condoms in a bedside table. She bit her lip. She wanted to tell him to skip the protection because it was taking too long. Too long? Maybe she had lost her mind. Unfortunately, she was enjoying it too much to worry.

When he crawled back onto the bed, he mounted her, plunging deep into her with one long stroke. She shuddered, clasping herself around him, and Michael pressed his face into the curve of her neck. His hot mouth opened over her jugular in a silent moan. He thrust into her again, filling her. Digging her fingers into his back, she gave a strangled cry. Ecstasy arced through her. He thrust into her twice more before his own climax rolled over him.

"You are so sweet to me," she murmured, running her finger through his hair.

"Sweet?"

She kissed his cheek. "I was starting to think I'd imagined you."

"Me too." He shifted off her. "Sorry that was so quick."

"You can make it up to me later."

"That so?" He pinned her hands over her head. "Demanding."

"I know it'll be a hardship."

"It'll be a hard something."

"I was hoping for that too."

He laughed and rolled away. Jumping off the bed, he said, "let's go get you some coffee or something. I want to keep you awake so I can play with you later."

She slid off the bed. His comment released a slither of anxiety in her chest. "From a gift to a toy?"

"Sure." He pulled his jeans back on, strolled around the foot of the bed and wrapped his arms around her. "Toy, treasure, breath, life, everything I ever wanted and all I need."

"Everything you ever wanted and all you need? That's a tall order." She forced herself to breathe before she passed out.

He put his hand on the top of her head. "No. Just about five six."

* * * *

Bear pulled out a chair for Maureen and Marc gave him a dirty look. Marc's date pulled out her own chair and plopped down. Marc needed to hook up with some classier women. Maureen smiled up at him.

Waking up next to her this morning had been heavenly. She'd been awake, reading a book in bed. Tonight he hoped to leave her so exhausted she slept until noon tomorrow. He settled in his chair and waved away the wine list. The restaurant had been Marc's choice and was way too fancy. Probably trying to throw Maureen, but in the pink dress he hadn't liked so much, she looked like she dined here every day. Cool and confident. The dress had been a good choice.

"So this is the wonderful Maureen," Marc said. "How do you like California so far?"

"I just got in last night so I haven't seen much." She folded her hands in her lap and leaned toward Bear. He draped his arm across the back of her chair. "Today, we just hung out at the house after we went to the grocery store to pick up some supplies. We didn't see anyone famous, either."

"Oh?" Marc cocked an eyebrow. "Who did you expect to see?"

"Nobody really, but Michael said Tim Allen shops there." Maureen took the napkin off her plate and shook it out. Then she laid it next to the plate instead of on her lap.

"Rick Allen," Michael corrected.

She shrugged. "Well then, I wouldn't have known him if he walked up and bit me. Tim Allen, I would recognize at least."

Marc's eyes radiated disbelief as he glared at Bear but said to her, "I'm pretty sure you could pick Rick Allen out in a crowd too."

"Maureen isn't really up on music. We spent most of today listening to CDs." He caught her eye. Most of the day when they weren't busy doing something else. A blush blossomed on her cheeks and he felt an answering tug in his groin. When had he thought that dress didn't look sexy on her? Every damn thing looked sexy on her.

A waiter invaded with menus and recommendations while his assistant came around to fill their water glasses and deliver bread. Maureen fiddled with her napkin again so he leaned over and kissed her cheek behind his menu.

"Don't let him bug you," he whispered.

"I'm not." She caught his eyes for a moment and then dropped her gaze. "Is it that obvious?"

"To me." He squeezed her shoulder. He wished he could tell her that meeting Sandy was going to be easier, but it wasn't. Sandy had all of Marc's disapproval and thirty years more practice throwing it around. "I don't care what they think and you don't need to."

She put her hand on his leg.

"What do you want?" he asked. His mom always had his dad order for her and it seemed classier than her ordering for herself.

She smirked gently. "Why don't you get me the fillet, medium rare."

"Good choice, my lady." He closed his menu and set it in the table.

"So what do you plan to do while you're here?" Marc leaned on the table, ignoring his menu. "Because Bear's going to be busy all week screwing up at rehearsals."

"Screw you." Bear sipped from his water glass.

"I thought I'd go see some museums or something while he's busy."

"We should go shopping," Marc's bimbo said. He really wished he'd been paying attention when Marc introduced her.

"That would be nice." Maureen smiled.

Bear doubted it, but he wasn't going to try and stop her. At least, not in front of Marc. "There's lots of stuff for Maureen to do while she's here. She wants to meet everybody and next weekend we're going to Disneyland."

"Disneyland." Marc's eyebrow cocked again. He was going to get a cramp doing that.

"My kids would never let me live it down if I was in Los Angeles and didn't go to Disneyland." She grinned.

"You have kids?" Marc asked.

"She has students." Bear gritted his teeth. "She's a teacher."

She squeezed his leg, reminding him to calm down. They'd had long conversations about him keeping his temper. His friends needed time to get used to her. Blah. Blah. Blah. She was right but he just couldn't figure out how she managed to keep cool.

"I'm happy to get to see Michael again," she said.

The waiter invaded again to get their orders. The assistant waiter dusted the table as if any of them had bothered to touch the bread.

"What grade do you teach?" Marc asked.

"Second." Maureen clasped her hands in her lap.

"How long have you been doing that?"

"Twelve years."

"You looking to hire a teacher, Marc?" Bear asked.

Marc turned his flat, assessing gaze on him. "I'm trying to learn a little more about your brand new fiancee none of us has met."

"Fiancee!" Marc's date gasped. "Can I see your ring?"

"I don't have a ring yet. Michael and I decided since everyone was so concerned about our sudden engagement, we would wait a little before making it official." Maureen held herself stiffly and didn't look at him. The subject had turned into a full-blown argument today. He'd been gung ho to go diamond shopping and she was just as determined to wait.

"I see." Marc studied her like a chess grand master witnessing a play he'd never seen before.

"This is a nice restaurant, Marc. Michael said you chose it. Do you eat here often?" Maureen surveyed the room. The whole place was lit by candles. Huge candelabras full of them hung from the ceiling. Whatever they might have saved on electric, they probably spent on having a team come in every day to change and light all the candles.

"No, our manager recommended it." Marc folded his arms.

So this was Sandy's game and Marc was just the first offensive. Marvelous.

"It is lovely." Maureen leaned back against Bear's arm. "Marc, why don't you tell me a little about yourself. I really want to get to know Michael's friends. He says you play guitar."

Stroking her shoulder with his fingers, he half listened while she steered the conversation. Marc was more used to being on this end of the interview anyway and now that she had more control, she had stopped fiddling with her napkin. Marc's date planted her elbows on the table, watching the two of them like she might watch ping pong. The assistant waiter came around to deliver their drinks and double check the bread and water.

"I think I should wash my hands before dinner," Maureen said when the waiter left.

Bear jumped up and pulled her chair out.

Marc and his date exchanged a look. "Uh, I guess I should go too," his date said. She started to get up and Marc stood to help her.

Maureen brushed a kiss across Bear's cheek, taking the opportunity to whisper, "Stay calm."

Bear nodded and watched her walk to the far corner of the restaurant with Marc's date on her heels. When he turned back to the table, Marc was already sitting down and scowling.

"What was that all about?" Marc demanded. "Are you going to jump up like a fucking jack-in-the-box every time she stands up?"

"It's polite and Maureen is a lady."

"I'll bet."

Staying calm was a tall order. Maureen had no idea. He took a sip of his wine and waited.

Marc twiddled a cigarette through his fingers. "You know what she's doing, don't you?"

"Trying to take me for everything I'm worth?"

Marc glared at him. "There is no way she's that clueless. She knew who you were the second she laid eyes on you."

"She's not clueless. She just isn't interested in music. The only preset in her car is NPR." He shrugged. "She likes dinosaurs, gardening and *The X-Files*."

"Dinosaurs, gardening and *The X-Files*." Marc tapped the cigarette on the table. "And you're just the sucker to fall for it."

"I'm not falling for anything. Dammit, why can't anybody believe we love each other?" He slammed his fist on the table, making everything on it jump. The other diners in the restaurant turned to stare.

"Because you've got a better chance of getting struck by lightning than of finding a woman who loves you for who you are instead of *who you are*." Marc stood up. "I'm gonna go get some dirty looks."

"You know that doesn't make any sense, right? A woman who loves me for who I am and not *who I am*?" he asked Marc's departing back. Marc gave him the finger over his shoulder.

Chapter 9

While washing her hands, Maureen tried to figure out how much to tip the bathroom attendant. She'd never had to navigate a situation like this before. Any of this. Nichole wouldn't be any help either. The other woman had started chattering the moment they walked through the lounge doors and had not stopped, even when they were in the stalls.

"So I think I'm going to be able to move in with Marc before they go on tour," Nicole babbled on. "He hasn't said anything, but these guys like to have somebody at home while they're on the road. He hasn't said anything about my expense account either. I kinda need him to get on the ball about that. I owe like a ton on my credit cards and any second now they're going to cut off my phone and then how's he going to get in touch with me? So when do you want to go shopping this week?"

The abrupt silence almost deafened her. Then the absurdity of what Nichole had said sunk in. The girl was in deep on her credit cards, about to lose her phone because she couldn't pay the bill and she wanted to go shopping? Was there a planet on which this made sense? She turned to the attendant to see if the astonishment was mutual, but the attendant maintained a passive expression as she handed Maureen a towel. "I haven't really made any plans," Maureen said. "Did you want to go Monday?"

"I can't, Monday. I have a mani pedi on Monday and I teach a strip class on Monday and Wednesday." Nichole applied more eyeliner, flicking the ends into exotic tails with practiced fingers.

"A what?" She tossed the towel in the wicker basket at the end of the counter. Maybe she should touch up her makeup too. When they left the house, Michael told her she looked fine, but based on Nichole, perhaps she should have worn more.

"A strip class. It is so much fun and really good exercise." Nichole slapped herself on the rear. "You wanna sit in? Rosie is in Vancouver shooting so there's a free pole and the boys always like the results."

With Nichole's comment, the scrambling for an excuse to miss the strip class stopped. *The boys always like the results*. Would Michael? Was he comparing her to Nichole and wishing she was a little more like that? But he'd spent a whole week with her unvarnished and he'd seemed to like it. Of course, that was back home. Maybe in his regular environment, he wished she were a little more wild.

Fishing a single out of her wallet, she cast another glance at Nichole. If that's what he wanted, he was with the wrong woman. This might be her only trip to California.

"I'm going back to the table," she said, dropping the single in the attendant's basket and hoping it was enough. She couldn't really read enough out of the woman's murmured thank you to tell.

"Ah hah," Nichole answered, applying lipstick like a fine artist.

Michael was alone at the table, hunched over his wine glass. When she reached to pull out her chair, he jumped up to get it for her.

"Where's Marc?" she asked.

"Smoking."

"He smokes?"

"Only when he's stressed." He draped his arm across the back of her chair.

"And he's stressed now?"

"He's getting divorced, he's dating this bimbo, he's appointed himself my father." He sighed.

Bimbo. That sounded promising in a twisted way. She put her hands on his cheeks. "You know he's only doing it because he wants what's best for you."

"You're best for me." He covered one of her hands with his and turned his face so he could kiss her palm.

"We'll have to give them time to see that."

He traced a small circle on her hand with his tongue. "Or we could bail and go home and have sex."

A shiver of delight ran beneath her skin. He was never shy about wanting her. Twelve years of spending most of her time with small children, and she'd almost forgotten what that was like. "You're being a bad boy again."

"That's why you like me." He grinned.

"Oh, you two are so cute together." Nichole stood behind her chair with a blissful expression. She slid into her seat. "So, Maureen, do you want to come to my class?"

"What class?" He laced his fingers through hers.

"Nichole teaches a strip aerobics class on Monday and Wednesday," Maureen said. "She wanted to know if I'd be interested in sitting in."

Michael's lips quirked as if he'd just eaten something he suspected was spoiled. "If that's what you want."

"I'll have to see what my schedule is like," she told Nicole. "I know Michael wants me to meet everyone while I'm out here and I don't know when they're going to be available."

"There's the band and the techs and they're going to be busy all week. Then there's Brian's wife, Bonnie. She's a bitch. And Ty's girlfriend, Liddy. She's sort of an airhead." Nichole ticked them off on her fingers. "Annabelle is pretty nice, but she works all week. I don't know Tori very well, but she seems nice, but you know I think she's on the set all week this week because she got a guest part in some show. Kim is always busy with her kids. Are you going to introduce her to Jason's sisters? The ones who live here? You could just go into the office to meet Tessa, but Connie might be difficult to get to. She's always pretty busy."

Maureen gave up trying to remember names. Hopefully, when the time came she'd be able to keep them straight. About the same time as the waiter and his assistant with their meals, Marc arrived at the table. He didn't appear any less forbidding but didn't say anything, either. She wished he would. The interview had been better than this icy silence. She had no doubt the meal she was eating was one of the best she'd ever have and she might as well have been eating an old canvas sneaker. Michael had hunched his shoulders, either to deflect Marc's chill or Nichole's constant chatter. Unwinding him tonight would take some doing. She could only hope tomorrow's meeting with his manager would go better.

* * * *

Michael parked on the front yard of a tidy little home in the hills. A few cars already crowded the drive. "So you know how to work the GPS?" he asked.

"Yes, but I don't see why I need it. I could just hang out at your house." After a couple of excursions through Malibu, the thought of trying to navigate Los Angeles made her head ache.

"You didn't come all the way to California to sit around my house all week." He climbed out and she waited for him to come around the car to open her door.

She wasn't in a big hurry to get out anyway. If the rest of Michael's friends were going to act like Marc, she'd rather stay home. Her own home.

No, she wasn't quite that put off. When Michael opened the door to help her out, she remembered why she was here. Being around him made her feel like the most beautiful, fascinating woman on the planet and she wasn't going to let a few naysayers get in the way. She straightened her t-shirt while he closed the door. From a five star restaurant to a backyard barbecue. He thought they wanted to rattle her, but she hoped it was more along the lines of fitting her into their normal lives.

He opened the front door and walked in. A wiry man with long dirty blond hair jumped up from the couch.

"Dude! This the new woman?" He stuck out his hand. "I'm Ty. She's hot. Congratulations on the engagement."

She shook his hand. "Thank you."

"Sandy's out back." Ty gestured with his head. "You want something to drink?"

"Nothing right now, thank you." She folded her hands together. Total acceptance shouldn't be throwing her as much as this.

"Come on." Michael tugged her hands apart. "Let's go see Sandy."

They walked through the living room and kitchen, and it wasn't what she expected either. The house was small, tidy and stunningly suburban. While she didn't make a habit of following lifestyles of the rich and famous, she'd expected them to be living in something a bit more palatial. He stopped to chat with a few people, introducing her each time, but the names evaporated the moment he said them. There weren't a lot of people there and she knew she should have been able to remember who was who, but couldn't.

In the backyard, he led her to the grill, where a stocky older man held court with a long-handled spatula in his hand. "Hey, Sandy," Michael said.

"Michael. And this must be your lovely lady friend." Sandy switched the spatula to the other hand. "Nice to meet you. You're not a vegetarian, are you?"

"No. I'm generally omnivorous."

Sandy laughed. "Good. I've got brats and burgers. What's your poison? Michael, get your lady friend a plate."

Michael left to do his assigned task, and she had to resist the urge to snatch at the back of his shirt to keep him close. On the phone, he had said Sandy was as adamant he was making a mistake as Marc. So why was the band's manager standing in front of her smiling like Santa Claus on summer vacation?

"Relay for Life," he said.

"What?"

"Your t-shirt. When I started teaching, the big thing for charity was donkey basketball. Beastly animals. Never did what you wanted them to. A lot like the boys, as a matter of fact."

"You were a teacher?" Michael hadn't come out of the house yet. Where had he gone for those plates? China? About fifteen people lounged around the yard, added to the ten or so inside. Ages ranged from children to Sandy's age, which had to be mid-sixties.

"Didn't Michael tell you? I was their high school business math teacher. Brian, Jason and Michael's, anyway. Michael says you teach second grade. How did you happen to meet him again?"

"His brother is my mechanic and my brakes were squeaking. He was at the garage when I took it in."

"Ah." Sandy half turned to the grill. "He said you had no idea who he was when you met him."

"I didn't. My interests tend to be things nine-year-olds are interested in. Dinosaurs, Disney movies. I never was much of a music fan."

Sandy selected a burger and put it on a bun. "What will you have? I know Michael will have a burger."

"A burger is fine."

Michael appeared and handed her a plastic plate, searching her face. He gave her a reassuring little smile and she returned it. Sandy didn't appear to hate her, but how could she be certain?

Sandy put the first burger on Maureen's plate and a second on Michael's. "You saw the table with the rest of the food by the back door and Cal is sitting under the tree," he told Michael.

"Yeah, I don't get enough of that guy all week." Michael put his arm around her waist. "Come on, Maureen."

He led her to a table laden with dishes.

"We weren't supposed to bring anything, were we?" she asked. Of all the dumb mistakes to make, not bringing a covered dish to a barbecue.

"No. Sandy usually orders what he wants and if you want to bring something, fine."

"You should have told me. We could have brought potato salad or something."

He gestured to the table. "Maureen, there's three different kinds of potato salad on this table. You want to go for four?"

"No, but I'm sure I could have thought of something." She chewed her lip. She had a lentil salad recipe half memorized.

He put his arm around her shoulders. "Don't sweat it. Nobody is going to kick you out for not bringing something."

"They're already searching for reasons to dislike me."

He kissed her cheek. "Nobody is going to latch onto this. What looks good?"

The killer corn bread would have been good too. "Do you know a lot of vegetarians?"

"No, why?" He picked a potato salad and scooped some onto his plate.

"Sandy asked if I was a vegetarian."

"He's manning the meat. I think Tessa is veggie at the moment and Cal and Kim and their kids, but otherwise everybody is a carnivore. Well, Candy goes through self improvement phases, but I don't think she's here today. She and Ty are on the outs again, or still. I'm never sure. Try some of this. It's Connie's and it's excellent." He pointed out the salad he'd put on his plate. "It's got bacon in it. See, not vegetarian."

Maureen took a sampling of food and then wondered who had brought what dishes. Would they be offended if she didn't try what they brought? Who did she have to worry about offending other than Sandy? And the other guys in Michael's band? And the guys who worked at his management office and with the band? Who at this party didn't fall under one of those headings? Maybe she should have become a vegetarian last week so she'd have a good excuse to skip a few things because no way she could try everything and she didn't know who would be bothered if she didn't.

"What?" he asked.

"What?" She met his eyes.

"You look like you're gonna have a nervous breakdown." He frowned. "What's up?"

"I'm starting to wish I was back at dinner last night. I never realized how many social land mines there were at a backyard barbecue."

"There are no social land mines. You're getting all worked up over nothing."

"Hey, Bear. S'up?" A pretty dark haired woman in denim shorts and a yellow t-shirt stopped beside him.

"Nothing much. Tessa, this is Maureen. Maureen, Tessa, our lawyer."

Tessa held out her hand. "Nice to meet you. I heard you were dating someone new."

"Yeah, will you tell her no one is going to ridicule or shun her for not bringing anything?"

"Michael!" She clenched her teeth.

Tessa laughed. "Don't worry about it, Maureen. Boys will be boys. How long will you be in town?"

"A week. I have to be back for school a week from Monday."

"Oh, so he's going to be sulking around again after that. Joy. Between him and my brother, I might have to walk off the end of a pier." Tessa rolled her eyes.

"I am not as bad as Jason." Bear scowled.

"When you get a good grouse on you are."

"Who's got a good grouse on?" another woman asked. She looked a lot like Tessa.

"Bear, when his woman leaves."

"Oh, I thought you were talking about Jason," the other woman said. She held out her hand. "I'm Connie. You must be Bear's girlfriend. Or did I hear fiancee?"

"Fiancee," Michael said before Maureen could stop him.

"Wow, so the rumor is true," Tessa said. "I thought it was just a rumor because Bear hasn't called me about a pre-nup. You will be having one of those, you know. Might as well get the scary bad conversation out of the way." She flicked Michael's ear.

"Ow!" Michael clapped his hand over his ear. "Big points for subtlety. We haven't talked about it yet."

Pre-nuptial agreement? A shiver ran down her spine and the yard started to sway as if she were on a ship at sea. That had never entered her mind. Pre-nuptial agreements were for people with a lot of money. Like Michael, who had just handed her a credit card and told her she had ten thousand dollars a month to spend. Hadn't she just been worried that she hadn't brought a covered dish? There was a lot more she wasn't bringing to this relationship. Most of it preceded by dollar signs.

"So what are you going to be doing while you're in town?" Connie asked.

"I don't know. Sightseeing probably. I just— Can you tell me where the bathroom is?"

"Go down the hallway beside the stove in the kitchen, first door on the right. Right across the hall from the basement door." Connie took the plate out of her hand.

Maureen fled into the house. The bathroom was free when she got there. If it hadn't been, her alternate plan had been to barricade herself in the basement. She locked the door behind her and leaned on it. Nothing illustrated what a strange land she'd walked into better than that one little hyphenated word. All her life, her aim had been to wait until she found someone she really liked. No rush. Better to die alone than live in the hell she grew up in. Once she found Mr. Right, she'd figured there'd be a wedding and then settling in to battle the usual demons of marriage, generally represented by money.

Her parents never fought about money. They had a budget detailing everything they spent in a year and they each contributed half. If there was some extra event or fee she'd needed for school, she'd told them and they made a decision. By high school, she'd been leaving written messages on the desk in the living room for them to get back to her about. Also by then, she had her own money and, as often as not, paid her fees. A mark of her adulthood was that she could manage her money without having to discuss it with anyone. How was she supposed to fight about money with him when he earned a hundred times more than she did? Did he expect her to sit back and take the generous allowance he gave her?

"Hey, Maureen. You okay?" he asked through the door.

"I'm fine. I'll be out in a minute." She ventured away from the door to peer at herself in the mirror. No wonder Connie had been so prompt with the directions. She looked like she was facing down an oncoming train. At the sink, she washed her hands and patted water on her face. She would have splashed her face, but she'd worn makeup to this shindig and didn't want to smear it. Sticking her head under the faucet would have really attracted attention at this very sedate rock and roll party, but would have felt sooo good. She dried her hands and braced herself.

When she opened the door, he leaned on the door across the hall, and as soon as she walked out, straightened. "Hey, Connie said she thought you looked—sick. Are you okay?"

"I'm fine."

He frowned. Obviously the words weren't matching the picture. He took her hand and led her further down the hall into a room and closed the door. It was a home office with a large framed poster of the band on the wall only it looked quite old. None of them could have been over twenty-five. "Listen, if it's about the pre-nup, you don't have to sign one."

"It's not— I'm— No." She pursed her lips to try and organize her thoughts before any more partials escaped. "It's not having to sign something. It's that it needs to exist. No, that's not right. I never imagined I'd be married to someone who needed one."

"Oh. They thought you didn't want to sign it." He laced his fingers through hers, making her want more contact.

"No, of course not. If that's what needs to be done, then that's what needs to be done. But I never plan on having to use it." She needed to be held, secured to him. She liked him and he liked her and that's what really mattered in the end.

He raised one eyebrow. "Really?"

"You might not have noticed, but I'm a 'til death do us part girl." She slid her arms around his waist. "I didn't wait this long for you just to split up in ten years." Stretching up on her toes, she kissed him.

He parted her lips hungrily, pressing her against the desk. When her feet lost contact with the floor, she wrapped her legs around his waist. His hard member pressed against her, filling her with heat.

She turned her head, trying to get a little breathing room. "Michael, we're at your manager's house."

"It's okay. He won't mind." He slid his hands under her shirt, making stopping a lot less interesting. Having sex in a strange house was more in line with what she'd imagined this lifestyle involved.

But it had nothing to do with her lifestyle. "I do." She planted her hands on his shoulders and pushed. At first, he resisted, but then gave in.

"Yeah, you're right." He smoothed her shirt down. "But I'm taking a rain check for later."

"At home."

He grinned. "I love it when you call it that. Like you already live with me." He leaned in to kiss her again, but she pulled back.

"Let's not get distracted. I'm already fighting one false reputation. I don't need a real one to go along with it."

He grumbled, helping her to her feet. "Are you sure you're okay?" he asked before he opened the door.

"I'm fine. I was just panicked for a minute."

Tessa lingered in the hall with a blond man. "Hi." Tessa almost succeeded in sounding as if she always hung around in the hall at these parties. Nothing unusual about it. "Maureen, have you met Brian?"

"Hey, good to meet you." Brian held out his hand.

Brian? She was never going to remember all these names. This one she should know since he was in the band. He played piano? No. Guitar? No.

"Hello."

"I'm in Bear's band. I play bass," Brian said.

Whatever the heck that was. He had a firm grip and warm friendly blue eyes. "Nice to meet you."

"Connie has your plate. Do you want to sit inside or out?" Tessa started down the hall.

Connie leaned on the kitchen counter with her arms folded guarding Maureen and Michael's plates. "Feel better?" Her tone was cool.

"Much. You know how it is when something hits you." Hopefully that didn't sound like a lie because it did feel like something had hit her in the gut.

Michael picked up her plate and carried it to the table. "What do you want to drink, babe?"

"Water is fine." She followed him.

"You sure? There's pop and stuff." He studied her eyes.

"Just water." She settled into a chair.

"I'm on it," Brian announced from the door. "Bear, beer?"

Tessa sat in the chair to her right and Connie at the other end. Michael took the seat next to her, nodded, and Brian dove out the back door.

"That boy flaps around like a torn sail in a hurricane when Jason isn't here to keep track of." Connie glared out the door after Brian.

"Maureen, you know the pre-nup isn't negotiable, right?" Tessa asked. "Nothing against you personally. It's just a formality. Any time one of the guys marries, I draw up a pretty standard form and both of you sign it."

"Tessa," he said, a warning in his tone.

The sliding door opened again and Brian walked back in. He deposited a can of beer in front of Michael and a bottle of water in front of her before leaning on the wall behind Connie.

Tessa ignored Michael. "We're not accusing you of anything, but there is no way Sandy is going to let anyone in this organization enter into any kind of legal agreement without protection."

"Tessa," he said again.

"I know it seems a little clinical and unromantic, but it really is as much for your protection as for his." Tessa steepled her fingers on the table. "We aren't betting against you and we hope to never have to use it."

"Of course." She peeked under the bun of her hamburger. Naked. She'd probably missed the fixin's tray when she'd gone rampaging to the bathroom. "I would assume something like that would be required. Not that I ever plan on using it, but do you recommend I have a lawyer check it for me before I sign?"

"What?" Tessa's steepled fingers sagged.

"Do you recommend I have a lawyer check it?" Maureen asked.

"She's got no problem signing, Tessa," Michael said. He reached for Maureen's plate. "You need stuff on this? Everything but tomato, right?"

"Thank you."

"You have no problem signing the pre-nuptial agreement?" Tessa and Connie asked at the same time.

"No." Maureen opened her water and took a drink.

"Jeez, you're kidding," Brian said. "Bon cried for a week."

"Bon was trying to break you so you wouldn't make her do it," Tessa told him. "Lucky for you, it was me she needed to break."

"Then what was that outside?" Connie asked. "Why did you go running for the bathroom when it came up?"

"I never dated anyone who needed one before." Maureen took another drink. "I thought I was dating a mechanic."

"You really thought he was a mechanic." Connie leaned forward while Tessa leaned back.

"Yes." Maureen shrugged. "He was wearing the coveralls and he had grease all over his face. He fixed my brakes and tuned up my car. Didn't you?"

Michael had just pushed through the door with both their plates. "What? Fixed your car? Yeah. You had about three more miles on those brakes before you went through a brick wall." He set her burger in front of her.

"Best blind date I never went on." She reached for his hand. He slid his fingers through hers like a puzzle piece finding its place.

"Imagine how thrilled I was when I realized I could have walked out of the repair bay and said, hi I'm Bear D'Amato from Touchstone and she'd have said, that must be nice for you, what can you do about my brakes?"

"I didn't know. I don't pay attention to that stuff. If anyone else here is famous, I apologize in advance for not knowing who you are." She picked up her burger.

"No one." Tessa gestured toward Brian. "Well, Brian, but they're in the same band. And Connie works on TV."

"Really?"

"Costuming for *Tinseltown, Idaho*." Connie shrugged. "It's a living. Too bad we're off this week. I could have taken you in to the set to watch filming."

"That would have been interesting."

"You realize this is what pissed Marc off." Tessa started toying with a paper napkin. "He hates not being recognized."

"What's this now?" Sandy came through the sliding door. "Boy! Get your foot off my wall."

Brian straightened and Maureen felt safe enough to start eating. Tessa explained her theory on Marc's mood, which Connie agreed with. Michael held the opinion Marc was being a jerk and no one asked Maureen what she thought. That relieved her more than anything else. This was what real acceptance felt like.

Ty wandered into the room and the conversation turned to what Jason's problem might be. Maureen finished her meal and glanced around for a trashcan. Spotting one in the corner, she grabbed Michael's empty plate and took it with her. When she came back, Michael grabbed her hand and pulled her into his lap. No one commented on that either, though Ty took her chair.

"Maureen, do you have any plans this week?" Connie asked.

"Not yet."

"We should do a spa day." Connie grinned at her.

"I want to come, but I bet my ogre of a boss won't let me off." Tessa winked at her then smiled at Sandy, who still stood at the door.

Maureen caught Sandy's shrewd glance in her direction before he shrugged. "Everything's pretty much under control right now. Why don't you take tomorrow and spend the day with Michael's new fiancee?"

A slight hesitation then Tessa squealed and clapped her hands. That told Maureen everything she needed to know. This wasn't what acceptance felt like. She was still on trial. They just hadn't already made up their minds against her like Marc had.

Chapter 10

"I think it went good." Bear shifted his grip on the steering wheel. He should have left a window open when they parked. The air conditioning couldn't keep up with the bake of a car sitting closed in the sun all day and he didn't need any help sweating. "Everybody liked you. And you've got a full week planned."

"I do. I hope I get to see you some." She had her hands folded in her lap and stared out the passenger window.

"I'll be home every night." Connie and Tessa were taking her to a spa tomorrow. That would give them time to talk. Tuesday, she was headed to a farmer's market with his drum tech's wife, Kim. Kim was pretty calm and she'd lived this lifestyle for a while now. Wednesday, she and Bonnie were doing something. That scared him a little. He loved Brian like a brother, but his wife was…unpredictable. She had plans for Thursday and Friday too. All the trips limited her need to drive in the city, which he knew worried her. Every day someone picked her up or he dropped her off on the way to rehearsal. This was what she wanted, right? If this was what she wanted, why was she being so quiet? "What's wrong?"

"Nothing." She turned to him with a blank expression.

"Right."

Her lips quirked. "I'm just not so sure they liked me."

"Of course they did. Everybody wanted to make plans with you."

"Because they're trying to check me out."

"And they're going to find out how great you are." He reached over and took her hand.

"All your friends here think I'm out for something."

"No, they don't." Unable to lie to her face, he kept his eyes on the road.

"Yes, they do."

"If this is about the pre-nup—"

"It's not." She slid her hand away from him. "It's more about me not measuring up to be good enough for you."

He turned and stared at her. "What?"

"Michael, watch!" She grabbed the dashboard.

As a midnight blue Lexus zipped across the lane in front of them, missing his bumper by microns, he slammed on the brakes. Tires squealed behind him and a couple of horns honked. "Fucker," he snarled. "What are you talking about?"

"Don't get that tone with me." She folded her arms.

"I don't have a tone with you." But he did. He tried to take a deep breath and couldn't. His chest and shoulders had braced for impact and hadn't relaxed yet. Impact from the other car or from whatever weird shit was going on in her head, he wasn't sure. "Okay, I have a tone. What do you mean you not being good enough for me? How could you not be? You're so nice and sane and normal."

"A little too normal and I know nothing about your life. I am completely clueless about everything you love." She folded her hands in her lap again and stared at them. The heavy sound of her breathing drowned out the radio.

"I love you."

"Michael."

"What? I'm serious. I don't care if you don't know all about music or cars or whatever. That just gives us more to talk about." He glanced at her. Still staring at her hands, she'd hunched over like she wanted to curl into a ball, but the seat belt held her back. "Come on, Maureen. What's the funk about?"

She shook her head.

He focused on the road. The tension in his shoulders and chest wasn't going away. The whole meeting had gone so well. Or had it all been wishful thinking?

No, not wishful thinking. Connie and Tessa never felt any compulsion to be political. Kim did, but Kim had dealt with some superstar diva wives during her marriage to Cal. Bonnie? Who the hell knew what Bonnie was thinking most of the time? Right now he was blanking on her plans for Thursday and Friday. "What are you doing Thursday?"

"Shopping with Liddy."

"And Friday?"

She sighed. "Shopping with Tori and a couple of her friends. I'm getting the impression all these women ever do is shop."

"That's what you need the expense account for."

"I guess so." She twisted sideways in her seat. "When we get married, where will we live?"

When. His tension started to ebb. "I don't know. I hadn't thought about it. I guess I figured you'd move out here with me."

"But my job is back there." She pointed eastish.

"Well, yeah, but Malibu has schools too, doesn't it?" It had to. If it didn't, Santa Barbara had some because Connie's kid went to school.

"I have twelve years toward retirement at home."

"Okay, fine. We live there, but it means I'm going to be away from home more because I'll have to come back here to work." He clutched the steering wheel tighter because he could hear that tone leaking into his voice again. Tension coiled back around his arms and chest too. "What are you doing, Maureen? Why are you throwing up roadblocks?"

"I can't be like those women, Michael."

"Like what women?"

"Nichole and Liddy and Tori. My brain will die."

"So don't. Who said you had to be?"

"We never talked about anything. We never discussed whether we wanted kids or if I would keep working or where we were going to live. There's a lot of things we need to decide."

"Fine. Talk. You want to have kids?"

"Don't get hostile."

"I'm not getting hostile. You're being crazy."

"I'm being crazy? I'm not the one who's shouting."

He thrust out his jaw. Turning into the neighborhood, he took a deep breath. "Alright, I'm not shouting. Do you want to have kids?"

"Do you?"

A growl rose in his throat and he fought it back down. If this were any more difficult there would be a dentist's drill involved. "I never thought about it. I like kids. I guess I wouldn't mind having one or two of my own, but it's not deal breaker. What about you?"

"I always thought I would like to have kids, but it's getting a bit late in life for me so I'd kind of given up on the idea."

"'Late in life'?"

"I'm thirty-four." She said it like she was telling him she wasn't a pedophile.

Still. Thirty-four? That made her at least four years older than him. Not that four years was a big deal. It didn't change her personality. In fact, it was probably one of the things that attracted him to her. She breathed stability and calm, but she was still fun and childlike. "Okay. You can still have kids at thirty-four." He caught himself on the verge of questioning. Everything he knew about women was being dashed on the rocks with her.

"For a few more years." She pursed her lips and narrowed her eyes, daring him to contradict her.

"Then we'll get on that right away." He reached for her hand. Pulling it to his lips, he kissed her fingers. "The trying will be fun."

She chuckled and her hand relaxed him his grip. "What about me working?"

"Work or not, it's your choice." He shrugged.

"You don't care?"

"Oh, I care. I'd rather have you home all the time, but I know if you don't have something to do, you're going to go bonkers." He turned into the driveway and hit the garage door opener. On the phone, all she'd talked about was her students. Teaching lit her up.

"And what about where we're going to live?"

"Like I said, my job is here and I can't do it anywhere else. If I stay in the band, I'm going to have to be here a lot."

"What about my retirement?"

"Baby, you don't have to worry about your retirement." He put the car in park and turned to her. "I'm your retirement."

"Because you can pay me ten thousand dollars a month to sit around looking pretty." Her jaw quivered.

"Don't get all hot again. The expense account is just for stuff you might need. I'm trying to take care of you. I want to take care of you. Let me." He put his hand around the back of her neck. "Please?"

She bowed her head. "No one's ever taken care of me before. It's hard to adjust."

He leaned his forehead on hers. "Take your time." Running the tips of his fingers under her jaw, he tipped her mouth up to his. Her eyes were open when their lips met and she kept her gaze focused on him. She seemed to see directly into his heart and he swore he could see into hers. She was everything warm, rich and wonderful that he'd ever imagined. As she captured his lower lip between hers, stroking it with her tongue, he wrapped his arms around her waist to pull her closer…

And the gearshift got in the way.

He cursed, shifting back. "I need a car with a bench seat."

"Yeah, the three you have now suck for making out in." Laughing, she opened her door, pulled the elastic out of her hair and tossed it at him. "Race you to the bedroom."

She really did mean race. By the time he got inside, she was running down the hall and her shirt was lying in the middle of the kitchen floor. In the dining room, her bra dangled from his snare. He pulled off his shirt and tossed it aside. Hadn't they been arguing ten minutes ago? Making major life decisions? Shouldn't she still be in serious conversation mode? Her jeans were crumpled in the hall with her panties still in them.

She knelt in the center of his bed naked, flushed and grinning. "Where have you been? I've been waiting."

"I'm sorry." He unzipped his jeans and crawled up the foot of the bed, bending her on her back. "How can I make it up to you?"

"You're off to a good start."

He studied her. Her hair wreathed on the bedspread, gleaming in the late afternoon sun. "You are amazing."

"Boy, are you going to be impressed when the spa gets done with me tomorrow. Connie and Tessa promise wonders."

"I'm already impressed." He stroked his hand down her side until he reached the curve of her waist. The way his hand fit perfectly there delighted him and it was one of the places he could touch her during the day. Flesh to flesh was so much better though. "I never want to be without you. You mean everything to me."

Her breath hitched. "Oh, Michael." Her lush, shining lips trembled. "I love being with you too."

"Whatever we have to do to make this happen, I'm willing to do it."

She blinked a couple of times. "I— I am too."

He swallowed around a lump in his throat and pressed a kiss on her shoulder, wishing he had more words to tell her what she meant to him. Her light fingers trailed down his back. He shivered, his cock straining for her. Ignoring it, he moved down her body and took her nipple into his mouth.

Her arms tightened around him as her body coiled with desire.

The rich scent of her filled the room. Heat and tides and sun. He didn't need to be in Southern California. He needed to be with her. Teasing the hard knot with his tongue, he drew a moan from her. His skin ached. Everywhere he brushed against her felt electrified. This woman. This amazing woman. He'd almost missed her. If he'd gone home that night when Tony did. If she hadn't stopped to have her brakes checked. If Tony had remembered to lock the door at the garage.

She laced her fingers through his hair. "Make love to me. I want to feel your whole body on mine. Please. I need you."

Brushing his mouth over her velvet skin, he savored the flavor of her sweat tinged with smoke from the cookout and the sharp tang of her anxiety. They liked her. They had to. He would make them like her. On his knees, he pushed his jeans down, and she reached over to the table, fished a condom out of the box. Sitting up, she ripped it open. As she rolled it over him with light, teasing strokes, she held his gaze. Bear struggled to contain the welling of lust and hope in his chest. She was amazing. Just amazing.

He slid into her with one long stroke. Clinging to him, she sobbed. He buried his face in the curve of her neck. Through his lips, he could feel her racing pulse. Her skin tasted so good. So fine and soft. She wrapped her legs around his hips, pulling him deeper into her. Nothing mattered but this woman. This moment. This life.

She called out his name and clenched around him, wringing his climax from him. It blindsided him, stealing breath and thought.

When sense came back, he was still lying on her with his face pressed into her neck and she was touching his hair.

"I must be crushing you," he whispered. Raising his voice took too much effort and would have shattered the still peace of the bedroom.

"No. You're fine." She spoke in a whisper too. "You always make me feel like the center of the universe."

"Maybe I'm amazed you let me love you and I have to put on a good performance to make sure you keep coming back."

She chuckled. "I'll keep coming back."

"Good." Very good. No matter what he had to do to keep her, he'd do it. Quit the band, sell his house and go into business with his brother. Or stay in the band and set her up like a queen.

And get a car with a bench seat. Bucket seats sucked for making out in.

* * * *

Maureen peered into the cup of "tea" that had been delivered to their table. The swampy green color didn't look like any tea she'd ever had, but it had been served in a clear glass cup and it steamed like tea. The massage she'd just come out of hadn't been like any massage she'd ever heard of before either.

"So how do you feel?" Connie asked.

"Good." She frowned, trying to find the lie in that. Nope. No lie. "I feel lighter." The spa experience was strange, but she could see the draw.

She also liked the company. Jason's sisters had gone out of their way to make her comfortable.

"You look great," Tessa said. "Doesn't she look great?"

"Those midwest winters are really hard on the skin." Connie picked up her tea.

Tessa shot her sister a dark glare before turning back to Maureen. "Not that yours was bad. You have great skin."

"No, that's not what I was saying." Connie put her tea down without tasting it. "What I meant was it's the end of winter and your skin always takes a beating in the winter. You do have great skin. I'd have never guessed you were thirty-four."

Tessa closed her eyes and groaned. Connie blanched.

"How did you know I was thirty-four?" Maureen asked. She sipped her tea. The bitter flavor complimented her mood. Up until now, she'd enjoyed her time with Tessa and Connie. Almost enough to forget they were checking her out.

Tessa held out her hand. "You have to understand, Maureen. It's my job to do a background check on you."

"A background check." Maureen took another sip of the tea. She liked it. At the moment, better than spying Tessa and loose-lipped Connie. How much did they know? Did they do an FBI check? Her bank records? Outstanding warrants or traffic tickets? Pull her teaching license paperwork to find out if she had any affiliation with terrorist groups? Good luck digging up any dirt. There wasn't any.

"Nothing really invasive. Just public records." Tessa gnawed her thumbnail.

"It really is nothing," Connie said. "You've got to understand, rock stars have two kinds of wives."

"Connie!" Tessa wailed.

Maureen sat back in her seat. Tessa had leaned forward like she wanted to reach across the table and snatch her sister bald. Connie cocked her head and curled her lip. For about five seconds neither of them said anything.

Then Tessa slouched back in her seat. "Fine." She took a drink from her tea, breathed a heavy sigh and shook her head. "Rock stars have two kinds of wives. There's the party wife. Usually married young and at the height of success, or at least the first success. She tends to take our boy for a wonderful ride and then take him for everything she can on the way out the door. Party wives never last."

"Bonnie has had her hooks in Brian for how many years now?" Connie raised one eyebrow.

"Yeah well, I still expect to see the back of her."

"You hope to see the back of her."

"Same thing." Tessa sneered. "Anyway, party wives are to be avoided. They're a cash drain. Sandy likes them to be stopped at the girlfriend stage before they do any real damage and I swear they end up being half my job."

"Didn't do such a great one with Desiree." Connie pushed her empty teacup away.

"She slipped through, but I've turned Bear away from three, Marc away from two others and Jason and Ty away from one each." Tessa ticked them off on her fingers. "My average is still good."

"You didn't turn Jason away from Stella."

"She played a very convincing game. I thought she actually liked him for his personality. I should have known nobody would like our brother for his personality."

Connie nodded. "You see, Maureen, we needed to know if you're rock star wife type two."

"Which is?" Maureen asked.

"The permanent wife." Tessa folded her hands on the table. "The permanent wife usually comes along when our rock star is over forty and settled. The career has leveled off. He's matured to the point where he's more interested in regular meals than rock and roll all night and party every day. She's in for the long haul."

"And what kind am I?" Maureen asked. Couldn't hurt to be plain about things. Subterfuge made her head hurt.

"You are definitely type two." Connie tapped her newly manicured nails on the table.

"We know that now, but when we first heard we didn't." Tessa started ticking off points on her fingers again. "You came out of nowhere. Rock stars mature, on average, about ten years slower than their peers so Bear is very young to be settling down. We've had to pull him off this particular cliff repeatedly. That last album tanked so he's a little vulnerable. And, he's Bear. He gets overexcited about stuff."

They made him sound like a seven year old, but the fact that they'd *pulled him off this cliff repeatedly* didn't sit well. How many times had Michael proposed?

"I'm really sorry about how all this sounds, but we had to do it. Nobody wants our guys to end up with a Heather Mills McCartney."

"Who?" Maureen drained her teacup.

"Especially not with Marc in the middle of his divorce." Connie spoke at the same time.

Tessa rolled her eyes and shuddered. "Thank God for Marc's prenup."

"What's going on with Marc?" Maureen leaned her chin on her hand. She'd check that other name later. Pretty soon she was going to have to get a notebook.

"He married his little party girl five years ago against all advice and she started screwing around on him during the last tour. She was using her expense account to pay for her boytoy's rent. Can you believe it?" Connie waved for the waitress.

"Oh, expense account." Tessa sucked her teeth. "We'll have to get you into the office to set that up. Is there a time you can come in?"

"I already have one."

Tessa frowned. "What?"

"Michael gave me a credit card when I got here and told me it was my expense account. That's what you're talking about, isn't it?"

Connie picked up a baby carrot. "Bear set up your expense account already?"

"I can't believe Helen didn't tell me." Tessa pouted. "I'm going to have a chat with Mrs. Wheals tomorrow. She should have mentioned it."

"She probably meant to and forgot. She hasn't been feeling too well."

"What's wrong?" Maureen asked. Twelve years of observing social structure in the microcosm of her classroom paid off. In this group's pecking order, Connie and Tessa ranked high and winning them to her side would ease her acceptance. If they were gossiping about the others in front of her and giving her privileged information, they'd accepted her. Marc should rank higher, but Connie and Tessa might be able to cancel him out. She'd still need to sway a couple of other people to her side though to cancel out Michael's brother. Two down, four to go.

* * * *

Maureen sat down in front of the TV. At noon she was meeting Brian's wife Bonnie for lunch and shopping, but that left her two hours to burn before she had to leave.

The outing yesterday with Kim had been successful. Kim liked her immediately and the farmer's market had been fun. Kim and Cal's two kids were older than Brian and Bonnie's, but they were home schooled so they had been along on the trip. Kim appreciated that Maureen could do on-the-spot math lessons in the middle of the market. Sadly, Kim was pretty low in influence.

Bonnie, however, had a lot of clout through Brian and wielded it like a club. Tessa and Connie had not had many nice things to say about her, which made Maureen wonder if she was something of a rival power. The few moments she'd had to talk to the other woman at the cookout hadn't yielded much information. Bonnie was brassy and loud and complimented her on getting Bear to propose so fast. She'd announced that she'd spent a year working on Brian and then had to get pregnant to seal the deal. Her phrasing had made Maureen's eyes itch. Reflecting on the conversation now, maybe this lunch wasn't a good idea. Michael wasn't happy about it.

The phone rang. She stared at it through another ring, debating answering. Then she grabbed it. "Hello?"

"Hi, Maureen? It's Bonnie. Hey listen, I have a problem."

Maybe she was canceling. What a shame.

"My sitter got the day wrong and I have a doctor's appointment this morning. I have been trying to get in with this guy for six months. I need you to watch the kids for an hour or so while I go. Can you?"

Maureen bit her lip. This could be a good way to get a solid in with Bonnie and Brian while getting in some practice being a mother. Michael had put Brian's address into the GPS navigation thingy this morning so she'd be able to go over there for lunch. "Sure."

"Great. I'll see you in a bit." Bonnie hung up.

Maureen grabbed her purse in the way out the door. This could be a perfect situation. With Connie and Tessa on her side, that gave her two votes to Marc's one. Adding Bonnie to the mix would give her Brian as well. Gaining full acceptance and cementing her reputation as wife type two would only cost an hour or so of babysitting.

Bonnie met her at the door. "I'm running late. Tess and Bub are in the living room playing. The sitter is going to try to come this afternoon and even if she doesn't, the housekeeper will be here. Thanks again." Bonnie slid past her and dove into her white Mercedes.

Maureen put her purse on the counter in the six square inches that weren't cluttered with dirty plates, junk mail and empty food cartons. When she walked into the living room, Tess stood up from a tea party set on the glass coffee table and the baby started to cry. The living room was a sea of toys with two leather couches, one white and one black, floating amid them. How long had it been since the housekeeper had been here last? Christmas?

"Who are you?"

"I'm—" Everybody here called Michael Bear, but what did the kids call him? And how was she supposed to define her relationship to him? Did it matter? The kids looked about four and two. "I'm your Uncle Bear's girlfriend."

"Bubbie's crying." Tess put her little hands on her hips.

"I noticed. Any clue why?"

"He doesn't like to be in his pen all the time."

"Out. Out. Out," Bubbie chanted, bouncing up and down.

Maureen studied the smaller child. Child psychology was a long time ago. "Well, we probably shouldn't let Bubbie out of his playpen with all these toys lying around."

"He tries to eat them. 'Specially my bobby shoes."

Bobby shoes? Oh, Barbie shoes. Maureen tipped over a wooden block and noticed something brown mashed around the red letter B. "We should pick up all the toys and put them away."

Tess surveyed the floor and then ran behind the white couch and dragged a huge gray plastic tub out. She scooped up toys with abandon, dumping them in the tub. The tub was clearly labeled *Barbie Dolls* in black Magic Marker.

Behind the couch, a pile of four more tubs were also helpfully labeled, in black Magic Marker. She toed over another toy, this one white plastic with a dark red smear on the side. Tess already had the first bin overflowing and was working on a second. "You know what might be fun?" Maureen said. "If we washed everything."

Tess cocked her head. "Can we wash Bobby's clothes? Some of her clothes are very dirty."

She didn't want to think about that. "We can. But first we have to sort all of Barbie's clothes out, because we have to wash them separately."

"Okay." Tess pushed over the full tub, giving Maureen a good idea how the living room had gotten to be such a mess in the first place. Bubbie started to cry again. Hooking his fingers through the mesh, he threw himself backward.

"Shut up!" Tess screamed at him.

"That's not helping." Maureen dragged out the other tubs and started sorting toys into the correct ones.

Tess ran to the playpen and screamed directly into her brother's face. "Shut up!"

Maureen hurried over and pulled her back. Second graders didn't do this. "Tess, stop. He doesn't understand. The sooner we get cleaned up so he can come out, the sooner he'll stop crying."

Tess frowned. Then she turned to her brother. "We'll let you out when we're done. You just stay there."

Bubbie kept bawling. His little face brilliant red and white marks on his fingers where he gripped the netting.

Was this what motherhood was really like? How had the species not died out? When her tub of wooden blocks looked about full enough, she carried it to the kitchen, dumped them into the dishwasher and turned it on.

In the living room, Tess had started singing really loud to drown out the sound of her brother crying. Tess did not have her father's singing voice. Or so Maureen assumed. The off-key caterwaul wasn't doing anything for the throbbing at the base of her skull. She needed to have to have another conversation with Michael about children.

Bubbie abruptly stopped screaming and Tess stopped singing in response. In the sudden silence, Maureen closed her eyes and thanked whatever gods had granted this moment.

Opening her eyes, she glanced at Bubbie. The kid was sitting in the middle of his playpen rocking back and forth with a smile on his face.

Tess frowned at Maureen. "Bubbie pooped his diaper."

Chapter 11

The back door opened. "What happened here?" a shrill, Latin accented voice demanded.

Maureen thought she should open her eyes and try to act like a grown up, but didn't have the energy. Besides, based on Tess' industrious braiding of her hair for the past half hour, she wasn't sure she could manage anyway. The regular, gentle tugging had been almost massage-like.

"Ahnyong, Sophie," Tess said.

Great, she'd managed to get through washing toys, eating lunch and two diaper changes and now she'd gone crazy. There probably wasn't even anyone here. Maureen opened her eyes. A thin oriental woman stood at the end of the end of the couch. Her flat moon face didn't have any expression, but Maureen felt safe in assuming puzzlement. She was puzzled too, because it didn't seem likely that this thin Oriental woman was speaking with a Spanish accent. It was possible, but she didn't remember that word Tess had said from her high school Spanish classes.

The woman, Sophie apparently, picked up Bubbie from where he was sleeping under the coffee table. "I will take," she said in a soft, not Spanish accented voice. She held out her hand for Tess. "Come. Naptime."

Tess left off her hairdressing and went with Sophie, cheerfully speaking some language Maureen had never heard.

She sat up, and her head did not thank her for it. The six Tylenol she'd taken in the last two hours had not dented her headache. A small, dark woman charged out of the kitchen. "What in the name of heaven is going on? Who are you? Where is the miss?" She paused, drawing back. When she spoke again her voice had taken on an awed tone one might use at a funeral. "What happened to your hair?"

She touched her head. Bo Derek she wasn't. "Tess was playing with it. All the toys are wet."

"I noticed. Why?"

"I washed them. They were pretty dirty." Maybe washing the toys hadn't been such a great idea.

The housekeeper put her hands on her hips. "Well, half my job is finished. Except I'll have to do a load of towels. Are those…"

Maureen followed the housekeeper's gaze. Tess had set up the clothesline for Barbie's clothes. Where the little girl had gotten the string and paperclips, she didn't know, but they worked. "We washed all of Barbie's clothes too. I'm afraid we used all the Woolite."

"All?"

"It got knocked over and a lot went down the drain." After it went all over the floor. On the upside, the bathroom floor was really clean. Her thighs tensed. Bathroom. "Can you excuse me for a minute?" She darted down the hall.

Since Bonnie left, she'd been afraid to leave the kids alone and hadn't gone to the bathroom. The bathroom mirror confirmed that Tess had made modern sculpture out of her hair. Tess didn't know how to braid, but she could twist and she had, in all directions. After she used the facilities and washed her hands, she tried to repair the worst of the damage. Walking back down the hall, she heard the housekeeper on the phone.

"She's not here. She left another woman here with the kids. Sophie and I were on the same bus. Thank you, Mr. Brian."

Maureen stepped through the kitchen door in time to see the housekeeper hang up the phone. "Mr. Brian and Mr. Bear are on their way. Would you like a cup of coffee?"

"Please."

"My name is Lucia." She hustled around the kitchen setting up the coffeemaker and clearing the counter. "Miss Bonnie just left you here alone?"

"She said she had an appointment she couldn't miss," she said and sank into a chair at the kitchen table.

Lucia made a noise and brought one of the toy tubs into the kitchen. She started filling it with wooden blocks, so Maureen helped her. "When did she leave?"

"About ten."

Sophie walked into the kitchen with another toy tub and began throwing plastic blocks into it.

"So you are Mr. Bear's girlfriend," Lucia said, breaking off her sorting to get Maureen's coffee.

"Yes."

"Mr. Bear?" Sophie asked.

Lucia raised her voice as if Sophie were hard of hearing. "This is Mr. Bear's new girlfriend. Maureen."

"Ah." Sophie nodded from the waist. "Nice to meet you."

"It's nice to meet you too."

"Here, sit down and drink your coffee." Lucia shooed her into her chair. "You've had a bad day."

She sipped her coffee gratefully. What six Tylenol hadn't been able to do, the presence of Lucia and Sophie did. Leaning back in the chair, she closed her eyes.

Someone spoke, and she jerked awake.

"And she just left? What the hell is this?"

"Are those guitar strings?" Michael.

She stood up, stretching. How she'd fallen asleep sitting up in a kitchen chair, she wasn't sure but she must have been that way for a while. Her coffee was cold and the newly clean kitchen smelled like roasting chicken. In the living room, Michael and Brian stood staring at Tess's rigged up clothesline. Sophie hovered at the bottom of the stairs, still impassive, but communicating anxiety through her grip on the bannister.

Lucia stood beside a vacuum cleaner with her arms folded. "Like I told you, Mr. Brian. When Sophie and I walked in, the miss was alone with the children. She said Miss Bonnie left at ten."

Michael looked up from the clothesline. "Hey, Maur." He crossed the room in three strides and wrapped his arms around her. "Tough day?"

"A little more than I could chew all at once." She leaned her head on his shoulder.

"Maureen, I'm really sorry about this," Brian said. "I don't know what Bonnie was thinking."

"You want a short list?" Michael asked.

Lucia harrumphed again.

"I really appreciate you stepping up. Thanks a lot." Brian didn't acknowledge Michael or Lucia.

She couldn't think of a proper response, so she nodded.

"Well, man, you do what you have to. I'm taking her home." Michael towed her to the front door.

As they passed the clothesline, she remembered what it was made of. Oops. "I'm sorry if we ruined anything."

"Don't worry about it." Brian fingered the clothesline. "Strings are cheap."

Outside, Michael opened the car door for her. "I have to go back to rehearsals after I take you home."

She swallowed trying to stop wishing he could stay home with her. Not for sex. No, for the first time with him, sex was completely out of the question. But to be held and catered to...

"Anyplace you want to stop? Pick up some food? I might be late."

Marvelous. Not only could he not stay, he might be at rehearsals late. Might as well get used to it now. According to Kim, this was a regular feature of life. She leaned her head against the seat. "Home, Michael."

"As you wish."

* * * *

Bear ushered Maureen into the rehearsal space ahead of him, already sweating. Yesterday when Lucia called, he'd ridden over to Brian's house and then driven his car back meaning both his cars ended up at the rehearsal space and she didn't have one at home. He wasn't excited about subjecting her to Marc again and didn't like the odds on introducing her to Jason, but she insisted it would be rude for her to just take the car and go.

"Hey, Maureen, Bear told you, right?" Brian charged over with his bass still around his neck. "Bonnie said she thought you'd be okay with the kids because you're a teacher. She said the doctor had an emergency and everything got pushed back and it took her forever to get out of the office."

"She explained when she called me yesterday." Maureen's voice was mild. Nothing like the bitter sarcasm from last night when he finally stumbled in from rehearsal.

He grinned at the floor, recalling her brutal imitation of Bonnie.

"What was her excuse for not calling to let Maureen know again?" Jason asked.

"Her phone died." Brian's lip curled into a sneer at Jason. "It's not an excuse."

"Because no one else had a phone she could borrow." Jason held out his hand. "Hi, Maureen. You haven't met me, but I feel like I already know you because Bear never shuts up about you."

"Jason, don't be a dick," Bear snapped. He put his arm around her shoulders. They weren't late, but everyone was already here, waiting for a bloodbath. And of course, Jason wanted to be front row center. Too bad Maureen wasn't going to give it to them. She wasn't like other women. She had class.

"Nice to meet you," she said over him, putting her hand in Jason's.

Jason closed his fingers around hers and pulled them to his lips.

Though she stiffened, she didn't pull her hand away.

"Enough, Jason." Bear growled.

Brian angled the neck of his bass between Jason and Maureen. "Come on, Jason. Cut it out."

Jason shrugged and wandered to the other side of the room where he went into conference with Marc, which Bear liked less than him kissing Maureen's hand.

"What are your plans for today?" Brian asked.

"I'm going shopping with Ty's girlfriend." She gestured in Ty's direction.

Ty was playing solitaire at the coffee table and hadn't bothered to come over to say hi. None of his friends had any manners at all.

"You're probably busy tomorrow too, huh." Brian fiddled with the stock of his bass, twisting the tuning keys.

"Yes."

"And then you're going back Sunday." Brian twisted one of the keys harder.

"Yes."

"Bonnie was kinda hoping you could do lunch another time, but it sounds like you're pretty busy." Brian kept winding that key. Bear pulled Maureen back a step, trying to judge exactly how far the string would fly when it snapped.

"I'm sorry." She managed to look genuinely disappointed even though there was no way in hell she was going over to Brian and Bonnie's house without a chaperon.

"Maybe next time." Brian gave the key one last twist and the string snapped.

Maureen flinched at the loud twang. Bear stuck out his arm to protect her and the string sliced through his skin. "Oh my God, Michael!" She grabbed his arm, pressing a tissue over the cut.

"Shit, I'm sorry. Are you okay?" Brian asked.

"It's nothing," Bear told her, though he couldn't say he didn't like having her fussing over him. He had no idea where the tissue had come from. It just had been there in her hand, like a magic trick.

Joey, Brian's tech, walked over, snatched the bass away from Brian and smacked him on the back of the head without a word.

She peeked under the tissue. "Michael, you need to wash this off and we'll put a bandage on it."

"I don't need a bandage. It's just a scratch."

"You still need to wash it off."

A determined glint had appeared in her eyes. She wasn't going to back down. He either had to take her to the bathroom with him or he had to leave her alone out here. Neither one was a great option. "Fine. I'll go wash it off."

"I'll show her around," Brian said.

Bear shot a glare at Brian and hoped he got the message. He had a stupid smile on his face like always so it was hard to tell. "I'll be back in a minute."

Which turned into ten because instead of the usual dozen people who came to rehearsals, there were twenty hangers on and every one of them found a reason to stop him to talk so they could gauge just how pissed off he was at Brian. He wasn't pissed off at Brian. Yes, Brian had married that self-centered bitch and wouldn't, for some inexplicable reason, divorce her, but Bear couldn't hold him responsible for her actions. By the time he got back into the main space, Brian and Ty were standing on either side of Maureen in front of his drum riser.

"We have to make sure the riser is big enough that he doesn't fall off the back," Brian was saying.

"Hey, that riser was way too small and that happened in high school." Bear put his arm around Maureen's shoulders.

"And you were drunk," Ty added.

"And I was drunk." He rolled his eyes at Maureen.

"How do you know the drum riser is even?" Jason called from one side of the stage.

"The drummer is drooling from both sides of his mouth," Marc answered from the other. "Why did the drummer go out with the second grade teacher?"

"Because he wanted to know what number comes after four." Jason rubbed his hands together. "Did you hear about the time the bassist got his keys locked in the car?"

"I think it's time for you to go home." Bear pulled Maureen to the door.

"It took two hours to get the drummer out," Marc said. "Speaking of bass players. How do you know when the drum solo is really bad?"

"I was hoping you could stay a little to see us play, but once they get going they won't stop until the audience leaves." He was kind of amazed she was letting him hustle her to the door. She hadn't even mentioned bandaging his arm.

"The bassist notices," Jason said.

"Don't let them bother you, Michael." She pushed open the door and latched onto his shirt to pull him out with her. Before he could ask what was going on, she'd pressed him against the side of the building, was kissing him with the frenzied desperation of a woman sending her man off to war. Her hands twined through his hair and she pulled herself up his body.

Bear bit back a groan. The whole day without her spun out ahead of him. There wasn't even anywhere to sneak off to for a few minutes alone. Besides, he didn't want to do that to her. As much as he wanted to have sex with her right now, he didn't want to drag her into a closet like a groupie. He slid his hands down the curve of her back to hold her tight to him. Air was too much to have between them. Air? Months and months of touring separated them. Thousands of miles and millions of people. He ran his tongue along the line of her pulse. Some of those people would be right around her. Like that Conner guy. Waiting for her to get weak and lonely.

He rolled her against the building, pinned her underneath him. "Will you miss me?"

"Yes." She shivered, stretching.

Her skin smelled sweet and fresh. Under that he could taste the tang of anxiety. She was working so hard to be accepted by his friends. Because she loved him. Because she wanted to be with him and wanted him to be happy. Desiree had been pretty invested in Marc's happiness too. "Will you wait for me?"

She giggled. "I'm only going shopping."

Oh yeah. She was going shopping. This was her idea of goodbye for the day. What was she going to do Sunday when she flew home? Maybe they should start on Saturday. "I know, but you might meet some gorgeous hunk at the mall."

Another giggle. "And what would I do with two gorgeous hunks? I think the one I have is plenty. Unless there's a really good sale."

He stepped back and helped her straighten out her clothes. She dressed like she was going to any mall in the Midwest. Jeans, t-shirt, sneakers. He'd warned her what Liddy was probably going to appear in and she'd laughed. Hopefully that humor and confidence would carry her because he didn't want her coming home feeling like second best to Liddy. Or worse, having picked up some of Liddy's style.

She put her hand on his chest. "Don't let them bother you."

"What?"

"They were teasing you a lot. Don't let it bother you." Adorable little crinkles formed at the corners of her eyes. She was worried. About him.

"The drummer jokes? That's nothing. They've been doing it for years." Bear resisted the impulse to pinch her cheek. The fact that she worried about him was so damn cute. Nobody worried about him. He was Bear the Invincible. If they did worry, it was about him damaging somebody else.

"You seemed upset."

"I just didn't want them to upset you."

Her sweet lips turned down. She wasn't buying that even though it was true. "Honestly, baby, those guys are my very best friends in the world. Even when they're assholes." He kissed her forehead. "Have fun today."

"I will." She fished the car keys out of her purse. "You'll be home for dinner?"

Now that was a nice conversation. Have a good time shopping. Will you be home for dinner? So fucking normal. "Yeah. If not, I'll call."

"Okay." She kissed his cheek. "See you tonight then."

He watched her climb into the Mustang and wiggle it out of the absurdly small lot. When she got straightened out in the alley, she stopped and waved. He waved back, feeling the tug in his gut. Better get used to it. Sunday he had to do it for a much longer stretch.

The door banged closed behind him. Marc stopped beside him, lighting a cigarette. "She finally go?"

Bear stiffened. "Yes."

"I admit she's got a good story."

"It's not a story."

Marc took a long drag. "She's cute too, in a wholesome way."

Bear ground his teeth. The asshole routine was rapidly overtaking Marc's status as a best friend.

"Tessa said you set up her expense account."

"You don't think she's doing all this on a teacher's salary, do you?" Maureen must have said something. Helen promised to keep it quiet because she had the taste to understand that he might have stumbled into something real for the first time in his surreal fantasy life. She didn't assume he was still too immature for a long term, serious relationship.

"Guess not." Marc flicked the ash off his cigarette. "She goes home Sunday?"

"Yes."

Marc glared at him, his dark eyes more world weary than they should have been. "You don't have to get all pissy and defensive."

"The way you guys have all been acting, I need to get more pissy and defensive."

The door banged against the wall and Jason leaned out. "Are you guys gonna get in here so we can get this shit going or what?"

Marc ignored Jason and flicked away his half finished cigarette. "I'm trying to save you some grief."

"Just because you two can't get your shit together doesn't give you free rein to rip up my life."

"Fuck you." Jason snarled. "I haven't done jack all to you or your new fuck toy."

Bear swung at Jason, who ducked. Marc grabbed his arms, yanking them back so Bear used the leverage to kick. Jason scuttled backward through the door. Crashing into Brian.

"What the fuck?" Brian yelled. "What are you doing?"

"You son of a bitch." Bear lunged toward Jason, pulling Marc forward. "Don't you ever talk about her like that. Just because some bitch fucked you over."

Jason leaped through the door, but Brian grabbed him.

"Hey! Dammit, will you guys just calm down," Brian demanded. "Little help," he shouted over his shoulder.

Everyone boiled out of the building. They'd come for a bloodbath. This might not have been the one they'd expected, but it would do. Cal grabbed Bear by the scruff of the neck and dragged him to the far corner of the parking lot.

"You're an asshole, you know that?" Jason shouted. "You always have been. The center of the fucking universe."

"Yeah, that's me all over. Because I'm the pussy still whining about the fact that some fucking clothes hanger dumped me in a magazine. And you." Bear pointed at Marc. "You married a fucking stripper. No wonder she started screwing her personal trainer on your dime. Brian married a bitch and Ty can't keep a girlfriend for long enough to learn her fucking name."

"Hey!" Ty threw up his hands. "When did this become about me?"

"I'm not stupid enough to make the same mistakes." Bear clenched his fists. "I'm doing it right."

"By meeting some woman and getting engaged to her within a week." Marc's jaw flexed like he was chewing steel.

"Yes. You just won't give her a chance because you think I'm a fuck up like all of you are." Bear tried to step around Cal, but the other man wouldn't let him.

"You know when a woman fucks with one of us, she fucks with all of us," Brian said. "We're a band."

"You are. I quit." Half a second after he'd said it, his guts turned to jelly and breakfast headed back up his throat. He'd known Jason and Brian since he was fourteen. Marc and Ty since he was seventeen. Half his life. They'd lived together in shitty, bug infested hotels, broken down vans and Sandy's basement. They'd fought over everything imaginable from women and money to the last French fry. Together they'd realized all their dreams.

And he'd walk away from them for Maureen.

"What?" Ty said.

"You can't. We're leaving for tour in ten days." Brian dropped his grip on Jason, who just stood there swaying like a tree in the wind.

"You son of a bitch." Marc stalked forward. "We'll sue."

Cal turned from keeping Bear back to put out a hand to stop Marc.

"Fine. Sue. I don't give a shit. I'm going home." Bear reached in his pocket for the car keys. If he left now, he'd be able to catch her before she went to lunch. She could cancel the stupid shopping trip. She didn't need to win anybody's approval anymore. Sunday when she flew home, he could go with her.

"Wait, wait." At the same time, he flipped open his phone. "We'll call Sandy. Let's everybody take a deep breath. Nobody is going to sue anybody."

Bear trembled. He wanted to go home to Maureen and have her tell him he'd done the right thing. When he dreamed of being a rock star, he'd never imagined most of his life would be dictated by a corporation and the fans and the rest of the band and various other strangers who wanted him to toe their line. He just wanted to be a guy with a wife and a mortgage and a job, to have conversations about what time he was going to be home for dinner and what they would be having.

"Hey, Sandy, Bear is threatening to quit the band. No, I don't think Jason did anything. I'm not sure what happened. He's right here." Brian held out the phone. "Sandy wants to talk to you."

"What?" Bear gritted his teeth, preparing for the tongue lashing of a lifetime.

"Look, son, I know how you feel. You boys are under a lot of pressure right now, but quitting is only going to make things worse. Why don't we all get together for dinner? We can hash things out and put a lot of these bad feelings behind us."

Not a tongue lashing, but Bear still felt fifteen. "I'm having dinner with Maureen."

"Ah, Maureen."

"What the fuck is that supposed to mean?" Bile boiled up his throat. Jesus, none of them could stand to let an opportunity to ding Maureen pass.

"Nothing, but I think I know what the argument was about now." Sandy paused and Bear could hear him clicking his pen on the other end of the line. "Alright, how about I come out there and we all have lunch? The six of us, like old times."

Bear searched the crowd, picking out his bandmates. Brian still looked panicked. Ty was peering around like he couldn't figure out how they'd gotten here. Marc stood with his arms folded and his permanent scowl firmly in place. Jason's swarthy skin had gone pale. Bear could understand that feeling. He'd thought quitting the band would be a relief, instead it made him feel like a raccoon trying to cross a busy eight lane highway. He couldn't imagine being without those guys, even if they were assholes. "All right."

"Good. I'll be there to get you boys for lunch at noon. In the meantime, I suggest you all practice and try not to talk about your personal lives."

"Good idea. See you at noon." Bear snapped the phone closed and handed it back to Brian. "Sandy's coming out for lunch."

"So you're not quitting?" Ty asked.

Brian whipped around like he wanted to throw his phone at Ty's head.

"Not today." Bear stuffed his hands in his pockets and started for the building. Fortunately, he could have done the walk blindfolded because relief was making him dizzy. He couldn't quit the band. What would he do without them? But if they were going to keep making him choose between them and Maureen, there was no contest. "We better get some work done before Sandy gets here or he's going to be pissed."

Chapter 12

Michael's warm hands cradled her face. He didn't say he wished she could stay. Didn't tell her he loved her. He didn't say anything at all. Everything had been said last night. Maureen felt threadbare with the lack of sleep. Yesterday, after they'd gotten home from Disneyland, she'd been so tired she thought she could sleep for a week, but sleep had never come. Instead they'd stayed up all night talking and making love until everything was used up.

Why did this feel so much like leaving home when she was *going* home? She had a house and a garden and a class full of kids who wanted to hear all about her big trip. The other teachers would want to hear all about her spa visits and her day on Rodeo Drive, as well as some other aspects of the trip. This week had given her enough ammunition to keep every person she knew emerald green with envy for the next several years. But if telling them meant leaving him, she didn't care if they ever found out.

"You're going to give that shirt back eventually, right?" he said.

"Maybe. Depends on if you try to quit the band again."

He chuckled, but it had the dry rattle of a recycling truck in Death Valley. "I'll be there to pick you up in five weeks. I'd say pack light, but…" He nudged her carryon with one foot.

"This isn't going to be like that movie where the girl showed up to meet the guy on tour and he didn't know what day it was, is it?" She resisted the urge to bite her lip. That movie was never meant to be a horror, but it terrified her.

"You've gotta stop watching that stuff."

Traffic flowed around them to the security screening. They'd been standing, forehead to forehead, his hands on her face and hers on his arms for ages. How much longer would they have to stand like this for her to miss her flight?

"You need to get going if you're going to get through security in time to make the flight." His thumb stroked her cheekbone.

What would happen if she missed it? Call school and tell them to get a sub for tomorrow. Get a sub for the rest of the year. She could travel with the band and make sure no groupies got their hooks into him and that he didn't forget what day of the week it was.

Abandoning her students and her house and her life. For a man. "I really have to go."

He took a step back, scooped up her bag and draped it over her shoulder. "Five weeks isn't that long."

"Not really. School will be out." She did bite her lip this time. State tests were coming in a couple weeks. She'd have a lot of hard work between now and then getting the kids ready. Then grades were due. And all the clean up she'd need to get on in her yard. Her to do list was about a mile and a half long. Subtract all the hours she'd spend sleeping and working and she'd have almost no time left to miss him. The length of a coffee break. Or recess on a nice day.

"I'm pretty sure if I kiss you again, I'm not going to let go." His lush mouth turned down and his jaw tensed. "Might be better if I just wave from here."

From there? He was a foot and a half away. But he was right. If she reached out for him again she wasn't going to be able to let go. Misery and panic clawed her chest. A well of hot tears boiled toward her eyes. "Yeah. 'Bye."

Spinning on one heel, she half ran for the x-ray area. She joined the line keeping her eyes resolutely forward, clutching the strap of her carryon. Even though her shopping sprees hadn't amounted to much, she'd had to leave a few things behind at Michael's.

Everything she left behind was old. He hated the idea of her in old Levi's when he could give her designer jeans. If he'd had his way, he'd have just supplied her with a brand new wardrobe from the socks up.

She hadn't let him buy her an engagement ring though. After their one big fight, the subject hadn't come up again but she'd caught him casting longing glances toward every jeweler they passed. Liddy, Tori and all Tori's friends told her she was nuts. Possession was nine tenths of the law. Whatever he bought for her would have a very nice resale value. Just the thought made her sick.

"Can you take off your shoes, please?"

"What?" She focused on the uniformed guard in front of her. She'd been so focused on not looking at Michael that she hadn't seen anything else.

"Your shoes." The woman pointed at her feet. "You need to take them off and put them in the tub. The carryon and purse need to go in a separate tubs."

She set her bag in a tub. Then she put her purse in another one. Slipping off her shoes, she put them in the third before shoving them all in the direction of the x-ray machine. In front of the metal detector, she paused. What would happen if it went off? Would they pull her aside for a more thorough inspection? Would it take so long that she would miss her flight? What if she refused?

"Miss, you have to go through the metal detector." Another security guard crowded her from behind and she moved forward. No alarms went off as she passed through. Swallowing around the knot of tears in her throat, she gathered her belongings and slipped her shoes back on. Only then, fully reassembled, did she dare turn back.

He stood where she'd left him. His broad shoulders slumped, but he raised a hand to wave. Her jaw shook and her feet were rooted to the floor. She couldn't go. She couldn't leave him. Her whole life she'd always been able to move on when the time came. She'd missed her high school friends, but at the end of school she'd gone on her way. Some of them she emailed occasionally, but not many. The same had been true in college. Every year she watched groups of children she had loved and cherished leave her for the next grade but she didn't spend the in-service day weeping over kids who'd left her, unlike many of her colleagues.

But now, the idea of leaving him shredded her. She wasn't going to be able to walk to the gate. Her knees would give out and she'd end up an undignified heap on the floor. People flowed around her as if she were just another obstacle between them and their destinations. Her destination was behind her. What was she headed toward?

Her students. Her house and friends. The life she'd made for herself, all by herself.

Chin lifted, she forced a smile then turned and walked toward the gate. In the lounge area, she dropped into a seat and stared into space. She'd known him for a month. Friday night they'd celebrated with pizza by candlelight. In that month, she'd been with him for only two weeks. The rest of the time had been over the phone. Now they faced a five-week separation during which, if movies were anything to go by, he'd be surrounded by women who would do anything for him. By his own report, he'd be lonely and bored most of the time with a few hours of happiness when he was playing.

And she hadn't let him buy her an engagement ring.

A woman sat down beside her. "Wow, just made it. They're going to start boarding any second." The woman focused on her. "Are you alright?"

She nodded, and couldn't form an expression.

"Ah, you traveling alone?"

She nodded again.

"First time?"

No. "Yes." She'd always traveled alone. Why was this so different?

"Poor dear." The woman patted her hand. "It gets easier with practice."

She forced a tight smile in lieu of speech, and the gate attendant called the first group to board.

"Well, that's me. Good luck, sweetheart." The woman stood and shouldered her bag. "Try to sleep on the flight. That always helps me."

While waiting for them to call her to board, she hugged herself. Five weeks. In five weeks, school ended and the tour passed close by. She was scheduled to join up with them for a month then he had a weeklong break. During the break he was going to come home with her. Five weeks apart, five weeks together. Then he left again. Depending on how things went, she might go with him.

On the plane, she stashed her carryon, buckled herself in, pulled the blanket over her head and closed her eyes. The lack of sleep last night and the massive depression shut her down so thoroughly, she knew nothing until the plane touched down. The man in the seat next to her gave her a wide-eyed look that made her wonder if she'd been talking in her sleep. If she had, he'd been treated to a better show than any programming the flight had. She'd dreamed about Michael.

Linda waited near the baggage carousel. "I wasn't sure where to meet you so I figured this would be a good bet. Are you okay?"

She shook her head. Half her brain still wanted to be asleep.

"You guys break up?"

She glared at her. Everyone was waiting with baited breath for him to dump her. "No. I slept the whole way back. I'm not quite awake yet." She wanted to be home as soon as possible so she could bawl in private. The three hours she'd gained flying out, she'd lost on the return trip. Darkness pressed against the huge airport windows, smothering her.

"So you visited your famous boyfriend in California and all you got was this lousy Tesla t-shirt?" Linda fell into step beside her.

"No." Maureen smoothed her hand down the front of the t-shirt. It still smelled like him.

"So what's the problem?"

"I miss him."

Linda shrugged. "Fair enough. I don't see a ring. You know there's a betting pool going at school about whether he'd ask you to marry him on this trip."

"He already asked." She should have let him buy her the ring. Even if he broke up with her it would have been physical proof that he'd existed. Something a little more permanent and serious than an old t-shirt for a band she knew nothing about.

"Excuse me?"

"He asked me weeks ago." She walked through the sliding doors and stopped at the edge of the drop off area checking for cars. The air was colder here too. Out in sunny California it had been too warm for her jacket. Now she wished she had it but it was stuffed in her bag.

"What do you mean, he asked you weeks ago?"

"He asked me before he left town."

Linda followed her off the sidewalk without looking in either direction. "You're kidding. Where's the ring?"

"I don't have one. We were keeping it quiet until everyone got used to us as a couple. I knew you'd freak out." Maureen stopped. Gravity was stronger here too. Her carryon weighed at least twice what it had when she got on the plane and she had no clue where Linda had parked. Linda wasn't giving hints either.

"Damn right. What do you mean, you got engaged weeks ago?"

"I mean, we got engaged weeks ago. He asked me before he left town. Remember that personal day I took a month ago? He asked me then."

"After he knew you for a week!" Linda's voice rang off the cement walls, sounding like her formerly squeaking brakes, which reminded her of Michael fixing those brakes.

"Yes, and this is why I didn't tell anyone. Where did you park? It's cold."

"I can't believe you. You were always so calm and level headed. When did you lose your mind?"

And this was her friend? She should have asked someone else to pick her up or taken a really expensive cab or something.

"You can't marry this guy. You don't even know him."

"It's not a done deal, Linda. I don't even have a ring. He asked, I said yes. We didn't run off to Vegas yesterday." Run off to Vegas. Why couldn't she have thought of that Friday night? They could have skipped Disney for Vegas and gotten hitched. He would have been all for it.

"I'm surprised you didn't."

"If I'd thought of it in time, we would have. Where is your car, Linda?"

Linda shook her head and stalked into the parking deck. "So what is it about this guy?"

"I love him." She bit back a sob. Love was such a tiny word for such a big emotion.

"Okay, but does he love you?" Linda didn't look back.

Maureen felt safe in letting misery bow her mouth. She pictured him standing in the airport, shoulders slumped, waving to her from the wrong side of the security checkpoint. He might be standing there still. Yesterday he'd spent the whole day at Disneyland with her. He'd never gone there before and had indulged her every whim all day long. Last night they'd spent all night indulging one another. Every time she looked at him, he'd been studying her with focused concentration. If he paid that much attention in rehearsals, he would have a lot fewer bruises. "Yes."

Something in her voice must have made Linda stop. When her friend turned back, Maureen closed her eyes and let her bag slide to the floor.

"You really love him," Linda said.

She nodded, covering her face with her hands.

"Oh, sweetie." Linda put her arms around her and she sagged.

She still felt torn to shreds. The woman at the airport before she got on the plane said sleeping would help. If this was helped, then they'd have had to take her off the plane in a stretcher if she hadn't slept.

"I'm sorry," Linda said. "If he really loves you that much it's meant to be."

"But what if he doesn't? What if he's not working with the same definition?" Sobs shook her. "What if a groupie gets her hooks into him? What if Marc convinces him to break up with me? What if he changes his mind?"

"Don't be silly." Linda stroked her hair. "I'm sure he loves you as much as you love him."

"I've never loved anyone like this before. I feel like I'm broken."

"You probably haven't, but I swear to you, you can get through it." Linda pulled her up until she got her feet under her again. "Let's get you to the car and calmed down enough to call him and let him know you landed safely."

"You think I'm being stupid, rushing into this."

"No." Linda brushed her hair off her face as if she were one of the kids instead of an adult. "I think for the first time in your life you're being a little impetuous and I can't deny you that. Come on. I have a box of tissues in my car."

* * * *

"Jesus, Bear, walk on your own feet, will you?" Rudy scuttled a few steps ahead as if that would help. He'd already done it three times between the bus and here and Bear still kept stepping on his heels.

"Where the hell did you hide her?" Bear scanned the venue. It was one of those outdoor deals. Most of the stage was already set, but instruments weren't out yet. Seven people crowded around the mixing board and he couldn't tell if any of them were Maureen.

Last night on the phone she'd been full of stories about the last day of school and the amazing haul of barrettes and coffee cups she'd gotten. No indication that she wouldn't be here today to tell him all those stories again in person, but he'd had vivid nightmares all night about getting here and finding out she'd changed her mind about coming or somehow gotten bored and gone home.

"I didn't hide her. She's right— Shit."

"Lost her already?" Marc said. Jason and Ty snickered. Brian veered off in the direction of the dressing room.

Bear followed Rudy's gaze to a section of seating up at the back of the pavilion. An empty section.

"Well, she was right there twenty minutes ago." Rudy pulled a radio off his belt. "Has anybody seen Maureen?"

In the crackle and hiss of the radio, Bear couldn't make out any of the answers so he dropped his duffel and started for her last known location. At least she'd made it. If she was in the same city, he was way ahead of the past five weeks. On one of the seats he found a paperback novel, an empty Coke can and a hair elastic with a purple silk rose on it. He slid the elastic around his wrist and turned back to Rudy. Rudy had the radio up to his mouth as he walked up the steps.

"...care if she volunteered. I needed her to stay put for ten more minutes and you guys have her running around like a goddamn gopher." Rudy moved the radio away from his mouth. "Joe sent her to check on the catering guys and Perry swears he saw her headed to the office."

"Michael!" Her voice echoed through the sound system followed by a whine of feedback.

Bear spun toward the stage. She stood at the edge next to Brian, a microphone in her hand like it was a live snake, and she was wearing the Tesla t-shirt she'd stolen from him when she left LA. Brian took the microphone and set it on the stage. Taking Maureen by the hands, he lowered her into the waiting arms of Joe, the lead lighting tech. Bear bounded down the steps wanting to yell at them to keep their hands off his fiancee, but seconds later she was in his arms and it didn't matter anymore. She tasted like heaven and smelled like fresh squeezed lemons. "You got it," he said when he had to come up for air.

"What? The case of body wash? Yes." She tangled her fingers through his hair, staring at him like she couldn't quite believe he was there. "You know it takes me about six months to get through one bottle. I now have enough to last me a decade."

"Good. When you run out, I'll buy you more." He kissed her again. The tangy sweet scent made him think of lemonade. He was never going to look at lemonade the same way again.

"Do the two of you need a few minutes alone in the dressing room?" Jason asked.

The thought had crossed his mind, but Maureen wasn't a groupie and he wasn't going to start treating her like one. No matter how much he wanted her.

"Whatever you need, you're going to have to do it someplace else," Joe said. "We have work to do."

He pulled her up into the seating area. "When did you get in?"

She led the way back to where she'd left her book. "Earlier this afternoon. I've already been to the hotel and dropped off my stuff. I picked up this book in the gift shop this morning." She held up the paperback, which she was half finished with.

"I'll try to keep you entertained a little more."

She put her arms around his neck and her warm soft body curved against his. "I hope so." Her lips met his again and all thoughts of lemonade and not treating her like a groupie evaporated. There was almost enough privacy between the rows of seats.

"Mr. D'Amato to the stage, please. Mr. D'Amato to the stage."

Almost, but not quite enough privacy. Onstage, Ty swung a microphone around by the cord as he talked to Jason, who already had a guitar in his hands. They were never ready to sound check this fast. Every day there was a minimum of forty-five minutes fucking around before they could get down to work. Today when he wanted a little time, they were all right on the ball. The bastards. "I'm sorry, Maur. I've got to get to work."

"It's okay." She brushed a kiss across his cheek. "I'll be here when you have a minute."

He had to circle the stage and go up from one side. By the time he'd settled behind his kit, the others were staring at him.

"Pooh Bear feel all better now that his honey pot is here?" Ty cooed.

Bear threw a drumstick at him.

"Let's just get this thing done." Jason sat down on the drum riser.

Bear watched her. As she promised, she sat down right about where he'd left her. She watched for a while, but most of the time she read. Was she already bored? The ride wasn't going to get much better. He had the whole run of *The X-Files* on the bus. They'd been watching them as they traveled. That should entertain her.

Maybe he could talk Brian into loaning her his electronic book thing too. Brian's weird taste in reading material might be a problem though. He probably had that thing loaded with freaky horror novels. Might be better if he got one for her and let her load it up with whatever she wanted. Brian always got new reading material wherever there was an internet connection when he ran out.

At the rate she was going through that novel she bought this morning, she was going to run out of gift shop offerings way too fast. Would she even want to watch the show every night? She might be happier at the hotel.

Five weeks he'd been dreaming about her being on tour with him and it had never occurred to him to figure out what to do with her when she got here. Beyond the obvious, of course.

Boy, he couldn't wait to get back to the hotel tonight and indulge in a little of the obvious.

As soon as they had the all clear on sound check, he jumped off the stage and headed for her. Behind him, Ty and Brian started singing *Pour Some Sugar On Me* only Ty replaced 'sugar' with 'honey' and Jason was catching on fast. They were going to be calling him Pooh Bear for the rest of the tour. He grabbed her by the hand and took her up out of the pavilion to the lawn area. Woods surrounded this venue so it must have some decent nooks to hide in for a few minutes. They wouldn't have long enough, but right now he needed a couple minutes alone with her. All he could find was a tree near a bank of bathrooms.

"Not very romantic," he said, pulling her behind the trunk.

"It's fine." She leaned on the tree, drawing him into her arms. "I missed you."

"You told me every day on the phone." He traced her lips with his finger. Warm and satiny.

"I know, but now I'm telling you in person."

When she'd walked away from him at the airport a month ago he'd thought he was going to die. He wanted to throw her over his shoulder and carry her back to his car. Watching her go through security and then down that long hallway until she disappeared in the distance, he'd thought of a thousand ways to latch onto her and dismissed every one. One of the things he loved about her was the fact that she had her own life separate from him. He kissed her.

She melted in his arms. All heat and welcome. Every curve, familiar and sweet. He tightened his arms around her, lifting her up. One of her legs coiled around his waist, and she slid her lips up his jaw and down his neck. "I missed you," she murmured.

"I missed you too, baby." He kneaded her shoulders. "Every day on the phone I wanted to climb through that line and touch you."

She chuckled and the dark chocolate cinnamon sound of it made his hair stand on end in the hopes that she might pet it back down. "What time do you get off?"

He knew what she meant, but he shuddered with desire. "The show is over at eleven, we'll have dinner and head to the hotel. We should get there about one."

Frowning, she nodded. It *was* a long damn time to wait.

He slid his hand down the curve of her spine. "Come on, let's go back and see what's going on backstage. They're already gonna be pretty rude."

She put her arm around his waist and leaned her head on his shoulder. "So what time does the show start, anyway?"

"Didn't we go over all this on the phone?"

"We did, but your voice is so much warmer in person."

He pulled her tighter. "Let's see. By now the guys in Eldrich should be here. I think we have a meet and greet with some local record store people."

"Like we did before?"

"Sort of. They're coming to us this time. There're some contest winners coming too." He guided her around the back and through the barricades. Why had he been worried about what to do with her? She wasn't a kid. There was plenty to keep her occupied.

"There was a contest?" she asked.

"On the band forum."

She made a little sound, but they'd arrived in the greeting area and he didn't have time to ask her about it because the meet and greet had started without them. About three dozen people grazed at the catering table or chatted up the other guys.

"You want something to drink?" he asked her.

"No, thanks."

"Hi, Bear." The woman who stepped in front of them sounded breathless. She had the expression of someone far too excited and in need of an oxygen mask. "Is this your new girlfriend?"

"Yes, it is and you are?" He held out his hand. A handshake, a photograph, and an autograph and on to the next one. At least he would have Maureen beside him.

The woman ignored the hand. "Your last girlfriend was prettier."

Bear blinked. "What?"

"She isn't as pretty as your last girlfriend. Everybody on the forum thinks so."

Maureen put his arm through his and met his eyes, impassive.

"Everybody on the forum doesn't know her yet," Bear told the woman. "Did you want a photograph?"

"I can take it for you." Maureen held out her hand for the camera.

Class. She had class.

* * * *

Maureen scurried through the backlot to the stage stairs. The caterers had arrived with dinner. The guys in Eldrich had left garbage everywhere every night and even though Rudy told her it wasn't her job to clean up, she did anyway. Leaping up the stairs two at a time, she met Tracy just offstage and the other woman handed her a towel.

Watching Michael come offstage was almost the highlight of her day. He always looked about twelve feet tall and electric. Marc swept past first, snatched a towel from Tracy and kept going. All night long he'd been one technical glitch after another. Jack, his tech, arrived to take Marc's guitar, hunched and miserable like he'd just run a marathon chased by whip wielding demons. Ty, right on Marc's heels, was in a much better mood. Instead of grabbing a towel, he grabbed Tracy and kissed her. Then he did the same to Maureen and headed for the dressing room. Brian accepted a towel from Tracy.

"Good show?" he asked Maureen.

"Great show." At this point, she was learning the difference.

"Who's the bassist for Def Leppard?"

She knew that too, but it wouldn't do to give the right one. "Fred Savage?"

Brian ruffled her hair as he walked away.

Michael scooped her off the floor and swung her around. Then he set her down and slanted his mouth across hers like he was starved for her. She rubbed the towel through his hair. Securing it around his neck, she leaned back. "Dinner's here."

He squeezed her tighter. "My dinner is right here."

"I'll have to take you up on that later. Come along before you crash." She twisted out of his grasp and took his hand. Over her shoulder, she saw Jason shuffling off last. She hadn't talked to him much, but she'd noticed that, unlike the others, he deflated the moment he stepped offstage. The others took a couple of hours. After particularly successful shows it might take until the next day before the glamour wore off. Not Jason.

"God, I'm starved." Michael pulled her toward the dressing room, falling into step beside Jason. "What the fuck was wrong with Marc tonight?"

Jason snorted. Ahead of them, Marc reamed out Jack at the top of his lungs. The sound echoing off the cinderblock walls grated on her, and Michael draped his arm around her shoulders as if to protect her. As they passed the two men, Jason split off and Michael cursed.

"You go on ahead, babe," he said. "I need to stay here to keep the peace. Tell Rudy, would ya?" He gave her a little push as he turned back to the confrontation.

These little blow-ups seemed to happen on a daily basis. The more time she spent hanging around with the roadies, the more of them she saw. It wasn't too much different than recess duty except the combatants could really damage one another and didn't end up crying. In two weeks on the road, she'd become as good at negotiating these little spats as Rudy or Gene, the road boss, and she didn't leave bruises like they might.

When Marc grabbed Jack by the shirt and hoisted him off the ground, she decided to intervene.

"Fucking cut it out!" Michael bellowed yanking Marc's hand off Jack's shirt with a tearing sound. Marc still clutched a scrap of material in his grasp and Jack backed against the wall, gasping.

"Like your shit doesn't stink." Jason reached across the group, giving Marc a shove.

Marc turned his attention to Jason. "Listen, you whiny bastard."

"Alright everyone, let's calm down." Maureen stepped into the middle of the group. Another thing different about recess. Those combatants couldn't keep arguing over her head.

"Fuck you. Who's whining now? It's not Jack's fault all your equipment is shit. Cheap bastard."

"Maureen, go get Rudy." Michael tugged her arm.

"Jason, this isn't helping," she said, and put her hand on his shoulder to hold him away from Marc. Her logic was flawed. Elementary kids didn't out reach her either.

"It's his job to keep the equipment in top condition and if he isn't doing it, he's fired." Marc leaned forward.

"You have had no trouble the whole tour until now. Everything just fucked up at once," Jack said.

"Everyone's tired and hungry. Why don't we deal with this tomorrow at sound check?" Maureen held on to her calm tone by force. In all the arguments she'd broken up, she'd never felt in danger, but this one teetered on the edge.

"We had to switch up the fucking set list because you're a fuck up." Marc reached for Jack again, but the other man stepped out of range.

Elementary kids also didn't swear quite so much. "The audience didn't even notice the change. Everything went perfectly smoothly," she said.

"Maureen, come on." Michael pulled her arm again. She had about ten more seconds before he picked her up and moved her out of the way.

"I'm a fuck up?" Jack clenched his fists.

"Yeah, you're a fuck up."

"Look in a mirror, dickhead."

Marc leaped forward, but Michael stiff-armed him before he trampled her. Maureen ducked away, walking up Jason's boots before he could move out of the way. Jack jerked backward into the wall. Marc slipped on the floor and landed on his rear.

Chapter 13

"What the fuck is going on here?" Gene bellowed. A little man with a big voice, he could keep the entire tour on the road through force of will. He waded into the fray and grabbed Jack by the shoulder. "I've got a hundred and fifty guys standing around with their thumbs up their asses waiting for you to get his shit off the stage so they can tear down. Get to fucking work. You four go eat your goddamn dinner. I don't want to have to listen to you bitch about how it was cold. Move it."

Then Maureen realized Jason was holding her up and she was standing on his feet. Elementary kids never, ever tried to go through her to continue the fight. Marc shot a glare at Jason and Michael before stomping down the hall.

"You okay?" Jason asked, setting her back on the floor.

Maureen nodded, but didn't shove Michael away when he slipped his arm around her waist and stared into her eyes.

"The divorce is final tomorrow." Jason shrugged.

"Great, so we have another day of this to look forward to?"

"At least two." Jason walked around them.

Michael brushed his fingers through her hair. "You sure you're okay?"

"Yeah. It just took me by surprise."

"Next time I tell you to go get Rudy, will you go get Rudy?"

She tried to laugh, but it came out pained.

He led the way to the dressing room. Everyone else was already eating while Marc pontificated on how women break up bands.

"Lennon was married before," Jason said.

"Yeah, but Cynthia wasn't as much of a meddling bitch." Marc's eyes found Maureen's. "The problem isn't the woman, it's the meddling."

"I don't think you can blame the whole break up on Yoko," Brian said.

She went to the microwave and heated up what they were all calling Maureen's Magical Elixir for Ty. Two parts honey and one part lemon, it ensured Ty didn't spend all night and part of the morning sounding like Kermit the Frog. Was this what Marc meant by meddling? Making sure the table was clean and fixing the elixir? Meeting Michael when he came offstage to give him a towel?

Michael kissed her cheek. "I'm gonna grab a quick shower."

Maureen delivered the elixir and brought their plates to the microwave so she could zap them when he came out. She didn't want to be at the table right now anyway. They were still on the subject of why the Beatles broke up. She would much rather they made Zen koans out of song lyrics. Discussing whether or not having a gun made Billy a hero was less of a personal attack than figuring out how the wrong woman could destroy a band.

"You really okay?" Jason asked. He leaned one hip on the table.

"Of course." She hadn't had much conversation with him. Marc hated her, but Jason hated the universe. He kept to himself and hardly talked to anyone except Brian.

"Marc is really being a dick to you."

"It's fine," she said, shrugging.

"It's not." He shifted closer. "Don't let him get to you."

"I'm not."

"Funny. Doesn't look like it." Jason lifted her chin with one finger so he could search her eyes. "You gotta let it go. Marc'll back off."

Michael's fist came into view about a half second before it connected with Jason's face. "Michael!"

Jason staggered backward into the catering table. Apples, oranges and pears bounced across the table and floor. Michael grabbed around her for him.

She caught his arm. "Stop it."

"I can't believe you're hitting on my fiancee," Michael snarled.

"I wasn't." Jason pushed himself upright.

"You fucking liar."

"He wasn't." Maureen adjusted her grip on Michael's arm. Then she realized he was wet and wearing only a towel. "He was talking to me."

"Jesus, man, what is wrong with you?" Marc demanded.

Michael swung around, nearly losing his towel. "You probably put him up to it."

Marc cocked one eyebrow. "Yes, the Cigarette Smoking Man called me last night and told me I needed to have Jason hit on your girlfriend to protect us from the aliens."

Maureen pursed her lips. She wasn't sure if she should take that as a good sign because Marc liked watching *The X-Files* or if he was making fun of her. Or if she'd been watching a bit too much herself and was getting a little paranoid. "Michael, you made a mistake. Why don't you just apologize and go get dried off and dressed so you can eat?"

Michael fixed his glare on her.

She backed up a step, bumping into the table. Her feet slipped out from under her. Jason caught her elbow before she went backward into the microwave. A hole opened in the middle of her chest. Did he think she was flirting with Jason? After two solid weeks of barely speaking to him?

Michael turned, managing to glare at everyone in the room as he stomped back toward the showers.

Shaking off Jason's supporting arm, she went after him. "Michael, I swear we were just talking. He came over to tell me not to let Marc bother me." Her voice echoed off the cavernous tile walls, its shrill tone making her wince.

Michael had stopped in front of one of the six shower stalls. He yanked off his towel and started drying himself off, keeping his back to her. "Stop treating me like I'm a kid."

"What? I'm not. Honestly, nothing was going on."

"*Michael, you made a mistake. Why don't you just apologize and go get dried off and dressed so you can eat?* You talk to me like I'm seven." He turned around, his expression still furious. "I'm not a kid."

"I know." She resisted the urge to back away again. She'd seen him angry before, but she'd never been on the receiving end. "I'm sorry. I didn't realize that's how it sounded."

"You talk to me like that all the time and it pisses me off."

"I'll try not to do it any more." To stop her hands from shaking, she clasped them together. "Jason and I were just talking."

"I know. Now." He rubbed the towel through his hair. "Besides, you I trust. Jason does stupid shit all the time." He threw the towel on the floor.

She stooped to pick it up, and he caught her hand. "Leave it. Somebody will get it." Towing her closer, he grinned. "I'm naked."

"I noticed. A little excitable too." Her heart fluttered as he pulled her into his arms and not in the preferable way. The anxiety from the argument still crackled through her nerves. She pressed against his hard, solid body.

"Too bad we can't skip dinner and head back to the hotel."

"You skip dinner and you'll run out of energy." The jittery anxiety wasn't going away.

"Can't have that." He ran his fingers through her hair. "Let's eat so we can go someplace more private." He grabbed his clothes and started dressing.

"I'll go heat everything up." She backed out of the room.

In the dressing room, everyone was almost finished and they were working on song lyric koans. She heated up their meals and had them on the table by the time he came out. Sitting next to him, she could hardly eat.

She'd thought she was used to the tension. Hah. Everyone chatted as if nothing unusual had happened even though Jason had an ice pack on his cheek. Before long everyone was being loaded into the bus for the long ride to the hotel. Michael settled onto the couch, still bandying around song titles so she sat down beside him. Resting her head on his shoulders, she tried to employ some of the tricks the roadies had taught her for sleeping anywhere, anytime. Nothing worked. She felt like she'd been drinking Mountain Dew all day long.

At the hotel, Michael pulled her into the room and pressed her against the door. "I love you and I want to be with you forever," he said.

Unable to meet his gaze, she looked down and bit her lip. "I'm sorry I treated you like a little boy."

"It doesn't matter."

"It does matter. Do you forgive me?"

"Of course I do." He brushed his fingers through her hair. "Baby, to be honest I don't think it was really about you anyway. Touring is rough. We bicker. You got caught in the middle and took it seriously."

"But I do treat you like a little boy sometimes." She stared down at his shirt. He had her trapped between him and the door. Not that she minded, but he did seem to like to have these conversations in close proximity.

"And sometimes I like it, just not so much in front of my friends."

"I can stop."

"Promise me you won't stop loving me."

She looked up. His dark eyes seemed a little fearful, but she didn't know why. She'd been the one screwing things up. Since the moment she met him, she'd been treating him like a child and he was no child. "I love you, Michael."

He cradled her cheek in his palm. "Good, keep it that way." He leaned over and kissed her. She pulled her body tight to his as if it would erase all her tension. His kiss deepened as he slipped a hand around, captured her nape. She shook with the need for him. Heat washed through her. Her skin came alive to the light brush of his fingers.

Waltzing her backward, he eased her onto the bed, trailing his hot mouth down her neck. When his hands touched her, they were hungry. He unfastened her jeans and slipped them off her in one motion with her panties and socks. Before she'd taken another breath, he was on her and in her. She cried out. Her body swelled around him, ready and hot. She arched as he thrust into her again. Clutching him, she was swept along by him. Loved. Cherished. Forgiven. He caught the back of her head, turned her lips to his and kissing her, thrust into her one last time. Over the edge she tipped, into a rich swirl of bliss.

Still buried inside her, he collapsed on her chest with his face pressed into the curve of her neck. "You're all I can think about. I can't believe I haven't screwed up on stage. I love performing, but I love our private shows too."

"You're not thinking about quitting, are you?" He hadn't mentioned it since that day in April, but that didn't mean he hadn't been thinking about it. "I know how much you love doing this. I don't think it's going to be easy for you to give up."

"I know." He nuzzled her neck. "I want that and I want this. All I want is everything. Is that too much to ask?"

How was she supposed to answer? The urge to promise him that he could have all of her nearly overwhelmed her, but she managed to keep her mouth shut. She breathed deeply and wrapped her arms around his shoulders. His hands roamed over her skin. Little tremors of pleasure rippled through her as he stirred inside her. He moaned against her flesh, starting to rock against her slowly.

He drew her ear lobe between his lips, sucked it gently as he stroked in and out. "God, I love you."

Maureen ran her hands down his back, feeling his muscles moving under his skin. Head lolling on the pillows, she was swept by his strength until rapture took her again and everything dropped away.

* * * *

Bear swore he heard *Swing* playing from somewhere on the other side of the room. Why their current hit would be playing in his hotel room, he couldn't imagine. He reached for Maureen, but she slid away. "Where you goin'?" he muttered.

"My phone is ringing."

"Your phone?" He opened his eyes in time to see her snatch her purse off the dresser and dump it out.

She grabbed her phone and flipped it open. "Hello? Denver, why?"

Bear sat up and brushed his hair off his face. The clock beside the bed said eight. They hadn't fallen asleep until after four. Who the hell would be calling her at this hour?

"What?"

Her tone sent a shiver down his spine. Today was their day off. Other than a flight to the next city, they didn't have to do anything all day long. He'd hoped to spend every possible minute in bed with her having sex and the silly conversations he was starting to enjoy almost as much as the sex. Her tone made that unlikely.

"How is that my fault? My class did well."

Bear threw off the covers and crossed the room. He wrapped his arm around her waist, but she didn't relax against him. "What's wrong?"

"A couple of board members are trying to blame the district's low test scores on me. This is insane. How can anybody believe it?"

"Easy," Linda said. "You aren't here to defend yourself. They aren't going to renew your contract."

"Oh my God." Maureen pulled away from him to lean on the dresser.

"What does that mean?" Bear asked. The stone in his gut already knew.

"It means I'm going to lose my job." She stared at him like she wanted him to fix it, but he knew if he told her to screw the job, she'd flip out. It wasn't a job to her. It was her life.

And she was his.

"I guess you have to go home and fight for it then," he said.

Three hours later, he climbed out of the taxi from dropping her off at the airport. He went through the hotel kitchen to avoid the fans at the front doors who waited for the band to leave for their chartered plane, which would fly out of a different airport in about an hour. Bear leaned against the back of the elevator. When she left him in LA, she'd been upset about going. This time when she walked away from him at the x-ray machines, she'd been so consumed with this bullshit thing going on at home she'd almost forgotten to kiss him goodbye. Had it even occurred to her yet that they were apart? Or did she know and not care?

The elevator doors opened on their floor and Marc stood waiting. He whistled. "Well, I'll be damned. Rudy said she left, but I didn't believe him."

"Fuck off, Marc." Bear stalked past him. "I'm not in the mood."

"So there really is something going on about her job?" Marc fell into step beside him. "Rudy said he thought she was going to lose her job."

"That's why she's going home. So she doesn't," he said as he swiped his keycard.

"She went home to save her job."

Bear turned in his door. "Yes, Marc, she went home to save her job. Despite what you think, she is not just sinking her claws into my wallet. And maybe if you hadn't been such a dick for the last two weeks, she'd have wanted to stay with me more and let the job go."

His throat closed. That wasn't true. Maureen would have wanted to go back no matter what Marc did. No matter what any of them did. Down the hall the other guys' doors stood open. Ty had been nice to her. He was nice to everybody. Brian loaned her his electronic reader during sound checks so she wouldn't burn through so many books. She actually liked his freaky horror novels. Even Jason had tried to be nice to her. Bear had screwed that up himself. Rudy, Gene, the crew, the guys in Eldrich, they'd all been really nice to her. No, Maureen had gone back because she had a life. The exact thing he loved most about her, took her away.

"Hey, man, I'm sorry. I was trying to help you play it safe. We're gonna swing through that area next week. I'll apologize."

Bear nodded. It might not help, but it sure as hell couldn't hurt. He'd been avoiding Marc since the tour started. Since he'd met Maureen, really. Right now it would be great to have someone to distract him. "I need to get my stuff together. You wanna hang in here while I do?"

Marc grinned. "Sure."

"What're you guys doing?" Ty strolled down the hall.

"I'm gonna watch Bear to make sure he doesn't slit his wrists because his girlfriend is gone." Marc smirked.

"Cool. Can I watch too?"

"You pass out at the sight of blood," Brian shouted out of his room.

"If he's going to pass out somebody better make sure he doesn't smack his head on anything," Rudy roared down the hall. "I am not taking any of you assholes to the hospital this tour."

Bear shook his head. Never took long to get back to normal. Inside the room, he strolled over to the dresser. She'd left behind her hair elastic with the purple rose. He wrapped it around his wrist. She'd be back. She had to be. And he'd still have the guys.

He'd have everything then.

* * * *

Maureen folded up the paper and threw it in the recycling bin. Then she picked up the stack of newspapers Linda had saved for her and dropped them on top. The editorial column had had eight letters today. Five of them reviled her as what was wrong with education in the twenty-first century. Two defended her as an excellent teacher. One was about garbage pick up. The ratio hadn't been too much different since this mess started.

She needed to get out of the house to keep her sanity, but in public she ran the risk of having someone confront her as the sole cause for the downfall of Western Civilization. Since she'd come back from the tour, she hadn't been able to buy her own groceries or go to the mall. All her library trips had been conducted through the pick up window at the main branch. She couldn't even go to school and work in her classroom. Once her "scandal" hit the papers, the governor had decided a massive investigation of the state's schools was in order. Kaitlyn thought he was jealous because she was in the papers more than he was, but that didn't make Maureen any more popular among the staff, now scrambling to pull records for an outside investigator.

The only bright spot was Michael arriving later today. The band started a weeklong break today and was using one of their precious days off to have dinner at Mama Lena's for no discernible reason. The restaurant was closed to everyone but friends and family of the staff.

Family. That was someplace she could go. Maureen grabbed her purse and headed out the door. Tony had written one of the editorial letters supporting her. Hopefully, it hadn't lost him too much business. His letter had also defended his brother as solid and reliable, nothing like the drugged out, party boy rock star everyone assumed. Based on that, hopefully Tony was up for a reconciliation. She couldn't do much about her problems, but she might help Michael.

As she pulled up in front of the garage, Eric saw her through the front bay door. He dropped the tool in his hand and ran for the back. That might not be a good sign. Before she climbed out of the car though, Tony was at her driver's door, pulling it open and reaching in for her hand.

"Miss Donnelly, I'm so glad to see you. You heard what's going on. I knew something like this was going to happen. Bear doesn't even know what kind of mess he can cause." Tony had her hand clasped in both of his. Any second, he was going to fall to his knees and beg her forgiveness. "He doesn't do it on purpose."

"It really isn't Michael's fault."

"Like hell it isn't." Rusty spit on the ground. He'd followed Tony out, Eric right behind him.

"It really isn't. I'm a scapegoat. The district's test scores were lower than expected and they needed to blame it on someone."

"That someone shouldn't have been you and if it wasn't for Bear, it wouldn't have been," Tony insisted. "You're a wonderful teacher. Everyone says so. At least they used to."

"I don't get why you don't just quit," Eric said.

Tony turned on him, growling.

The sixty thousand dollar question. Just quit. "I can't. I'll look guilty and I'll never be able to get another teaching job."

"So? Bear makes a lot of money." Eric shoved his hands in the pockets of his coveralls.

"Shut up. She's not going to stop teaching. She's a great teacher." Tony spun around. "You're not going to, are you?"

What was he getting at? Why did he care if she kept teaching? "Nicky isn't going to be in my class next year."

"I know, but if Bear— If you and Bear split up."

She bit her lip. Tony's pause had volumes in it. Tessa and Connie had been certain Michael was too young to settle down. Tessa claimed to have turned him away from three disastrous marriages. Just because she'd passed their test didn't mean Michael had. Greasy insecurity slithered through the back of her mind, towing behind it the answer to the sixty thousand dollar question.

And she didn't have the energy to deal with that right now. "Michael's coming to town today."

"I heard."

"I'm sure he'd like to talk to you."

Tony folded his meaty arms. He looked like an older, tired version of Michael. "I'm not sure I want to talk to him. Especially not now."

She hadn't planned on having an audience for this conversation or even knew what she was going to say. "It's hot out here. Can we talk inside?"

"There's no air conditioning," Eric said.

Rusty turned toward Eric and pointed toward the garage. Eric rolled his eyes and stomped back inside with Rusty following him.

"Miss Donnelly, I know what you're trying to do."

"It is fairly transparent and you might as well start calling me Maureen. I am going to be your sister-in-law." Who knew for how long, but that was beside the point.

"Maureen." Tony pursed his lips.

She held up her hands before he started to speak. "I know you don't think it'll last. I'm not sure it will either. But I do love him and I plan to stay with him."

"I believe you. Unfortunately, I know him. When he was a kid we used to call him Flip-O-Matic because one day his favorite ice cream flavor was chocolate and the next it was vanilla and the day after that it was cherry or some other fucking thing. The only things he's ever stuck with in his life have been drums and that band, and I don't think the band gave him a choice."

"He's stuck with you."

"I don't count."

"You're his brother."

"So he had no choice."

Maureen sighed. "I just don't want to come between you and him. Especially if I'm only temporary." Her words cut though her like a laser beam, but she kept the pain off her face.

"Bear has been trying to get something between us since we were kids. It's not your fault."

"I really wish you would talk to him. It bothers him that you aren't speaking."

Tony scuffed his steel-toed boots on the pavement. "He say something?"

"Yes. Many times. He's going to be at Mama Lena's tonight at six. I know he'd be happy to see you."

Tony shrugged. "I'll talk to Pam."

"Thank you, Tony."

"Yeah, good luck. You need it."

Maureen climbed back in her car. She suspected a promise to talk to Pam meant he would be there. They were already on the guest list. Driving back to her house, she decided not to tell Michael just in case.

A strange white car sat in her driveway. She let her car coast. Maybe it belonged to a particularly persistent reporter wanting to get her side of the story or twist her side of the story, depending on what would sell more papers. Two people sat on her front stoop, smoking.

Michael and Marc.

Her foot slipped on the brake. Her car bucked and Michael turned to look. He stood, flicking away the cigarette and met her in the driveway.

"Hey, baby, those brakes giving you trouble again?"

She threw her arms around his neck. Temporary. She needed to be reminding herself she was temporary. "What are you doing here?"

"We flew in early." Michael buried his face in the curve of her neck. "I missed you, baby."

"He bitched and moaned until we agreed to fly right after the show instead of waiting until morning," Marc said.

Maureen breathed deeply. He smelled wonderful—and like he needed a shower. They must have flown straight from the stage. And he tasted like an ashtray. "I can't believe you're here." She glanced over his shoulder. No, she could believe he was here. Marc was another story altogether.

"He came to keep me company on the drive down." Michael turned to Marc.

"Uh yeah, I wanted to apologize to you, Maureen." Marc shuffled his feet and took another drag on the cigarette. "I was sort of a jackass to you and I'm sorry."

Michael looked pleased with the apology. What had he had to do to get it though? "Apology accepted. Did you guys want to come in? Are you hungry?"

"We thought we'd take you out."

"That might not be a good idea. I never know when people are going to show up with rotten vegetables." She slid her hand into Michael's big warm one, and his fingers closed around hers. The whole scandal had seemed insurmountable until he'd shown up. Now she could conquer the world, with or without the help of the newspaper.

"It's that bad?" Marc asked.

"It's not good. Michael, when did you start smoking?"

"I didn't."

"You were smoking when I pulled up." She stepped around her car door so he could close it.

"Oh yeah, I was kinda— I'll get the butt out of the yard." He bumped her door closed and loped to the middle of the yard to retrieve the cigarette butt.

Marc dropped his cigarette and mashed it out. Then he picked it up and peered around as if trying to figure out what to do with it. "Did you call Tessa?"

"Why would I call Tessa?" she asked.

Michael walked past and took Marc's butt on the way to the trashcan at the side of the house.

"She's a lawyer. What they're doing might not even be legal."

"No, they've been very careful." Maureen started for the door. "I've talked to my union lawyers. The reasons they're giving for not renewing my contract are that I'm in danger of losing my teaching license due to not meeting relicensing requirements and some nebulous number of complaints they haven't produced."

"Are you in danger of losing your license?" Marc followed her.

"No. I need four more credit hours to renew. I've been working on a Master's Degree, but I took the last year and a half off because I was house hunting. I had planned to start back this summer, but I met Michael." It had seemed like a perfectly plausible reason at the time.

While she was house hunting, she hadn't had the money or the mental focus to be sitting through graduate level classes and getting decent grades. Spring semester she'd taken off to save up and relax. Then she met Michael and the idea of not being able to see him over the summer because of some stupid seminar…

"So when do you need to have these credit hours?"

"I have until next June to get one, maybe two classes." She unlocked the front door.

"So that part's trumped up." Marc followed her inside with Michael behind him.

"Yes." She kicked off her sandals by the door.

"What about the complaints?"

Maureen headed for the kitchen to put on coffee. At least she had food in the house this time. "They've dug up about a dozen complaints from parents over the course of my career."

"Is that a lot?" Michael asked.

"Some teachers get a dozen complaints in a year." She sat down in the chair next to Michael and leaned her head on his shoulder.

"Might not be a bad idea to get your own lawyer. This all sounds like bullshit." Marc pulled out his phone. "This isn't Tessa's field, but I'll call her and see if she knows anybody."

"You don't have to. I have the union lawyers." Maureen tensed. Was it the coffeepot making noises or her stomach? She really should have had breakfast this morning.

"I'm not sure the union lawyers are going to do their best for you." Marc put the phone to his ear.

"I can't afford my own lawyer." She glared at him. Might have been better to have him as an enemy.

"I can. Don't sweat that." Michael squeezed her shoulders and stood up. "I'll get the coffee."

Maureen clasped her hands in her lap. Her stomach was making an impressive bid to crawl up her throat. Marc chatted with Tessa, giving her the details. He wanted to help, which was nice. Michael poured coffee for all of them. He wanted to pay for the lawyer.

Between them, they were making her depend on them and she was only temporary. Michael was going to get bored and move on right about the time she'd come to need him. She already needed him. The kitchen started to sway. The bitter scent of the coffee scorched her nose. "I think I'm going to be sick."

Michael chased her down the hall. "What's wrong?"

She threw herself into the bathroom and slammed the door behind her. Pressing her hands to the wall, she fought for breath. When had she stopped being the one who controlled her life? She'd stopped in at the garage to get her brakes fixed and ended up speeding down hill. The school board wanted to fire her because they didn't like her lifestyle. Michael, who'd gotten her into this lifestyle, wanted to hire a lawyer to fight them. The lifestyle really wasn't anything more scandalous than any other person's; it just happened six hours later and involved more travel, but no one would ever believe that. If she went with him, she'd be wholly dependent on him for everything, knowing he was going to get bored and cast her aside. If she walked away, she'd be trapped here dealing with the aftermath and she'd be without him.

She'd be without him.

"She pregnant or something?" Marc asked in the hall.

"Fuck off." Michael knocked on the door. "Baby, what's the matter?"

Chapter 14

Maureen yanked open the door. "I asked you to stop calling me that." Michael and Marc both reeled back.

"Okay," Michael said. "You gonna come out of the bathroom now?"

She clutched the door. Her lip started to tremble so she clenched her teeth hoping to make it stop.

"I'm gonna go outside." Marc strode down the hall as fast as his long legs would go.

Michael stepped closer and put his hand on her cheek. "Maur, what's the matter?"

"How long is it going to take you to get bored with me?" Her stomach, unable to escape through her throat, started in the other direction.

"I dunno. Never?" He slid his hand to the back of her neck. "I love you, Maureen."

"You've been in love before."

"So have you. How long is it going to take you to get bored with me?"

An excellent question. Was he worried about the same thing? She let him pull her closer. "At the moment, I wouldn't mind a little boredom."

"Me either." He leaned his forehead on hers. "Remember when we talked about the pre-nup and you said you didn't want to use it? I don't either. I'm a 'til death do us part kinda guy."

"I missed you."

"I missed you too."

She kissed him, drawing him tight against her. The power of his broad shoulders fed her, making her stronger. Opening his mouth with her tongue, she explored him. The rich, exotic flavor and heat. He groaned, the sound vibrating through her.

"We are not in my manager's bathroom," he murmured around her lips.

"Marc is outside." With the cold tile wall behind her and the hot man in front, she didn't want to move.

Michael slipped his hand under her shirt. "Where are your condoms?"

"Bedroom, but I'm on the pill."

"I'm clean if you are." His fingers worked between them, but she couldn't tell if he was unbuttoning his jeans or hers.

"I'm a second grade teacher."

He kissed her neck. His zipper opened. "I've heard what a wild bunch you second grade teachers can be."

She pushed out a breathy laugh. Her heart throbbed and her skin ached. She caught his mouth again. Drawing his lower lip between hers, she sucked until he shuddered.

"Evil woman." His hands twisted to open her jeans and the sensation of the heavy cloth tugging between her legs sent a shock through her.

"Bad boy."

He laughed. "I live to serve."

"Maybe you should be serving me on your knees."

He dropped to his knees, pulling her jeans down with him.

She squawked and tried to jump back, but only flattened herself against the wall.

"Be careful what you ask for." He grinned at her, lifting one foot to slip off her jeans.

"I'll keep that in mind." She searched for something hold onto. The towel rack was on the opposite wall. The door handle was too low. The shower curtain wasn't strong enough. He kissed the inside of her thigh and her knees gave. His hands wrapped around her waist, holding her up. The whole relationship in a nutshell. In over her head with nothing to hang onto but him.

As he trailed a line of kisses up the inside of her thigh, she closed her eyes. She didn't need more support. Michael was enough. More than enough. His tongue delved into the crease at the top of her leg.

"Michael," she moaned. "Please."

He chuckled, sending a whisper of hot breath across her skin. "How many licks does it take to get to the center of a Tootsie Pop?"

"Bad boy."

He pressed his face between her legs, his tongue seeking her heated core. She drowned in the tide of sensation and emotion boiling within her. All her life she'd been looking for this. Someone who cared about her and wanted to take care of her. Someone who would worship her and play with her. Someone who loved her. She'd never expected that same person to set her into a raging conflagration. His lips and tongue teased her to a dizzying height and then slowed. She teetered on the edge, whimpering as he stood.

"Baby? Maureen?" He kissed her lips softly. "I love you, Maureen."

"I love you too, Michael." She opened her eyes.

"Then why are you crying?"

She hesitated, on the edge of the joke. It would have been easy to complain he'd left her unsatisfied, but that wouldn't have been the truth. Right now, half naked in her bathroom, he needed the truth. "Because I love you and I miss you and I want you so much."

He sighed. Brushing his hand down her cheek, he said, "Me too."

Those two words carried more impact than all the times he'd said he loved her or any of the conversations that started "I miss you."

He lifted her off the floor, spreading her wide, and thrust into her.

She clutched his shoulders. He filled her with long, easy strokes. The tiny room echoed with the sound of their breathing, but nothing more needed to be said. Nothing more could be said. She coiled and burst apart in his embrace, held together only by his arms. A moment later, he shuddered, squeezing her tight.

He ran his fingers through her hair. "I'm serious, Maureen. I want what my mom and dad had. I want what Tony has. Everything in my life changes based on the season and the time of day and the band and the fans and the record company. I want some regular programming."

"Regular programming?"

He shrugged, which she felt more than saw. "Discussions about dinner and where we're going for vacation and if your car needs gas. I want to know someone somewhere is thinking more about what's good for me than what I can do for them. I want you."

She closed her eyes and leaned her head on his shoulder. That, she believed. She could also believe his family called him Flip-O-Matic when he was a kid. For a long time, she couldn't think of anything to say at all and when she did, she was less than inspired. "Where is Marc?"

"Outside." Shifting back, he set her on the floor. "We have a system."

"I don't want to know." She grinned. They would have a system. The whole band had systems and signals worked out for everything else. She pulled her clothes back on and splashed water on her face.

"Hey, Maureen?" He stepped behind her and put his hands on her shoulders, studying her in the mirror. "This wasn't exactly the welcome I had planned."

"Doesn't matter. You're here and that's what counts." She turned around. "You can make it up to me next time."

He kissed her cheek and led her outside.

Marc sat at the picnic table in the backyard staring at her lilac bushes. He'd even brought out their coffee. "Tessa called. She knows a guy who knows a guy who knows one of your union lawyers. They're gonna take a closer look. She said it sounded like a royal crock." He turned to look at them. "The question on everybody's lips is, why bother? Take their dismissal and relocate. You could get a job in LA in a heartbeat. Hell, you could get three jobs in LA in a heartbeat."

Maureen sat down at the picnic table and Michael settled next to her. The same question twice in an hour. Despite Michael's assurances, she didn't want to put all her eggs in his basket. Right now he thought he wanted regular programming, as he so eloquently put it, but next month? Next year? Yes, she could get a job in California, but she'd have to tear up the roots she'd so carefully cultivated here. And that regular programming he cherished so? How much of it was her second grade teacher lifestyle?

All of that would go out the window when she wasn't a second grade teacher anymore. How attractive would she be to him then? She licked her lips. "I have to fight for this job because if I just walk away, the people who have fought for me and all my former students will think I never really cared. If I leave, I have to go on my own terms."

Marc nodded like that made sense. "Well, we'll figure it out." His phone started to ring. "It's Tessa." He flipped it open.

Michael put his arm over her shoulders. "See, we'll take care of everything."

She swallowed. That was what she was afraid of.

* * * *

Bear kept his arm tight around Maureen's waist. Mama Lena's was packed and most of the people who came up to talk to them supported her against the school board. How was her job even in danger? Most of the city wanted her to stay and saw through the phony baloney excuses the board was using to get rid of her.

Marc had some plans. He knew how to bring all the firepower they had to keep her in her job.

At least it's a nice place, Bear thought. *Since I'm going to be living here.*

She smiled up at him. For that, he'd live on the moon. Too bad he wasn't as sure about her. Sex this afternoon had been—well, it was weird. For a while it looked like he was really gaining ground after she had her little snit and locked herself in the bathroom, but the more he thought about it, the weirder it got. When they were together she was his, but the moment a little air got between them she wasn't. This woman had the ability to pull back to amazing distances without moving more than a few inches. One of these days he was going to call from some real, physical distance and she would be on the moon without him.

"I think somebody's here to see you."

"They're all here to see me." He glanced in the direction she gestured.

Tony, Pam and Nicky stood by the door. Four or five hundred times, he'd reached for the phone to call Tony since he left town. His brother. The only family he had left and the best way to stay close to Maureen when he wasn't in town.

He grabbed her hand and pulled her across the crowded room. "Tony!"

Nicky pulled away from Pam and ran to him screaming, "Uncle Bear."

He let go of her hand to scoop up his nephew. "Hey kid, how's your summer?"

"The school wants to fire Miss Donnelly and mom wants me to go to private school."

"Nicky!" Pam scolded.

Bear set the boy down next to him. "Glad you guys could come."

Tony shook his hand. "Yeah. You're my brother. Even when you're an idiot."

"Same to you." Bear put his arm back around Maureen's waist.

"This thing they're trying to do to you at the school is ridiculous." Pam scowled. "I don't understand it. Everyone told us you were the best teacher in that school. Mrs. Farrinacci told us to get you for Nicky when he was in kindergarten."

"Angela Farrinacci?" Maureen asked. "Didn't she retire?"

"She lives two houses over. She used to sit for us."

"Really." Maureen made a face. "I thought she hated me. I worked with her for four years and I don't think she ever talked to me."

"She had nothing but nice things to say to us."

"Wow. Thanks. Why don't you guys come get something to eat? Come on, Nicky." Maureen guided Pam and Nicky to the buffet table.

Bear caught Tony's arm before he followed them. "Hey, about before..."

"Whatever. Don't sweat it. You still owe me for that door." Tony shrugged.

"You know where to send the bill. You planning to send Nicky to private school?"

"Talking about it."

"I can foot that." Bear stuck his hands in his pockets and watched Maureen and Pam get swallowed by the crowd. He should tell Tony what he was thinking. They were family and he never wanted to have an argument like that again. Ty circled past with one of the local girls, which reminded him he hadn't apologized to the band for trying to quit back in April. He couldn't even begin to tell Maureen how much he loved her. What good was the English language when it didn't cover the important stuff?

"Your funeral," Tony said. "I was kinda surprised when Maureen showed up at the garage this morning. I mean, I wrote a letter to the paper for her. Well, Pam wrote it, I just signed it."

"Wait." Bear turned from his observation of Maureen. "She went to the garage this morning? There something wrong with her car?"

"No. She wanted to make sure we were coming tonight. She said it bugged you that we weren't talking."

Bear frowned. He didn't remember saying anything about it to her. Well, once or twice. She must have read his mind. Maybe with Maureen around, he didn't need English. "Yeah, it did."

"Bugged me too." Tony folded his arms.

"You gotta help me hang onto her. Between this mess with the school board and the tour, I'm to not going to get to see her enough."

"And enough would be…"

"All the time, but there's gonna be months when I can't see her at all. I need somebody to take care of her car and make sure she's okay." Maureen's head wove through the crowd, moving away from him. She'd stuck close to Pam, and he assumed, Nicky. Good, they were bonding like sisters-in-law should.

"You know she's been doing that just fine for a long time now."

"I know, but I want to be the one to do it now." He clenched his teeth to keep the whine out of his voice. If she didn't need him, she was going to slip away, bonds or no bonds. She wouldn't even use the damn expense account. If she didn't rely on him for money, what did he have to make her rely on him for?

"You just want me to make sure no other guy moves into your territory."

"Duh."

"All right." Tony sighed. "You're going to ruin her life. This thing with the school board is just the beginning."

"I don't want to ruin it. I want to change it for the better." Since she was already doing that for him.

* * * *

Bear opened his eyes and looked around. Not a hotel room. Not his bedroom either. Maureen's house, but no Maureen. He sat up and rubbed his hair off his face. "Maureen?" He threw his legs over the side of the mattress. "Maureen?" he called louder.

Shuffling to the dresser, he found a pair of jeans and a t-shirt. She'd made space for him so he could unpack his suitcase. Amazing, how nice it was to take clothes out of a drawer instead of a suitcase. Dressed, he wandered out to the kitchen. She wasn't there either but she'd left a note on the table.

Good afternoon, sleepyhead. Had a meeting with lawyers and school board. Lunch is in the fridge if you don't sleep through that too. Then scrawled across the bottom, *Car having snit. Took yours.*

Car having snit? He called the garage. "What's wrong with Maureen's car?"

"I don't know. What's wrong with Maureen's car?" Tony asked.

He opened the refrigerator door. Lunch was a do it yourself sandwich. Room service it was not, but she had put everything on the same shelf for him. "Maureen had to take the Satellite today. She said something was wrong with her car."

"Did it not start again?"

"What do you mean, again?" He relocated his lunch fixin's to the counter for easier assembly.

"Last fall she had trouble with it. It wouldn't start and then by the time the tow truck got there it would. It's an electrical problem."

"You didn't fix it?"

"It's an electrical problem. Damn thing will probably start now."

Shoving the bread and meat back in the fridge, he slammed the door. "Why did you let her keep driving that junker?"

"I know you haven't known her long, but you did notice she's a little independent? Plus there's that stubborn streak."

"The one that's three feet wide and runs up the middle of her back? I noticed that." Bear slapped the cheese and the top slice of bread on his sandwich. She'd put out carrots for him too, but he skipped those in favor of the chips on top of the fridge. "It's been doing this for a year?"

"It started a year ago, but hasn't done it much. At least, not that she's called me."

"I'll bring it down and put in on the diagnostic."

"Knock yourself out. I can't find the problem."

"I know. Electrical," he replied as he settled at the table with his sandwich and the chips. "What she really needs is a new car."

"No kidding, but try to talk her into it."

"Yeah."

"I found a guy to make the badge for the Satellite."

Badge? Oh, the name on the side of the car. "Great. Thanks. I'll be in later."

"Okay, 'bye."

He hung up. Her car was serviceable enough, but soon it was going to be more expensive to keep on the road than getting another car. If it had an electrical problem, it wasn't going to be reliable. What if she needed to get to school and couldn't because it decided not to start? Or if she got stranded? Trying to run down an electrical problem was a nightmare. If he was here with her, between albums, he'd have the months needed to test things and wait for them to fail. In six days? Six days he'd planned to spend with her and not under her car? The first thing out of her mouth when he told her she needed a new car would be *why*?

He needed to just go buy her a car.

* * * *

Maureen tried to be attentive to the meeting. It was her fate, after all. But it was dragging on forever with her lawyer insisting on full disclosure of everything the board had against her and the board refusing. Most of the board. Ginnie Labbe looked ill at the whole proceeding. She should. Maureen had taught Ginnie's youngest son seven years ago before he'd been diagnosed ADHD. They'd had to work very closely to get Jeff into third grade and diagnosed.

She'd much rather be home with Michael. Two weeks, she'd sat around with nothing to do but follow her own notoriety in the paper and the very week Michael had off, the school board decided to meet. For hours.

Her lawyer stood up. Maureen jumped up with her. The guy who knew the guy who knew Tessa turned out to be a woman. Theresa Hanson had belonged to the same sorority as Tessa only several years earlier. "I'm very sorry to hear this, ladies and gentlemen."

That sounded bad. Maureen wished she'd been listening.

"An unjustified dismissal is going to create a lot of hard feelings, both with the union and in the community," Theresa said.

"Are you threatening us?" The board president stood, leaning on his fists on the table.

"Not a threat. Merely a warning. Miss Donnelly." Theresa waved her ahead, so Maureen walked out of the room.

Dismissal. Unjustified or not. This wasn't going to look good on a resume. Michael might have to support her when she couldn't get another job. Ever. The small of her back hurt from sitting up straight on the hard plastic chair for so long. "It's not going well."

"No." Theresa pursed her lips. "I'm sorry. There may be nothing we can do. Your contract is up for renewal. They can choose not to renew it for no reason at all. The only thing keeping them from doing that is the flap in the paper. Enough people support you to make it unpleasant for the board in the future."

"Which isn't going to help me at all when I'm fired."

Theresa sighed and opened her mouth. At that moment, her phone rang. She held up a finger and answered it, moving a few feet down the hall for privacy.

The conference room doors opened behind Maureen and she turned. Six of the board members walked out in a self-satisfied mob. A couple of them glanced her way, but didn't stop. Smug bastards. She hoped they all got voted out next election.

Ginnie Labbe walked out last and alone.

"Ginnie!"

Shoulders bent and deep lines around her eyes and bracketing her mouth, Ginnie waited at the conference room door for her. When had Ginnie gotten old? She had thought they were the same age. "I'm so sorry, Maureen."

"Isn't there anything you can do?"

Ginnie wilted another two inches. "You don't understand. The city's schools ranked near the bottom in the state. The voters were furious. We needed a reason."

"And you picked me?"

"You had been in the paper because you were dating Bear D'Amato. Parents don't want to think of their kids' teachers having a private life at all, let alone such a public one. One with so much scandal attached to it."

"Michael and I have hardly been scandalous."

"Not you, but rock musicians in general. The drugs and the drinking and the wild parties and the sex."

"Are you kidding? Michael doesn't take anything harder than aspirin. I've been to exactly one party with him. It was a backyard barbecue."

"But you went on tour with him." Ginnie made an uncertain face.

"Believe me, it's not like in the movies."

"People think you aren't going to be focused on your job because you're thinking about your boyfriend."

Maureen put her hands on her hips. A hundred instances where other teachers hadn't been focused on their job because they'd been distracted by their personal lives boiled behind her lips, but she didn't want to start naming names.

Theresa put a hand on her arm. "Maureen, you really shouldn't be talking to board members without counsel."

Ginnie took a step backward. "I'm really sorry, Maureen."

"I got her son through second grade. He's in high school now," Maureen told Theresa.

"It's not fair. I don't think the board expected you to fight." Theresa guided her down the hall toward the stairs. "What you need to do right now is be an exemplary second grade teacher."

"It's the middle of summer."

"I know. You'll just have to keep as straight and narrow as you can. Be home every night by nine. Dress conservatively in public. Play down your involvement with Mr. D'Amato."

"Michael is visiting me this week. I was supposed to go back on tour with him and now I won't get to see him again until school starts. How did this become an issue of my morals?" As she pushed open the outside doors, the heat settled around her like a weight.

"I don't know, but it did. We need you to appear as squeaky clean as possible."

"I am squeaky clean."

"Then I guess you'll just have to be all you all the time. The board meeting is in four days. If they vote for non-renewal, we'll file for defamation of character. That's all I can do for you." Theresa patted her arm. "I'll talk to you on Tuesday."

"Thanks." Maureen crossed the parking lot to Michael's car. She'd intentionally parked far away from the building so no one would see the mismatched muscle car. Every car she'd been parked near had moved and no one replaced them so now the Satellite sat all by itself, almost on a pedestal. Or a stage. She drove home, certain the heavy growl of the engine was attracting all kinds of unwanted attention.

Someone had carelessly parked dead center in the middle of her driveway. Who could be visiting? Parking on the street, she hurried up the drive to the house to have them move so she could hide Michael's car in the garage. Maybe now that he wasn't fighting with his brother Tony could store it for him.

She threw open the front door. "Michael!"

He walked out of the kitchen grinning. "What do you think?"

He'd shaved, but that wasn't unusual. The t-shirt and jeans she'd seen him in before. His hair hadn't been cut, as far as she could tell. "Think about what?"

"Your new ride." He shifted from grinning to beaming.

"My—" Her mouth didn't close as she glanced over her shoulder.

"Nice, huh? I wanted to get you the Candy Red, but none of the dealers in the area had that in stock so I figured the Grabber Blue would be good. We can switch it if you have your heart set on a different color though." He draped his arm over her shoulders, pulling her outside to the front of the car.

From this angle, she could see the little horse on the grill of the light blue convertible sitting in the middle of her driveway. "It's a Mustang."

"Yeah, a GT Premium. You want to take it for a spin?"

She pointed at the car. "That is not my car."

"Yes, it is."

"No, my car— My car. Where is my car?"

"In the garage. You said it wouldn't start this morning."

"It's an intermittent problem." Her voice had risen to a shriek, but she couldn't stop herself. He bought her a car. A loud, gaudy, not conservative, un-second grade teacher-like car.

"I don't like to think of you having that intermittent problem so I took care of it."

"You took care of it. Are you out of your mind?" She pressed her hands to her temples. Were the neighbors listening? He bought her a car. "Oh my God." She stomped into the house.

"What is the problem?" He walked through the door and slammed it behind him.

"You bought me a car."

"I thought you'd be happy."

"What are people going to think?"

"That you have a rich boyfriend who wants to spoil you a little. Shit, it's not like I bought you a Mercedes."

"There's no difference."

He sneered. "There's at least ten thousand dollars difference."

"Oh my God. I don't want to know how much it cost." She started to run her hand through her hair and got her fingers caught in her barrette. "Ow. Damn." She ripped it out, taking a few strands of hair at the same time, and threw it across the room.

"Maur, you need to calm down. Did you have a bad meeting or something?"

She gripped the back of the couch. "This is not about the meeting." One of her fingernails snapped on the fabric, sending a sharp pain through her, and tears sprang to her eyes. "Have you not been paying attention?"

"Yes, I have been paying attention," he roared. Surely the neighbors could hear that. "I'm trying to help you fix things."

"Fix things? By giving me an extravagant gift?"

"I thought it was logical. Your car is a piece of junk. I got you a better one."

"A better one. Too much better. Everyone in town is going to know you gave it to me."

"So?"

"Michael, I am fighting for my life here."

His face hardened. "No, you're fighting for your job. There is a difference." He stomped past her and out the back door.

She wrapped her arms around herself. Through the curtains, she could still see it. It was a nice color and he knew cars so it must run well. Tony said electrical problems were almost impossible to fix. Miles of wires throughout the car. The problem could be anywhere. It could get worse or stay the same. No telling. A new car would solve the problem.

Michael had tried.

And he'd failed so incredibly, spectacularly badly. On a scale only Michael could fail. Why did he have to do something marvelous at exactly the wrong time and make her feel so awful for being angry? Any woman in her right mind would have been thrilled to have her boyfriend go out and buy her a car. He'd done the most thoughtful thing imaginable. He was taking care of her.

If she just walked away. Saved everyone the trouble of fighting it out. She could get another job in California or not if she wanted. He wouldn't even notice supporting her. A lot of hard feelings in the community would be averted. This mess was going to linger in the air like the stink of burning rubber. She could stem that now by simply giving in, taking his gift and packing her things. Theresa could coach her on what to say to soothe feelings on all sides. He would be thrilled to have her waiting for him at home when the tour ended. Kim would be pleased to have someone to go to farmer's markets with. Connie could fulfill that promise to take her to the set. Tessa would be glad to know Michael was marrying rock star wife type two so she could cross him off her to do list. Everyone would be happy.

She might even be happy once the dust settled.

The back door opened, he came inside and put his hands on her shoulders. "Baby, I'm sorry. You're right. I didn't think it through. I should have bought you the kind of car you needed instead of the kind of car I wanted you to have."

She turned and wrapped her arms around him. "I'm sorry I didn't appreciate it." In his arms, she was secure and safe. His hard chest supported her against all the slings and arrows life wanted to throw. "And I'm sorry I yelled at you."

"So was it a rough meeting?"

"The board is still stonewalling. The lawyer says all she can do if they don't renew my contract is file a defamation of character suit. Ginnie Labbe told me the kids' parents don't want to think of a teacher having a personal life at all, let alone such a public one."

"A public one?"

"With you."

He swallowed, but didn't say anything.

She pressed her cheek against his chest. Why were they making her choose? Her whole life she'd been waiting for someone to love and when he came along he was wholly inappropriate for the life she loved. Why couldn't she have fallen for some nice accountant who came home at night and didn't mind a little gardening on the weekends if it didn't interfere with football?

He guided her face to his and kissed her. It felt like goodbye so she sank her fingers into his shoulders to hang onto him. He responded by kissing her hard, taking possession of her mouth as his arms tightened around her. Welcoming the deep exploration and the tight hold, she melted into him. This man cared about her. He cared about her more than anyone in the world ever had. He wanted to do everything for her.

Why was that so frightening?

He lifted her up and carried her back to the bedroom. Laying her in the middle of the unmade bed, he stripped off her clothes before taking off his own. She couldn't speak as he explored every inch of her, kissing and licking, tasting and touching. In turn, she touched him, admiring the velvet softness of his skin in the afternoon light. The well developed muscles sliding under that skin, trained for strength and yet capable of such tenderness. His dark eyes held her. Every odd wrinkle or bulge she'd always thought were imperfections, he studied like art. His every sigh was music.

She brushed her fingers down his arm and around his elbow, placing a kiss in the inside. Then she followed the blue veins along his forearm to his thick, powerful wrists. Drew his palm to her mouth, kissed it, traced the creases with her tongue. Which one was the life line? The heart line? Where did they cross?

His other hand trailed up the inside of her thigh sending out soft waves of pleasure as she took one of his fingers into her mouth. His incredible, talented fingers. On stage, she'd watched him spin drumsticks between his fingers before dropping them effortlessly into his palms to pound out a thunderous beat.

His lips brushed her nipples, pulling a gasp from her. A slight breeze blew hot air through the curtains, making them move and letting in a shaft of sunlight across the bed. Outside she could still hear the twitter of birds and children playing on the next street, but all of it was so far away. So insignificant.

Only he mattered. Nothing else. She needed to tell him and hear him assure her that only she mattered to him.

"Michael?"

"Shh." He closed his mouth over hers again to keep her from speaking. The slow movement of his hands spoke more eloquently than words. Nothing else mattered. This moment in time, this small room, this touch.

She tangled her fingers through his hair. Sweat slicked their skin. She could taste it sliding into their mouths as they kissed. The sharp, salty flavor reminding her that this was real and not some wonderful dream.

He groped toward the table. Yanking open a drawer, he pulled out one condom. She wanted to tell him to skip it again, but this was another part of his taking care of her. He'd done it since the moment they met. Telling her she couldn't drive the way her brakes were and then taking her out to dinner before driving her home. Fixing them for free. Admitting who he was instead of taking what he wanted and disappearing. Buying her a car because hers had an unfortunate tendency to not start.

She took the condom and tore open the package. Rolling it on, she eased him onto his back then straddled him. He hadn't wanted her to speak before. No words could meet the moment anyway. Lowering herself onto him, he groaned. His strong hands closed around her hips, guiding her rhythm. She planted her hands on his chest for balance against the tide of sweet desire moving between them until it crested over her. Her breath caught in her throat as she heard his answering groan. They were linked. Eternally.

Slumped onto his chest, she tried to breathe. His heart hammered under her ear.

"Maureen? I can take back the car and switch it for something a little more you. A Saturn or a Taurus or something." He stroked his finger through her hair. "And I'll talk to Tony about storing the Satellite at his place. It probably doesn't look good for you to have it in the street here. He can unload your car for you too. Sell it to somebody who doesn't mind fucking with it."

She nodded.

"When is your school board meeting?"

"Tuesday night. First Tuesday of the month."

"Do you want me to go with you?"

Maureen chewed her lip. Trying to think clearly right now was too hard. "I'll talk to my lawyer and see what she thinks."

"Good idea." He tangled his fingers through her hair. "I want to help, baby. Tell me what to do. I'll do whatever you ask."

He would. If she told him to leave town, he would go until it all blew over.

But she didn't want him to go. She wanted a hand to hold. All her life she'd managed everything on her own and now—

Now she needed him.

Chapter 15

"I'm really not sure about this," Theresa said.

Maureen clutched Michael's hand in her lap and hoped he hadn't heard. The school board meeting had been scheduled for a former classroom in the old school building the board used for offices, but the number of people arriving caused it to be moved to the auditorium. She'd been here a number of times for in service, but never felt like she'd swallowed two cups of lead before. The auditorium wasn't air-conditioned and the fetid heat made the room feel like a scummy classroom aquarium forgotten over summer break. Someone had set up a long table and a couple of folding chairs on the stage. When the school board filed in, a hush fell over the crowd.

Michael sat beside her. He cleaned up very nicely. The neat blue button down shirt and khakis were a far cry from the coverall he'd been wearing or the shorts he usually performed in. Theresa had objected to his being here, saying he would draw unwanted attention. So far he hadn't. Most of the attention had been focused on her, good and bad. Tony and Pam sat on Michael's other side. Crowded around her like a personal security barrier, the parents of her former students and many of her colleagues sat in the rows in front of her and behind.

The list of boring housekeeping dragged on while the crowd grew restless. She closed her eyes when they got to the list of renewed teachers. She'd always thought this was a pointless waste of the board's time. Listing off the names of all the teachers up for renewal and then voting yea or nay? They always renewed everyone so why not do it all at once? Michael put his arm around her shoulders.

"Andrew Dean."

A chorus of "yeas."

"Maureen Donnelly."

For a beat, nothing. Then like the clang of funeral bells, "nay, nay, nay, nay, nay, nay."

"Yea."

She opened her eyes at the collective gasp.

Ginnie Labbe stood at her seat, gripping the table like it might fly away. "I would like to lodge...a formal protest...about this vote." She sounded like she had hiccups or perhaps it was the fact that she couldn't believe what she was doing. She had the wild-eyed look of someone possessed. "I have personally worked...with Miss Donnelly...and believe that the board is...in error. I would like to call for a second...second— Second vote."

The other board members scowled at her, but the crowd had started yelling, both in support and opposition. Police officers stationed at the walls, straightened. Police. At a school board meeting. Because of her.

The board president pounded the gavel. "I will have order." His voice had an edge of panic to it that she could have told him was defeating the purpose of his words. The best way to get order was to stay calm. "I will not have chaos at this meeting."

"You started it!" someone shouted from the back of the room.

The president stood up. "This meeting is now going into closed session."

The other board members followed him backstage. Maureen wondered what he was going to do when he found out the only way back into the school was through the auditorium. Not very good planning on his part. Behind them, the crowd got louder. They sounded more like the crowd at one of Touchstone's concerts, only angrier.

"We need to get out of here." Michael pulled her to her feet.

She swayed, staring at him. "Why?"

"The crowd is getting ugly and I don't want you in it." He turned her and propelled her by the shoulders over Theresa and out into the aisle. The outer aisle was already filling with people, but he shifted in front of her and cleared a path to the door towing her behind. Before she realized where they were, the metal doors were clanging behind them and he was pulling her down the sidewalk to the parking lot.

"Wait a minute," she said, yanking her hand out of his. "We can't just leave."

"We have to. This looks dangerous." His eyes scanned over her shoulder.

"There isn't going to be a riot at a school board meeting." She glanced back at the people already spilling out of the building. At the moment, they did look more like a mob than the audience of a school board meeting.

"Let's just go." Tony waved his hands like he was trying to herd them forward.

"Come on, Maureen." Theresa grabbed her arm. "You shouldn't be here right now. Let Michael take you home. I'll meet you at your place."

Pam and Tony hurried off in the direction of their car and Theresa went to hers. Maureen allowed Michael to take her to the sedate gold Saturn he'd bought for her.

"This isn't happening," she muttered.

"I'm sorry, baby. It's happening."

"I didn't just lose my job." She turned to the window. They were one of the first cars to leave. Four police cars and two vans were parked in the fire lane. Some people straggled to their cars, but a larger group congregated on the cement apron in front of the main doors. She could pick out half-remembered faces from parent teacher conferences past.

Michael reached for her hand as he turned onto the road. "We'll go home and regroup. You knew this might happen. What's next? The defamation suit?"

"I just lost my job." Her throat closed. "This must make you really happy."

"No, baby, it doesn't." He glanced at her. A second later he glanced at her again, frowning. Then he pulled off into a restaurant parking lot. "Why would you think this would make me happy?"

"You get what you want now." Arms tensed, she fought the urge to pull away from him. She couldn't do that now. Without him, she had no income. She'd lose her house and her car. She'd never get another job.

"Maureen, you're getting all freaked out. I never wanted you to lose your job. I wanted you to be happy and I can't seem to pull it off."

Tears gathered on her eyelashes, and she blinked. "We'll be together now as much as you want. I could finish the tour with you." He wouldn't. Now that he had her, he wouldn't want her around all the time. Now she was an albatross. He'd get tired of her much faster. She should have tried to make friends with Marc's ex while she was in California. And a couple of the other band members' exes. Those women were going to be her peers soon.

"Maureen, hey, snap out of it." Michael caught her face between his hands. "We're not going to be together that much because you're going to win this defamation suit and they're going to have to give you your job back. And in December when the tour ends, I'm gonna come here and we'll decide what we're gonna do from there. Okay? Everybody's going to your house. We'll talk it out. We'll make a plan. I told you I was going to do whatever it took to make this work and I am."

She nodded. Reality weighed around her, dragging her into the seat. She was wholly dependent on him and trapped. His phone rang. "You better get that." Then she leaned her head back on the seat and closed her eyes.

* * * *

Bear stared at her through another ring. She'd detached herself. It was freaky to watch. He pulled out his phone and answered it without looking. "What?"

"Is it over? How did it go?"

Marc. From the sound of things everyone was with him. Bear heard Tessa raving in the background. "They didn't renew and things were getting hot so they moved the meeting behind closed doors."

"I can't believe it. Maureen's lawyer said the police were there."

"You talked to Maureen's lawyer?"

"Tessa's on the phone with her now."

Which explained Tessa's raving. "So why are you calling me?"

"Because we want to know what's going on and we're all on the wrong side of the country at the moment, so spill."

"Poor baby, stuck in LA thousands of miles from all the action." Bear glanced at Maureen. Her head had lolled to one side and her lips were parted. How could she fall asleep at a time like this? "I don't know anything. They voted to not renew her. One of the board members complained and asked for a revote. The crowd started to get hot. The board walked offstage and I got her the hell outta Dodge."

"That ugly?"

"We have fewer cops at our shows."

"Shit. How's she doing?" In the background Brian was demanding the phone. Funny, a couple of months ago they were all suspicious of her and now she was one of their own.

"She was freaked out a minute ago, but she just fell asleep. I think it's too much for her. We're all meeting at Maureen's." Inside her purse, *Swing* started to play. "Shit. Her phone's ringing and I don't want it to wake her up. Talk to you later." He snapped his phone closed as he dug for hers. "Hello?"

"Uh. Is Maureen there?"

"She's asleep."

"Oh. It's Linda. You guys left before I caught you."

"Yeah, I was sort of afraid somebody was going to produce a rope so we could have an old fashioned lynching."

Linda snickered nervously. "So what's the plan?"

"We're meeting up at Maureen's."

"We being?"

"Theresa and my brother and sister-in-law."

"Okay. I'll swing by the grocery store and pick up some refreshments and meet you there." Linda hung up.

Great. It was going to be a party. Bear put the car in gear and drove back to her house. Pam and Tony were waiting in the driveway. Theresa had parked on the street. Pam swooped in and took over care of Maureen before he could even get out of the car. The lawyer started discussing strategy for what to do next with Tony. Or rather, the lawyer talked and Tony nodded a lot.

Bear went to the kitchen and put on the coffee pot. Maureen had a coffee fixation like no one he'd ever seen. Even in this heat, she'd want a cup of coffee. He checked the ice trays to make sure there were some ice cubes in case she wanted it cold. Linda arrived with a couple of plastic containers of cookies. He gave her a plate to put them on and went to take drink orders. Theresa had the table covered with her briefcase, masses of loose paper, a tablet computer and two phones. She was making notes in her tablet and talking so fast Tony looked like a bobble head doll. There was a knock at the door and when he answered it, the women outside said they worked with Maureen. As they joined Theresa's audience and Linda took over door duty, Bear retreated to the kitchen to wash glasses because if people kept showing up, they would run out.

It felt like hours had passed before Theresa announced that she needed to go. Maureen had reappeared some time earlier looking more like herself. Theresa had worked out a complete battle plan and issued orders. Bear walked her to the door, leaving Maureen to talk to her friends.

"Can I ask you a question?" he asked after she'd stepped through the door.

"What's that?"

"How much of this is my fault?" He clenched his teeth, hoping she would laugh and tell him he was being an egomaniac.

Instead, Theresa pursed her lips. "I don't want to get involved in your love life."

"I know, but I'm asking. If she didn't know me, would she be having any of this trouble?"

"No. You're famous and you've drawn attention to her. People are making a lot of assumptions about what your life is like and, by default, what her life is now like and they don't want that for their children." Theresa shifted her briefcase to the other hand. "I'm sorry. It is what it is. The damage is done. You can't undo it. All we can do now is try to be as normal and reliable as possible."

"I have a top ten song and a top ten album and I'm in the middle of a huge tour right now."

"Yeah." She thrust out her lower jaw, which made her look like a matronly bulldog. "That's a problem. This story is starting to get picked up by major news organizations because of your involvement."

He wanted to bury his face in his hands, but didn't. Wouldn't look good to the lawyer. "Thanks."

"For giving you bad news?"

"For giving it to me straight."

She nodded and walked down the drive to the street, and he turned back to the party, which was now breaking up. Tony extracted a promise from him to come to the garage tomorrow and Pam invited them to dinner tomorrow night. Maureen's co-workers were pleased to have met him, but subdued by the news. None of them seemed to blame him for it. No need. He was doing enough of that for everyone.

If it wasn't for him none of this would have happened. If he'd stopped it after that first pizza, she'd have carried on with her life, taken the classes she needed to keep her teaching license, never been in the paper. She'd have been happy.

But he'd had to get greedy.

He closed the door behind Linda and turned to Maureen. She stood clutching the back of the couch like she'd just experienced her first major earthquake. He held out his arms. "Come on, baby. Let's go to bed."

"We should clean up."

Bear glanced around the room. A couple of glasses sat on the dinner table by the empty cookie plate. Clean up would take twelve seconds. "I'll get it in the morning."

She nodded and went to him, sinking into his embrace. For a long time, she clung to him before she let him guide her down the hall to the bedroom.

* * * *

Maureen spun her spoon on the table. The world had taken on a haze since last night and she couldn't penetrate it. Kaitlyn and Linda had asked her out to lunch to get her out of the house. Theresa thought it would be a good idea for the public to see that she wasn't cowering at home. Maureen was dubious. She'd rather be at home, in bed with the covers pulled over her head.

"Maureen, are you with us here?" Kaitlyn asked.

"No," Linda said. "She's on tour with Michael."

"Michael is at the garage today. He goes back out in two days." Seventy-two short hours. Less because the flight to Tampa was an early one.

"You're not going with him?"

"I can't. I have to stay here and be a model citizen." She stuck out her tongue.

"When is he coming back to town?"

"At the end of August. They have a two week break right when school starts because Brian's daughter starts preschool and he wants to be there."

"Aw." Kaitlyn sighed. "That's so sweet."

"So he'll be here right when school starts."

Maureen shrugged. "Or I'll be there. Nothing keeping me around." No job. No way to get a job until after the dust settled. Her last paycheck would arrive around the end of August. After that she'd be digging into her savings or asking Michael for handouts. Would the bank accept the credit card he'd given her for house payments?

"Slut."

Maureen looked up. She vaguely remembered the woman standing at the end of the table, but her hair color didn't look right. The hard, angry set of her expression did. "Excuse me?"

"I knew you were a slut when you had my Logan, but nobody believed me. Well, now they do."

"Logan Szabeki's mom," Maureen said.

"I'm not surprised you remember. As much as you hated my son."

"I didn't hate your son, I hated his behavior."

"My son did nothing wrong in your classroom. The other kids blamed him for everything and you let them." Logan's mother put her fists on her hips and narrowed her already squinty eyes. Maureen couldn't remember her last name. She knew it had been different from Logan's, but nothing else.

"Logan Szabeki," Linda mused. "Did he just spend six months in juvie for boosting a car?"

Theresa had hoped Maureen's friends would shield her from the worst of the public. Maureen decided she should have warned Theresa about Linda.

"My son is a good boy." Logan's mother stamped her foot.

"Your son is a del—"

"Linda, let's just go. It's all water under the bridge." Maureen stood. "It was nice to see you again." She gave Logan's mom a bland smile and walked away. They hadn't paid the bill yet and she had to wait at the hostess desk for them to get it.

"This is unacceptable." Linda stomped toward the car. "Now the parents of every brat you ever scolded for picking his nose is going to feel justified in calling you a bad teacher."

"I don't know if you should be saying that out here." Kaitlyn glanced around. "Someone might hear you."

"They need to hear me. Like teaching their little monsters isn't hard enough without them being convinced their kids are perfect. I hate to break this to you but even the perfect ones screw up. They're kids. It's in the job description." Linda hit a button on her key fob and the horn started honking. "Oh darn it. They need to make these buttons bigger." She jabbed at the key fob again to no result, and Kaitlyn snatched it out of her hand.

"Just because you're under investigation doesn't mean you get to act like a big baby. Maureen's taking it better and she's lost her job." Kaitlyn turned off the panic button and unlocked the car doors before handing it back.

"What do you mean, under investigation?" Maureen asked.

"Oh, we all are, it's nothing." Linda opened her car door. "Do you guys want to go to the mall or something? Is there a half decent movie playing?"

"The state is questioning some of Linda's education credits," Kaitlyn said.

"What? Why didn't you tell me?" Maureen turned to Linda.

"Like you need the extra stress. It's nothing. I did a seminar. The state is questioning whether or not it counts. Let's go to a movie. It'll be cool in the theater." Linda climbed in her car and slammed the door.

Maureen hurried around to the passenger side and jumped in. "Linda, if you lose your license, you're going to lose your job."

"Well, if they decide to disallow that seminar all the sudden, there's about two hundred and fifty other teachers who are going to be in the same boat."

Maureen leaned her head on the seat. "This is all my fault. I should have listened to Michael."

"Michael."

"He told me to just quit and go live with him. He wanted to run away and get married over spring break. If I'd listened none of this would be happening."

"Oh stop. You're not the center of the universe. If you weren't in the middle of this it would have happened to someone else. Now, let's go find a movie." Linda started the car.

Maureen squeezed her eyes closed. Not only had she managed to ruin her life, she'd ruined hundreds of other peoples'. Very slick.

* * * *

Tony and Bear stepped back to admire the car. The candy apple red gleamed under the heat lamps. In a couple of days it would dry and he could ship it home. Unless he came back here on the next break and talked Maureen into a little cross-country driving trip.

"Well, it looks better now that it matches," Tony said.

"Jackass. It looks fantastic."

"Alright, fine. It looks fantastic. You can't do anything with it now. How about you help me out with some of the real work?"

Bear rolled his eyes. "That's the only reason you want me here. So you get free labor."

"Mom and Dad told me that's what you were for when they brought you home from the hospital." Tony walked out of the garage and around the front of the building. "They said, 'Tony, he looks little now, but when he gets big he's gonna work for you for free.'"

"Right."

A car squealed into the front lot. Right about where Maureen's was the first night he met her. Bear grinned. No matter what happened, that was still an incredible stroke of luck. A skinny guy jumped out and stormed over to where he and Tony had stopped on the sidewalk.

"You! This is your fault," the guy shouted.

Tony peered at Bear and then pointed at himself.

"No, not you. Him. You son of a bitch. My daughter has been crying all summer. All. Summer."

Bear shrugged at Tony. "Do I know you?" Bear asked.

"You're Miss Donnelly's boyfriend. The famous guy. You're the reason she lost her job."

Bear ground his teeth. That would be him. "I'm doing everything I can to get her job back."

"Yeah, and what are you going to do about Lindsey?"

"Who's Lindsey?"

"My daughter. You don't even remember her. We met you at the museum. My daughter had Miss Donnelly last year. She has been crying all summer because of what's going on in the papers. She's written letters."

Conner. The guppy from the museum with the spelling genius daughter.

"This is your fault. She's been crying all day. My wife has been on the phone yelling at me like it's my fault. When it's your fault."

Tony stepped in front of him. "We had no control over any of this. If you have a problem, you need to take it up with the school board."

"I have." Conner snarled.

Maureen would have been a lot better off with the guppy. The guppy wouldn't have lost her job for her.

"Tell your kid we're doing everything we can," Bear told him. "And tell her I'm sorry."

Conner huffed for a second before stomping back to his car. Hopefully, he was headed off to buttonhole one of the assholes on the board. They deserved it slightly more than he did.

"Well, he is right." Tony raised an eyebrow at him. "Hurricane Michael."

Chapter 16

Maureen stared out the window. Dinner with Tony and Pam had hardly been distracting. She doubted the declaration of nuclear war would have been distracting at the moment. Linda was in danger of getting caught in her tidal wave. How many other teachers she knew hadn't mentioned it to her? How many she didn't know? According to Theresa, there were months of waiting and preparing for the trial to get through too. What was she supposed to do? She'd registered for a class at the university, but one class was hardly going to absorb all her time. A couple of parents had contacted her about tutoring.

Theresa recommended she stay in the community so she was a constant presence. Michael would be on tour until December with intermittent breaks, unless they added more dates. The thought of that made her stomach clench. She wasn't sure she could handle the next couple of months alone. A few more might kill her.

Bear cleared his throat. "Maureen, I've been thinking."

"You're breaking up with me."

"No." He turned, giving her a horrified look. "No! What kind of a heel do you think I am? I'm not breaking up with you. I'm never breaking up with you." He caught her hand in his.

"I can take it. Honestly, at this point I wouldn't blame you. I'm a huge liability."

"No, no you're not." He pressed her fingers to his lips. "I'm not breaking up with you. I was just thinking that it might be easier if I left early."

"Because it's easier to break up from a distance." Relief coursed through her. Relief? This should be the worst thing that had ever happened to her. He was leaving. But now that the other shoe had dropped, she could move on. She'd always known it would. Someone like him could never stay with her. Especially considering what a walking disaster she'd become.

"I am not breaking up with you, but I am getting you bad attention. If I leave town, that should die down."

And I'll be alone again. Naturally. I need to sign up for another class. I can use the credit card Michael gave me to pay for it. Until he cuts it off. "Of course. You're right."

"I'm right?"

"Yes. You're right." The searing pain behind her sternum would go away. Maybe she needed to take a full load of classwork. She'd always wanted to take an archeology class.

"I'm ruining your life by hanging around here."

"Yes." She pulled her hand away from him and folded it in her lap. "I understand."

"But I'll come back. If things have cooled down at the end of August, I'll come back then. If not, you and me can take the Satellite home. We could drive it back to LA together."

"You don't have to feel guilty about this."

He clutched the steering wheel. "Well, I do."

"It's the most logical choice."

"Jesus, would you get mad at me or cry or something already? You sound like you were raised by Vulcans."

She studied her hands in her lap. She couldn't say she hadn't seen it coming. The moment she met him she'd known he was going to walk away. Exciting, funny, sexy guys like him didn't hang around with dull elementary school teachers. And at that point she hadn't realized how many excellent reasons he had to go. "Michael, I don't want to make this harder than it is."

"It's not that hard." He turned into her driveway. "Okay, it's really fucking hard. I'm going to miss you and I'm going to want to see you every day and I can't. But I will see you and I will marry you and we will make a life together."

Maureen reached for her car door. "I know that." The limp lie felt like the best alternative at the moment.

"Let me get the fucking door." He threw open his door and stomped around the car. Opening her door, he lifted her out and held her. "I love you, Maureen. Things have sucked lately and I wish I could stay here and help you through it but even your lawyer says I'm making things worse by being here. If I go away, things will get better. I really want things to get better for you. I want to make your life perfect."

The orange street lamps made it hard to see, but his sincerity shone through his gaze.

"Marry me, Maureen."

"You asked me that once."

"I know and I'm asking you again. Marry me."

"Okay."

"Christ. She says okay." He cupped her face in his hands. "You remember when I told you I was willing to do whatever it took to make this work?"

"Yes."

"That is what I am doing now. If me going away for a little while now will mean we can spend the rest of our lives together later then I'll do it." He groped in his pockets. "I still don't have a ring for you, but this might work better." After another moment's search, he pulled his Mustang keychain out. A simple key ring with a short chain from which the pony emblem dangled like a charm. Picking up her left hand, he draped it over her ring finger. "There. You need me, you just hop in the Satellite of Love and you come find me. Okay?"

She turned her hand, studying the key ring hanging from her finger. It was escape and promise in one. Sobs gathered in her throat. Clutching her fingers around the key ring, she threw her arms around his neck.

* * * *

"Hey," Marc answered on the first ring.

"I'm in Tampa." Bear flopped backward on the bed. This room was his home for the next three days.

"Oh."

He stared at the ceiling. Leaving Maureen at the airport this morning, he'd realized what it must have felt like for her to leave at the end of spring break. Getting on the plane required a supreme act of will.

"I'm assuming Maureen isn't with you."

"No." Maureen was home by now and had been for a couple of hours. He hoped she wasn't crying. She'd cried a lot last night, and screamed at the universe for making life so hard, but she'd never once questioned his need to leave.

"What happened?"

"It was getting pretty hot and I was attracting a lot of negative attention. I was ruining her life just by being there."

"The story got picked up by CNN dot com. Legitimate news."

"Great."

"So you guys broke up?"

"No, we're just...separated." Separated sounded too much like almost divorced. He closed his eyes. Was that little girl still crying? Was her father still looking for somebody's neck to wring?

"You know what, I'm not doing anything here. I think I'll come out early too."

"Yeah, I know how much you want to spend another night in a hotel room."

"About as much as you do. I know, we can go to Disney World. How clean cut and straight laced would that be?"

The image of Marc walking around Disney World wearing mouse ears made him laugh. It helped stem the pathetic desire to gush over the fact that his friend was willing to fly in early just to hang out. "Might be fun. Give CNN dot com something to report. I'll be here when you get here."

* * * *

"...and I've filed a libel suit against the newspaper on your behalf."

Maureen swam out of the fog of her reverie. The house was too quiet and it distracted her. "What was that last part?"

Theresa peered over the top of her bifocals. "What part?"

"The last thing you said."

Theresa consulted her notes. "I filed a libel suit with the paper. They claimed on numerous occasions that the school board possessed a number of complaints against you, but the board had never produced a single one."

"But if the board said it, it's not the paper's fault."

Theresa peered over her bifocals again. "It's the reporter's job to track down proof. Without proof they never should have gone to print."

"But that reporter could be fired."

"And should be. She wasn't doing her job."

Someone else on the verge of losing their job because of her. Was the poor reporter sitting at her desk worrying about when her last paycheck was going to arrive and how she was ever going to get another job with this on her record? "Theresa, this is too much. I want justice, not revenge."

"Maureen, justice is what you're getting. You did your job well and without fail for many years. Then along came a couple of people who wanted to shift blame for something beyond your control to you and a couple more people who didn't do their jobs."

"It feels like revenge."

"If you wanted revenge, we'd have to add some zeroes to the damages." Theresa smirked. "I see that you're tired. Your boyfriend left?"

"Yes." That was why the house was too quiet. Even when Michael was out, his temporary absence made noise in the house.

"I never sleep well when my husband is out of town." Theresa shuffled together her papers and put them back in her briefcase. "I always think if I walk around another corner, he's going to be there and, of course, he isn't. How long will he be away?"

"He may come visit about the time school starts. Depends on what the situation is with the trials."

Theresa raised an eyebrow. "Really? He would stay away to improve your chances in court?"

"He left early to improve my chances in court."

"Well, that's awfully supportive of him."

No, it was just awful. She folded her hands on the table and tried to calculate how many minutes were left until he called again. Too many.

"What do you plan to do with your time? It can get very depressing just sitting around waiting."

"I'm going to take some classes. I've been working on a Masters degree. Or I might run away from home and join the circus."

Theresa laughed like she believed Maureen was joking. "Well, I'm glad to hear you have plans. I'll talk to you again in a week and let you know how things are progressing."

Maureen showed her out and then leaned against the door. It was awfully supportive of him to leave to help her, but she'd much rather have him here supporting her. She fished the keys out of her pocket. They hadn't left her since he had. Last night when she'd been trying to sleep in her too big bed, they had been on the table, lit by the neighbor's security light.

This was stupid. He loved her enough to leave even though he didn't want to. She loved him and didn't want to be apart from him just to prove a point. Even if she won, she lost. She searched the house for her cordless phone. It was on the bookshelf. "Hi, Linda," she said when her friend answered. "What are you doing?"

Linda hesitated. "Nothing."

Maureen chose to ignore the hesitation. "Theresa just left. We're suing the newspaper too."

"Really?"

"They printed that the school board had complaints and the school board isn't producing them."

"Yeah, well, should have checked facts, I guess."

"It's really frustrating that I'm guilty until proven innocent." Why had she called Linda? Kaitlyn wouldn't have gotten her all wound up. Jeanette would have asked if she wanted to come over and swim to distract her. Kathy would have taken her shopping. Linda was just going to get her angry.

"What's worse is that it's nobody's beeswax. So you're dating some super hot musician. What does that change about your teaching?" Linda asked.

"I know."

"It's like they want to fire you on an ethics violation and you haven't had the good taste to show up to teach stoned. This isn't the nineteenth century. Teachers don't have to conduct all their dates on the front porch where the whole town can see them."

"I know." Now she knew why she'd called Linda. She needed a reason.

"You have a right to your life."

"I do. And I'm a good teacher."

"You are a great teacher. Your class had the best scores in the building on the stupid tests. If they're gonna fire somebody over that, then they need to fire whoever had the class with the lowest scores."

"I don't think that's necessary."

"No, but neither is what they're doing."

She paced behind the couch. "True. And if they were going to fire someone over ethics violations—"

"Oh, oh, the coach at the high school."

"Uh huh."

"I don't know why they let him near girls. If he isn't doing something yet, it's only a matter of time."

"I know." She adjusted a pillow. "So you think I have a pretty good chance in court?"

"If there is any justice in this world, the school board and the paper will settle because if you go in front of a judge with your record, you'll will mop the floor with them."

"Can you watch my house?"

"Why?"

"I'm going to go on tour with Michael."

Linda laughed. "You go. Send me postcards."

Maureen threw a few things in a bag and tossed it in the car. Running back into the house one last time, she located the tour book he'd given her so she would know where he would be. The directions to the hotel and the venue would work just fine once she got Tampa. This time when she parked in front of the garage, Tony walked out.

"Hi, Maureen, what's up?"

"I need the Satellite." She climbed out with her bag in her hand.

"What…for." Tony's eyes fell on the bag. "I thought you were supposed to stay in town to look good for your lawsuits."

"I'm going to let my lawsuits handle themselves. Where's the Satellite?"

"Around the side. Are you sure this is a good idea?"

Maureen walked around the side of the building to the weedy lot where he parked cars while he waited for their owners to come pick them up. Her old car sat there with a For Sale sign in the window. The Satellite was parked next to it. "I'd rather lose and be happy than win and be miserable." Overheated air washed across her face as she opened the Satellite's door.

"It's a long drive."

"Fine."

"Shouldn't you call ahead?"

"I'll do that when I get closer." When she sat in the driver's seat, it fit like a glove. Even before she started the engine, she knew what it would sound like.

"Well, wait a minute." Tony shifted from one foot to the other. Rusty and Eric leaned around the side of the building to watch the excitement. Tony kept stalling, and when she reached for the door handle, he jumped to attention. "I just got the badge this morning. I figured Bear would want to put it on himself. Let me get it for you."

Maureen started the engine. It did have a lovely, heavy purr. A lot like Michael.

Tony came back around the building with something in his hand. "Here. Bear will know what to do with it."

Maureen traced her finger over the little piece of plastic that spelled out the words "Satellite of Love" in aerodynamic sixties type.

"And if you get tired, you pull off and get some sleep. At a nice hotel, not a motel." Tony pushed her door closed. "There's no hurry. The Tampa show isn't until tomorrow anyway."

"Thanks, Dad." Grinning at him, she slipped the car into gear.

* * * *

"What the fuck is that?" Jason demanded.

Bear turned toward the sound. It sounded suspiciously like his car. What would his car be doing in Florida in the underground parking at the venue? The whole band was here now. Marc and Ty came out early and they'd spent yesterday at Disney World. Though he hadn't been able to talk Marc into the Mickey ears, he'd found a great barrette for Maureen. Brian and Jason had arrived just in time for sound check. Afterward they'd come out to the bus to check things over because Rudy swore something was wrong. Nothing looked out of place.

Except the candy apple red nineteen seventy-two Plymouth Satellite coasting past the parked rigs and stopping in front of the bus.

Bear glared at Rudy, who was smirking. "You dick. You knew."

"Of course I knew. How do you think she got in here?"

Maureen climbed out of the car and leaned on the roof. "Hi, baby."

Bear ran around the car, grabbed her and spun her around. Setting her back on her feet, he leaned his forehead on hers. "What are you doing here?"

"I missed you."

"I missed you too."

"What about your lawsuit?"

"Everything will work out the way it's supposed to. Besides, there are schools in California. Here, Tony sent this." Maureen angled her hand between them and opened it.

He had to lean back to see what she was holding. Satellite of Love. Perfect. Bending her back, he kissed her. She was still summer and fine wine and the audience screaming for a second encore in the pouring rain.

Perfect.

Meet the Author

For my seventh birthday my brother gave me The Eagles' Hotel California and I was completely enchanted by the title track. No clue what it meant, but I loved it and my fate was sealed. Unfortunately, as a hard core introvert, performing onstage in any capacity was off the table as a career choice. So I turned to writing and spent many boring college lectures detailing the adventures of Touchstone in the margins of my notebooks. Years later I decided to do something with them and wrote what became Heaven Beside You. These things do tend to get out of control with me. A fun side project that kept me entertained while I was teaching English in Korea turned into a series that I was working on through a stint in Chile, the US and the Middle East. And I'm not slowing down.

When not writing, I like to travel so much that I recently had to have pages added to my passport. I also enjoy eating, reading and listening to music. Often simultaneously.

www.ingramcontent.com/pod-product-compliance
Lightning Source LLC
Chambersburg PA
CBHW020446270626
47155CB00022B/1707